LIFER

Beck Nicholas

Published by Month9Books
Cover by Victoria Faye
Cover Copyright © 2014 Month9Books

Month9Books

For Mum. In my heart always.

LIFER

Beck Nicholas

Chapter One

[Asher]

I mark my body for Samuai.

My right hand is steady as I press the slim needle into my skin. It glints under the soft overhead light of the storage locker, the only place to hide on Starship Pelican. Row upon row of shelving fills the room. Back here I'm hidden from the door.

It's been seventeen days since Samuai passed. Seventeen days of neutral expressions and stinging eyes, waiting for the chance to be alone and pay my respects to the dead Official boy in true Lifer fashion. With blood.

The body of the needle is wrapped in thread I stole from my spare uniform. The blue thread acts as the ink reservoir. It's soaked with a dye I made from crushed feed pellets and *argobenzene*, both swiped from farm level. The pungent fumes sting my eyes and make it even harder to keep the tears at bay. But I will. There will be no disrespect in this marking.

My slipper drops to the floor with the softest of thuds as I shake my foot. I raise it to rest on a cold metal shelf. Samuai always held my hand when we met in secret, but I can't bear to examine those memories now. The pain of him being gone is still so fresh.

The first break of skin at my ankle hurts a little. Not much, since the needle is nano-designed for single molecule sharpness, and it's not as though I haven't done this before. Recently. The tattoo for my brother circles my ankle, completed days ago, a match for the one for my father. My memorial for Samuai had to wait for privacy. The blue spreads out into my skin like liquid on a cloth. The dot is tiny. I add another and another, each time accepting the momentary pain as a tribute to Samuai. Soon I've finished the first swirling line.

"Are you mourning my brother or yours?"

My hand jerks at the familiar voice, driving the needle deep into the delicate skin over my Achilles. Davyd's voice. How did he get in here so quietly? I wince, clamping down on a cry of pain. No tears though. Nothing will make me disrespect Samuai. I remove the needle from my flesh and school my features into a neutral expression before I turn and stand to attention.

"Davyd," I say by way of greeting. Despite my preparation my throat thickens.

My response to him is stupid because he looks nothing like Samuai. Where Samuai radiated warmth from his spiky dark hair hinting of honey and his deep, golden brown eyes, there is only ice in his brother. Ice-chiseled cheekbones, tousled blond hair, the slight cleft in his chin, and his gray eyes. Eyes that see far too much.

But he's dressed like Samuai used to dress. The same white t-shirt and black pants. It's the uniform of Officials, or Fishies, as they're known below. He's a little broader in the shoulders than his older brother was—to even think of Samuai in the past tense is agony—and he's not quite as tall. I only have to look up a little to meet his gaze. I do so without speaking.

I shouldn't be here, but I'm not going to start apologizing for where I am or his reference to my forbidden relationship with his brother, until I know what he wants.

"Is that supposed to happen?" He points at my foot, where blood drips, forming a tiny puddle on the hard, shiny floor.

His face is expressionless, as usual, but I can hear the conceit in his voice. I can imagine what the son of a Fishie thinks of our Lifer traditions.

Today, I don't care. Even if his scorn makes my stomach tighten and cheeks flame, I *won't* care. Not about anything Davyd has to say.

"It's none of your business."

One fine brow arches. Superior, knowing.

He doesn't have to say the words. The awareness of just how wrong I am zaps between us. Given our relative stations on this journey—he's destined to be a Fishie in charge of managing the ship's population, and me to serve my inherited sentence—whatever I do *is* his business, if he chooses to make it so. He's in authority even though we're almost the same age.

In order to gain permission to breed, Lifers allowed the injection of nanobots into their children. These prototype bots in our cells give our masters the power to switch us off using a special Remote Device until our sentence is served. At any time we can be shut down. I'm not sure how exactly, only that each of us has a unique code and the device can turn those particular bots against us. It's an unseen but constant threat.

I keep my face blank and my posture subservient, but my fingers tighten around the needle in my hand. How I long to slap the smooth skin of his cheek.

For a second, neither of us speaks.

"Your brother or mine?" he asks again. Softly this time. So low, the question is almost intimate in the dim light.

I inhale deeply, welcoming the harsh fumes from my makeshift ink. The burning in my lungs gives me a focus so the ever-present emotional pain can't cripple me. My brother and my boyfriend were taken on the same day, and I'm unable to properly mourn either thanks to the demands of servitude.

I can't let it cripple me. Not if I want to find out what really happened to Zed and Samuai.

"Does it matter?" I ask. Rather than refuse him again, I twist the question around. He would never admit to having interest in the goings-on of a mere Lifer.

"No." His voice is hard. Uncaring. He folds his arms. "But it's against ship law to deface property."

It takes a heartbeat, and then I realize *I'm* the property he's talking about. My toes curl because my fists can't. I see from the flick of his eyes to my feet that he's noticed. Of course he has. There's nothing Davyd doesn't notice.

It's true though. The marks we Lifers make on our bodies are not formally allowed. It is a price we pay for the agreement signed in DNA by our parents and our grandparents. They agreed to a lifetime of servitude, and their sentence is passed down through the generations for the chance at a new life on a new planet. I am the last in the chain, and my sentence will continue for twelve years after landing.

We Lifers belong to those above us, body and soul, but no Fishie or Naut—the astronauts who pilot the ship—has ever tried to stop the ritual. In return we are not blatant. We mark feet, torsos, and thighs. Places hidden by our plain blue clothing.

If the son of the head Fishie reports me, it will go on my record no matter how minor the charge, and possibly add months to my sentence. A sentence I serve for my grandparents' crimes back on Earth after the Upheaval. Like others, their crime was no more than refusal to hand over their vehicle and property when both were declared a government resource.

I swallow convulsively.

I don't want that kind of notice. Not when we're expected

to land in my lifetime. Not when I hoped to find answers to the questions that haunt me.

The first lesson a Lifer child learns is control around their superiors. I won't allow mine to fail me now.

"Did you want something? Sir?"

If there's a faint pause before the honorific, well, I'm only human.

He lets it pass. "The Lady requires extra help at this time. You have been recommended."

"Me?"

His lips twist. "I was equally surprised. Attend her now."

The Lady is the wife of the senior Official on board the Pelican, and both Samuai and Davyd's mother. She's a mysterious figure who is never seen in the shared area of the ship. I imagine she's hurting for her dead child. Sympathy stirs within me. I've seen the strain my own mother tries to hide since Zed died, and I don't think having a higher rank would make the burden any easier to bear.

It's within Davyd's scope as both Fishie-in-training and son of the ship's Lady to be the one to inform me of my new placement, but I can't help looking for something deeper in his words. There should be a kinship between us, having both lost a brother so recently, but Samuai's death hasn't affected Davyd at all.

"Who recommended me?"

He shrugs. "Now. Lifer."

I nod and move to tidy up, ignoring the persistent pain in my ankle where the needle went too deep. My defiance only stretches so far. Not acting on a direct request would be stupidity. I will finish my memorial for Samuai, but not with his brother waiting. It's typical that Davyd doesn't use my name. I can't remember him or his Fishie friends ever doing so.

It was something that stood out about Samuai from when we

were youngsters and met in the training room. It was the only place on the ship us Lifers are close to equal. I was paired to fight with him to first blood, and he shocked me by asking my name. "Asher," Samuai had repeated, like he tasted something sweet on his tongue, "I like it."

In my heart there's an echo of the warmth I felt that day, but the memory hurts. It hurts that I'll never see him again, that he'll never live out the dreams we shared in our secret meetings. Dreams of a shared future and changes to a system that makes Lifers less than human.

When I've gathered the small inkpot and put on my slippers, I notice a smear of blood on the slipper material from where I slipped earlier. It's the opportunity I need to let my change in status be known below.

"Umm." I clear my throat. *Please let the stories I've heard of the Lady be true.*

"What?" asks Davyd from where he waits by the door, presumably to escort me to his mother. The intensity of his gaze makes me quake inside. It's all I can do not to lift my hand to check my top is correctly buttoned and my hair hasn't grown beyond the fuzz a Lifer is allowed.

"My foot attire isn't suitable to serve the Lady." I point to the faint smudge of brown seeping into my footwear. It is said by those cleaners who are permitted into the Fishie sleeping quarters that the Lady insists her apartment be kept spotless. She's unlikely to be pleased with me reporting for duty in bloodstained slippers.

Davyd's jaw tenses. Maybe I've pushed him too far with this delay. I hold my breath.

But then his annoyance is gone and his face is the usual smooth mask. "Change. I will be waiting at the lift between the training hall and study rooms."

He doesn't need to tell me to hurry.

He opens the door leading out into the hallway and I expect him to stride through and not look back. Again he surprises me. He turns. His face is in shadow. The brighter light behind him shines on his tousled blond hair, which gives him a hint of the angelic.

"Assuming it's my brother you're mourning," his voice is deep and for the first time there's a slight melting of the ice. "You should know…He wasn't worth your pain."

Chapter Two

[Blank]

I awake naked, walking.

Midstride, I stumble, awareness flooding my senses.

I squeeze my eyes shut, protecting them from the rising sun's glare, and cover my ears to block the whine of distant machinery. I inhale, and grimy smog fills my sinuses and coats my tongue like a thick city soup. There isn't enough oxygen.

Gasping, I bend at the waist. Fall to my knees and black gravel bites into the tender skin. The plastic shrub I use for support is cool and spongy. I cough up a globule of soot-covered phlegm.

Still short of breath, I climb to my feet with stiff, aching muscles. Where am I?

Better question: who am I?

A glance down tells me I'm male, but beyond that the answers start to form, but slip away before I can grasp them. I'm left with the barest outline of an echo of a memory.

Everything I need to function is there, but 'me' is missing. Whoever the hell he was. A nearby sign tells me I'm in a preserved garden. So I can read. I continue trying to assimilate everything. The surrounding walls stretch high above me, bordering a small patch of cloudy sky above. The opening makes me feel exposed. Unsettled. It is a sensation probably made worse by my lack of clothing.

Briefly there's a woman on an overhead walkway. She is older, wide-eyed at my nakedness, and then gone into one of the buildings. A belated surge of embarrassment sweeps through me, staining the skin of my upper body red and heating my cheeks.

I shiver when the heat fades. The wind chills my hairless skin. I need to find something to wear. In my search, I'm drawn to a clearing in the middle of the garden. Here, the noise is muffled and the metal structures and imitation trees with their plastic scents give way to a huge, dark red, weathered tree trunk, encircled by fortified glass. I look up, way up, to where green leaf-dotted branches stretch out like a twisted staircase to the sky.

It's alive.

I press a hand against the glass and imagine I can smell its fresh scent. Here and there small lower branches are stunted and shriveled, the glass cage obviously not designed for growth. Shriveled like I'm going to be if I don't find clothes soon. I shake my head, bumping it against the cool glass. Fine water droplets inside run to the small patch of soil at the base of the tree.

Water.

I need water.

On the other side of the tree, dirty liquid trickles over a path of rocks to wet the soil. With urgency I couldn't muster before, I stumble on shaky knees toward the source. I notice white, dry spots on my hands, elbows and knees.

I haven't had water for days. The thought arrives and then lodges in my brain as fact.

I collapse at the edge of a small, murky pool. The brown surface shows the sky far above and a young man. Me. I scan my reflection. Shaved head. Dark, shadowed eyes. Skinny with prominent cheekbones. Nothing special. No spark of recognition fires within me and I avert my gaze from those eyes then lower my head to drink.

Before I can slake my thirst, I see the body.

Blinking, I peer into the gloomy spot in the middle where the shadows from the buildings are at their deepest and vines trail from overhanging rocks. The half-submerged figure doesn't move. Only wrinkled toes, decorated in a swirling pattern of blue ink, rise clearly from the water.

This isn't good.

I wade in, my chest constricting as the icy water envelopes my feet, then my ankles. It's knee deep when I reach the feet. I touch the cold, waxy skin of those patterned toes and a shudder spreads through my numb body. Any thought I could save them disappears. Swallowing bile, I grab a foot with each hand and drag the body to land. It's heavy, way heavier than it looks. My muscles protest the work, but I have to do something about it.

Once the body is out of the water I can see it's a young boy, on the edge of adolescence. He's pale with blue lips and only the whites showing where his irises should be. His head has been shaved, leaving only dark bristles.

The constriction in my chest cramps tighter. I have to close my eyes to press my fingers against the purple bruising on his neck to be sure.

No pulse. No life.

My thoughts swirl like the pattern on the boy's toes. What happened? It doesn't look natural. Are they coming back for me?

Blood and feeling return to my extremities. Escape. I need to get away from the crime.

My crime?

I pause and then dismiss the notion. I have to believe I didn't kill this boy, but I can't afford the time to mourn him either. Now is all about survival. I move to slide him back out of sight when the rough material of his jacket stops me.

He has clothes and I need them.

I feel like I should hesitate more, but survival rules. I strip the body of his zipped jacket and blue pants. I leave the boy in a t-shirt and underwear for modesty and try to cover him as best I can. The items are heavy and wet in my hands. I gag, unable to bring up anything from my empty gut other than the taste of bile as I wring as much water as I can from the garments.

Once dressed, I hesitate. I need to get outside these walls, find food and drink, and then figure out who I am. Still, I linger. It's harder than I expect to leave the boy. "You are not my problem," I growl to the shape in the shadows.

The garden is secluded. I've seen nobody since the elderly woman above. I can stay here, report the body to the authorities and maybe be accused of a crime I didn't commit. With no memory I'd make an easy fall guy. Every time I think of authority a heavy weight on my chest makes it hard to breathe. There's too much I don't know.

"Sorry kid."

A rusty padlock secures the first door out of the garden, but the next hangs on one hinge. It's open. The heavy wooden door, with its peeling brown paint, moves freely. Beyond is a dark tunnel with faint light at the end. I pause at the entrance, my reflection stretches out on a shining, sticky stone floor. Then I stride into the squelchy darkness without looking back.

Bang.

I spin and drop to a crouch. My hands fly up to protect my face.

I'm tense. Ready to fight. The hammering of my heart makes it hard to hear but I hold perfectly still, listening for a possible attacker's next move. I scan the framed garden behind me. There's a gust of wind and the big wooden door bangs against the concrete wall behind.

I fight a laugh and exhale. Only the wind.

Back on my feet I stride through the tunnel. With the after affects of adrenaline pumping through me I feel more comfortable than any time since I woke.

Empty shop fronts suggest this was once a mall. Lettering on the windows is so faded I can't tell what they sold. The light grows until I step out into a narrow alleyway between two tall buildings. Light streams through rubble on either side. The walls are blackened and I'm surprised gravel doesn't tumble from them. I inhale dust and long-forgotten smoke with every breath. Something happened here. Something huge and deadly.

But not recently.

Brown and white moss grows in the corners of the fallen walls. Piles of bird droppings decorate the taller remnants of concrete and stone. The disaster that spared the garden behind me happened too long ago to have killed the boy or taken my memories. And my loss seems way too specific to be accidental. All I'm missing is me, but everything else remains.

There's movement at the end of the alleyway. People maybe. Water. Food. Answers. I head in that direction, slowing to climb over a stack of crates and boxes overflowing from a large dumpster that blocks half the alley. Fumes rise like an invisible wall across the small space, thick and drenched with urine. Suspicious stains decorate the nearby walls and there's a box of rotting food scraps dumped on top of the rest of the rubbish.

"Hey."

I freeze. This time I'm not imagining the threat. The voice with the strange, thick accent is coming from a green-robed figure in the shadows of the bin. Shorter than me. High, young voice. Smooth jaw. His only weapon is a light baton swinging from his hands.

I can take him. Instinct gives me a confidence I have no right to feel considering the blank where my history should be.

"Hey," I reply. I balance my weight on both feet and let my hands hang loose at my sides. Ready for action but not threatening.

"Name and business," he says.

He's talking like he owns the place. "Who's asking?"

He steps closer, moving further into the light. "Name. And. Business."

Of all the questions, I'm pretty sure he's not going to like my answer. My amusement must show on my face because he lifts the baton, which upon closer examination looks like a plastic rod, and points it at me.

"I'll use it." The end shakes and his sleeves fall away, revealing slender brown hands. Young hands, like the dead boy's.

The situation isn't funny anymore. I hold my hands out, palms up. Classic supplication. "Look, Buddy. I'd tell you if I could."

"I'm not your buddy." His volume is rising. "You need to tell me."

"Settle down. I can't, really, I can't."

"You mean, you won't. I'm not just a little kid. I'll make you come with me." His chin juts. "Then Keane will make you talk."

"No." I take half a step back. The kid says 'Keane' like it's a god but no one can make me tell them something I don't know. "I'm sorry."

His chest puffs out and he flicks a switch on the end of the weapon. "If you don't come with me peacefully, I'll fire."

Chapter Three

[Asher]

The door clicks closed and seals behind Davyd, leaving me alone with his comment's echo. Samuai *was* worth the marking of my skin.

"You're wrong," I say. I know what Samuai and I shared. I know it was special and true and would have lasted.

But he's no longer here. I'm talking to myself. And wasting precious seconds.

I slip out of the storage area and head for the Lifer sleeping quarters. My hope of passing through unnoticed ends when I see Kaih. Her blond, shaved-short hair and baggy clothes don't detract from her blue-eyed beauty. Probably because it shines from within.

Lately, I avoid her innate goodness even though she is my closest childhood friend. She longs to help, to make up for what I've lost, and probably to tell me everything's going to be okay. I can't bear the lies. No matter how well intentioned.

"Asher?" It's amazing how much sympathy and question she manages to load into my name. Underneath it is a hint of hurt.

Guilt at having to cut another conversation with her short slows my steps, and I muster a smile. "Sorry. I can't stop. New orders."

I don't wait for the inevitable questions and see her lift her fingers to bite her nails. Something she only does when she's upset.

Automatically, I duck, entering the Lifer's sleeping space as the doors seal shut behind me. Here the ceiling is low enough I can brush it with my elbows bent. Several small screens on the walls show the countdown until estimated planet arrival. My gaze lingers on one flickering display. In a week another year will fall, making all us Lifers another year older and closer to serving out our sentences. Above, they celebrate the end of the year with a huge ball. Preparations are already underway. Down here, it will be another day.

The light from the regular banks above never feels bright enough to pierce the gloom, and the five steps between each Lifer's bed and cupboard never feel far enough to pretend we have our own space.

As usual it's mostly deserted. Some would still be in the galley, while others would have already returned to their assignments at the Farm or Manufacturing quarters. Those with free afternoons would be in the training rooms. Only those on night shift lie in their beds trying to get a few more hours sleep.

For their sake I am quiet, weaving easily between the beds to mine. It is a path I know because I have always slept right here. There's nothing to make it stand out from the rest—that would be asking for attention from the Fishies who occasionally inspect down here.

I walk past the empty bed where my brother once slept without pause. The time for sitting there and replaying our last joke or last fight is gone. Now I need to honor him with truth and, if necessary, justice. I didn't come down here to mourn.

In the bed next to mine lies the reason for my delay. I pad over and kneel beside her.

"Mother," I say. Her breathing's heavy, but with her back to me I'm not sure she sleeps. Her head, with its dark, close-cropped hair exactly the same shade as mine, doesn't move. I touch her shoulder, feeling bone. She seems frailer in rest than she ever would in the training rooms. "Elex," I try again, using her name.

She turns in a fluid motion. The soft overhead light glitters off her shining dark eyes. Was she crying? The thought cramps my belly and brings a lump to my throat, but then she's pulling me into her arms in a warm but brief embrace.

"Asher, what are you doing here? Is something wrong?" The usual authority is back in her voice. The authority she hides when a Fishie or Naut is present.

I exhale relief. Mother is far too strong to let grief crush her. She survived my father's loss nine years ago in the failed rebellion. Now she will not let what happened to Zed destroy everything she's worked toward. There are far too many lives depending on her decisions.

The report on my brother's death was short. It said there was a malfunction in the training room resulting in no oxygen for seventeen minutes. Zed and Samuai were fighting a practice bout. It was too late by the time they were discovered. Strangely, no one saw it happen. No one saw anything.

"I have a new placement," I say softly.

She sits up and pats the bed next to her. "Tell me."

Where we work is assigned by the Fishies and supervised by Neale, who graduated to the role of Staff Captain after my father's death. However, it's the unspoken rule amongst us that my mother be informed of any changes. It's necessary for her to know where everyone is in case their post creates an opportunity to gather more information. Information on what happens in the quarters of the Officials and even more importantly, the thirteen Astronauts, who keep the spaceship on course for its final destination. This is where my father failed. He simply didn't know enough. My mother will not make the same mistake.

I settle close to Mother. The confidence she radiates from her slender frame and her soft honey scent used to make me feel safe. Since Zed and Samuai were pronounced dead, there's no such thing as safe, but the comfort still draws me. I fill my lungs, trying to recapture that feeling.

"I have been told to report to the Lady."

"No. You can't. I'll tell Neale." Her face hardens in a way I've never seen directed at me.

I don't understand. It's stupid but this makes the tears of grief harder to keep at bay than the pain of the needle. I was so sure she'd be eager for me to go. Now more than ever, we need information or we'll never know what happened to Zed.

"The request came from above. It's an opportunity to spend time on the upper levels. I thought you would be pleased."

She must hear the confusion in my voice because her mouth softens a fraction. "Yes. You're right. It could be important."

I wait, but she says nothing more. "So I should go? Because Davyd is waiting."

She's silent for a long moment. Has she heard me? I can't linger here when Davyd expects me. I don't want to make a mistake so soon. Not when the post could give me the answers I need about those I've lost, as well as information for my people. Not when I want the chance to prove Davyd wrong about his brother.

"If the Lady," her lip curls at the title, "needs someone so desperately, we could send Sela or Kaih." She names my friend and another Lifer girl a little older than me. Both excel in the training rooms where we challenge each other or provide sparring partners for Fishies and Nauts.

"You don't think I can handle it."

She pats my knee. Placating. Condescending. "I'm surprised, that's all. The other girls attend the meetings, they know the kind of information we need if our plans are to be successful."

And I don't.

Of course I support the idea of the rebellion, but I'm not interested in the chest-thumping we're-gonna-kill-the-Fishies mob. There has to be a way we can coexist on the new planet that doesn't involve more loss of life. It was a dream Samuai shared.

"I can gather information. I'm not stupid."

Instead of rising to the argument in my voice, my mother remains steady. "Asher, it's not that simple. You are not the first."

"What?"

"To serve *her*." Mother's hands clench.

I hesitate. I didn't know. "The other girl?"

"Never returned."

Fear slides a lightning trail down my spine. More deaths in service to our forced masters. More reason to do everything I can to get the information I need.

"I might not seek the fight, but I'm no coward."

"I know, but after what happened…"

The memory of Zed sits between us, heavy and painful. I know she's hurting. I am too, and I need to do something about it. Zed would have expected it of me, his adored big sister. I stand. "Davyd said I was recommended specifically."

"Davyd said?" There's an edge to her voice as she parrots me.

My throat gets hot and I'm thankful for the dim light, I know what she's getting at. While we never spoke of it directly, she knew about my feelings for Samuai and I'm certain she didn't approve. She couldn't be more wrong if she thinks I'm just going to transfer my affections to his brother.

"Do I report or do we miss the opportunity?"

She blinks at my rough tone. "Report." Her hand brushes my

arm and her voice lowers. "But be safe."

I nod.

I change my slippers, feeling my mother's gaze on me. It's like her worry settles as an extra cloak across my shoulders. For the first time I'm not sure of her reasons. Does she fear for me as a mother who has lost her only son? Or as the leader of the Lifer rebellion who would wish for a better-trained gatherer of intelligence?

I can do this.

But I don't say it aloud. As I'm about to exit the Lifer quarters, I glance over my shoulder. It should be too far to tell, but when I make out the shape of my mother standing by her bed, I *know* she's still watching me.

As I wait for the lift, there's a flutter of anticipation in my belly. I'm taking action at last. I put my mother and her unsettling reaction out of my mind.

He's right where he said he would be, watching one of the sparring matches in the huge training room through the big windows by the lift. I cross quickly to meet him, resisting the urge to apologize for the time I've taken. My steps slow. I've avoided this place since Zed and Samuai died.

Davyd doesn't look away from the fight as I approach. It doesn't bother him that our brothers died in a fight like this one.

There's a scuffle down the hall between two Lifers waiting to battle. The sounds of raised voices and fists on flesh send a few Fishies scurrying past us toward the upper levels. Fishies are now choosing to fight only amongst each other, scared of the pain their servants inflict. Except Davyd. He thrives on the battle.

This match is between two Lifers but I can't make out their faces as they move in the blur of low gravity. It's set up to mirror our destination planet. We are allowed to train here if none of our superiors have booked the room, and only hand to hand combat. Obstacles are allowed; however, these combatants created a dangerous looking game space. Collisions with the polymer constructs are inevitable. My stomach churns in time to the spinning of the two combatants.

I look away but can't avoid hearing the crunch of impact. Game over.

"Ready?" As usual, Davyd seems unaffected by other people's pain.

"Yes."

I stare straight ahead as he presses his wrist against the blood scanner. Moments later the lift dings and the doors slide open. Access to this part of the five-level ship is strictly regulated. It takes seconds to ascend to the level above, but it's taken me over sixteen years to get up here.

Davyd and I don't speak on the short walk down the hall. Mostly, I'm trying not to obviously gape. My usual working shift rotates between the Farm, the sewing subsection of Manufacturing, and the minimal class time young Lifers are permitted.

This is my first time in this part of the ship and it might as well be another planet. It's bright and open. The hint of brown in the wall color adds a sense of class and warmth I've never experienced in the sterile rooms below. It reminds me of the mansions in the Earth recordings we're forced to watch periodically about before the Upheaval. I couldn't reach the ceiling here if I was standing on Davyd's shoulders. Airtight seals remain around the doors like we have in the lower levels. But there's no lingering scent of animals or chemicals.

In fact, there's a slightly sweet smell. Not exactly like the honey I associate with my mother, but something. I inhale deeply, trying to place where I smelled it before. It's a little like the compound plants they feed the rabbits and the chickens but less earthy.

Whatever it is, I like it.

The hum, the buzzing of machines and pumps recycling water I've barely noticed because it's existed in the background my whole life is gone. I strain to listen. No, the sound is not gone completely, instead muffled to whisper quiet.

The pressure to remember everything to report back to my mother drags my footsteps on the shiny floor. While cleaners are required to work on the ship's upper levels on a regular basis, their access to the private quarters of the head Fishie and his Lady is intermittent.

Davyd halts at a set of double doors.

It's all I can do to stop in time so I don't smack into his chest. That faint smirk is there again when I look up. Can he guess why I was distracted? Or does he assume it's general wonder at the life of my betters?

Focus. I need to do this better, heed the warning in my mother's words. Too many people are relying on me. I need to do this for my brother's memory.

Instead of blurting out a question or quip about Davyd nearly causing a collision, I wait for him to speak.

He looks over his shoulders at the doors and then back to me. "The Lady is—" His pause is long. Loaded with something I can't read. "She's unwell. We are concerned. Do as she asks. Whatever it is."

"Of course."

"Don't upset her. Don't ask any questions."

There's tension in the set of his shoulders as he presses his arm against another wrist scanner that I didn't notice in a small panel above the handle. The doors swish open.

My breath catches.

"Yes. It's bright," Davyd mutters.

Bright is an understatement. Every wall's painted a hyper

yellow and the color presses in on my eyes until it hurts to keep looking. The white of the furniture provides only a small relief. The chemical odor in the air suggests a recent painting.

Does Mother know already? Such an odd paint request would be news in Manufacturing, and the work detail should go up on the rosters, yet I'd not heard a whisper. It must be that the color scheme of the Lady's rooms doesn't matter to the rebellion. Or a Lifer didn't do the work.

I glance at Davyd's hands and they're clean of yellow. Not him then. I can't picture him with a paintbrush anyway.

The Lady herself bursts into the room from another door before I can step over the threshold. She wears a flowing green dress and I imagine a summer meadow from the Earth recordings. I'd mentally prepared for an invalid, or at least someone weighed down by mourning her son.

This blond-haired woman radiates energy and life in a whirlwind of movement and a wide, guileless smile.

"Asher, you're here at last, come in."

She knows my name? I take a wary step, keeping my head bowed. My gaze flicks to Davyd's for direction on how I should greet his mother. He responds with the slightest of shrugs. I should have known he'd be less than helpful.

The Lady takes the decision out of my hands. She embraces me in a hug and squishes me. Shock stills me. Her soft body envelopes me, and I have to force myself not to step back to breathe. Up close she reeks of the scent I noticed in the hallway. What was pleasant is now overpowering.

My nose must wrinkle or something because she giggles. A high, creepy tinkling sound. "It's flowers, dear."

"Flowers, my lady?" I'm not sure of how to address her. When she doesn't answer I add, "Ma'am?"

"Call me Lady." Her mouth curves up. "These flowers are

from plants inedible to us and the animals. Not useful in the slightest. Just beautiful flowers." She giggles again. "What a wonderful thing."

I know what flowers are in theory, but I didn't expect them to smell so nice. My work detail has covered every inch of the Farm. There, the food we don't produce chemically is grown, and I have never seen anything as frivolous as flowers for no purpose.

What power must Lady have if she can order the growth of flowers for their appearance? Where did she get the seeds?

Seeing my interest, she hooks a thumb over her shoulder toward a white low table. In the center stands a tall vase. Green stems holding yellow blobs of sunshine, or at least that's what they remind me of, lean askew out the top. Their color almost matches the walls. No wonder I didn't notice them before. I take a step toward the curious sight before I remember my role and the need to be on my best behavior.

After all, Davyd hasn't moved from his station at the door. Silent and intense as always. I'm on trial, and I don't know what I need to do to pass.

But Lady doesn't seem to mind. She pushes me gently toward the table. "You may look."

It's an order. Crossing to the flowers allows me to reassess. It's taking time to get my mind around the work I thought would be involved in caring for a sick person and the reality. In my mind, I replay the scene in the hallway. Davyd hesitated before he used the term unwell. Maybe this over-the-top exuberance from his mother is the reason.

"Thank you for escorting Asher. We'll be fine from here," says Lady.

I glance up from pretending to examine the flowers in time to see Davyd shake his head. "I'll stay."

Lady's mouth flattens. "Shouldn't you be following Maston

around?" Her question has a biting edge.

I freeze. Maston is the head Naut. He's a figure of legend in the Lifer levels of the ship. The Control Room where the Nauts work is completely out of our scope. I have to stifle a shiver. My father died trying to reach it.

Lifers can't change their place in our society; at least not until we land and can serve out the sentences passed down through the generations. But we aren't the only ones. Fishies will never be any more than the bureaucrats running our lives. The ultimate power lies with the Nauts. They are the thirteen people we all depend on. The Nauts rule all of us. That Davyd associates with Maston is exactly the kind of information I need for the rebellion.

He'll end up a Fishie. It is law. So why is he following the head Naut around?

Davyd ignores her question. He leans back against the wall, all leashed power and brooding intensity. Clearly he's not planning on going anywhere.

I meet his gaze. It radiates suspicion. Lady might use my name and act like I'm here as a guest, but Davyd has no intention of leaving her alone with me. However, he's not in charge here.

"You may go." Lady dismisses Davyd with a flick of her wrist.

He doesn't respond.

She turns to face her son and I imagine he flinches, but that would be ridiculous. Nothing and nobody bothers Davyd. It's why he rules the training room. Be it a mental or physical foe, he excels at beating them. The only one who came close was Samuai.

My heart cramps at the thought of Samuai's nonchalant grin after a bout. Samuai didn't care about the fight like the other boys on the Pelican. And I loved it about him.

"Go. Now." Command strengthens Lady's voice.

He does. The doors close with a quiet swish but there's a slam implied in the way Davyd strode through them.

Lady stares after her son. It's obvious she was once a beautiful woman, before time and the luxuries of Fishie life took hold. Beneath the soft cheeks, there's a hint of Davyd's cheekbones, and her smile has something of Samuai about the shape of it, warmth I can't help being drawn to. Her hand lifts, as though she's about to reach out after Davyd, but that doesn't make any sense. She told him to go. Not thirty seconds ago she demanded he leave. Lady stands statue like, her side toward me.

What now?

It is not my place to do anything other than wait for my next order. I have no idea why she wanted me, specifically, here. I don't know what she expects.

Her jaw wobbles. The slight movement draws my attention to the weak folds of skin at her neck and the heavy layer of cream and powders she's smoothed on her face. Whatever this ultra-chirpy display is, I'm beginning to suspect it is just another mask.

She turns. Bright and bubbly like before. She claps her hands together. "Now that he's gone I have a surprise for you."

Chapter Four

[Blank]

My hands curl into fists and adrenaline ramps up my heart rate. "I don't think I can do that, buddy." I keep my voice low and controlled.

The green-robed boy steps closer. He's almost within reach. Now I see his face beneath the hood. His dark eyes are wide and his lips are a pale straight line. "It's set to bone."

That doesn't sound good. Something like fear licks my insides. Hot and sour. Still, I'm not about to head off with some kid. I don't want to meet Keane, who'll make me talk. As far as I know, I don't have anything to say.

I close the distance between us in a single step. His arm wobbles. He hesitates. Just like I knew he would. This kid isn't a killer. If he's someone's hired help they're getting ripped off.

I knock the weapon aside as he fires. A tickle grazes my side. There's no pain, only the pounding of my heart and the kid's sharp intake of breath. Although weaponless now, he's not hopeless. His fingernails go for my exposed eyes, but I lift my left knee even as I grip his slight shoulders, drawing him toward me in one easy move.

Incredibly easy move. Like I've done it a million times.

But I don't have time to think. I act. My knee finds the boy's groin.

"Oof." His warm breath sprays my face. His green eyes bug and his hands go from my face to wrap around his privates. He hits the ground sucking for air. Sweat forms in fine beads across his forehead.

I step back. My heartbeat slows to normal.

Logic tells me to run, but now he's incapacitated I need to make sure I haven't done real damage. Images of the boy in the water stalk me.

The kid dropped his weapon and I pick it up while I wait. Recalling the strange tickle in my side moments before I landed the blow, I rub my hand there to make sure I'm not hurt but it's not even sore. The weapon is as light as it appeared and there are several settings. Skin. Bone. Blood.

By the time I look up again, the kid seems to be breathing normally. His gaze hasn't left me, and he scrambles back until he hits the wall.

"You okay?" I ask.

He nods slowly, still wide-eyed. I figure from his expression that most people in these parts don't check on victims after a fight. One hand's checking the injury. I'm guessing it's going to hurt for a while. His Adam's apple bobs.

"Are you?"

I wipe my brow and am surprised when it comes away bloody from where he tried to scratch my eyes out. Then the pain follows. Nothing I can't handle.

"Fine."

He chews his lower lip. "I meant your side."

"The tickle?"

"I must have missed." He sounds annoyed.

He didn't miss. I'm sure of it. I'm tempted to ask more about the weapon, but I don't want to reveal just how strange a stranger I am. I pass the weapon between my hands, reminding him I have it. "You always treat strangers this way?"

He doesn't seem to hear what I say. His focus falls to the weapon and he pales. "Don't shoot."

"I'm not going to—"

That's enough for him. He's up and running down the alleyway in an awkward hobble. His boots slap against the concrete like a round of applause at my mercy. He's fast and I'm not completely positive I could catch him. And I've no idea what I'd do if I did. I can hardly haul him around with me. So I either silence him permanently, or let him go.

I don't follow.

I'll have to deal with the fallout from his report to the Keane person if it happens. I refuse to sit and wait for retribution.

Happy not to have added to the body count, I turn back toward the wide street where people are moving. I head toward it at a casual pace, belying the skip of my pulse. I'm just an ordinary guy out for a walk. Except my stomach is tight, I have no memory of who I am, and I've left a dead kid in a shallow pool behind me.

I linger at the corner. In front of me is an open square, dominated by rows of rough stalls selling everything from dark green leafy vegetables I can't name, to polished-up vehicle parts. At the stall nearest to me, an old lady hawks a deep fried delicacy. The honey-brown coating glistens in the early morning sun as she places it to cool on a wire rack. My gut emits a loud growl. I glance around to make sure no one hears.

The roads away from the square lead up and down hills that look like a frozen wave in the earth. Buildings are cracked, windows gaping. People's faces don't reflect the destruction surrounding the market oasis. No one looks my way. They are all far too busy. Buying. Selling. Hurrying about their business.

I exhale a breath of relief. I don't even look too out of place. Others wear jackets and pants like mine, and still more people wear dark green robes like the boy's. I avoid looking at them for too long.

One woman stands out. She wears a gray one-piece uniform and moves with an air of command that I retreat back into the alleyway, even as I observe. Her gaze scans the market and she avoids those in green robes. Curious. I'm not having much luck working out who's in charge here. The woman stops at the old lady's stall and points. The old lady hurries to respond and then holds out her hand for payment. It's knocked aside by the woman and the old lady cowers.

If gray shirt is what passes for authority, I'm better off keeping my head down until I know more, considering I've left a body in that garden. When she takes a bite of the deep fried food and juices drip down her chin I stifle a groan.

I should be frantic to solve the puzzle of my mind, but the hunger clawing at my belly dominates everything else. I double-check the pockets of the jacket I'm wearing. Fortunately they're empty, so my disrespect ends at stealing the dead kid's clothes. I'm not tempted to take his money as well.

Standing here isn't going to get me the sustenance I need. The sooner I explore the market, the sooner I'm able to escape those in green robes. Hopefully before the boy reports in and they start looking for me.

Wary and watchful, I move into the market proper, my eyes scanning for an opportunity. But there's nothing. No leftover food. No credit sticks dropped on the litter-strewn ground. In a few minutes, I reach the other side and the stalls give way to another road. A two-foot chasm buckles the center of the roadway. As I watch, a motorcycle flirts with the edge before accelerating away.

The row of bars and restaurants on the other side of the broken road glow with welcoming neon signs. The food odors drifting in my direction make my mouth moisten.

Maybe I can work in exchange for food and water.

I cross the road, shoulders hunched. I'm taller than those around me and don't want to stand out. I walk straight past the first building. The exotic couples in the images out front and the darkened windows make me suspicious of the services offered inside. I'm not that desperate.

The next establishment offers 'Food, brew, and good times' according to their sign. I don't even get in the front door before a muscled guy with a black moustache informs me, "No credit. No entry," in a tone I don't care to argue with.

The next place is called 'Gan's Gaming Bar.' The plain black and white sign looks new and the mottled gray windows block the view inside, but the absence of both naked women and intimidating doormen makes it worth a try. The big glass door opens silently.

Inside, a dozen cubicles line each wall, and big soft couches divide the room. Each cubicle holds a different game. In some, the players dance furiously, watching their movements on the screen. Others use real-looking weapons to fight a hologram enemy. Still others tap at a modified keyboard. There's something for every age and taste. Young, scantily-dressed men and women move through the crowd, exchanging drinks and drugs for a swipe of a credit stick. The bar buzzes with activity even at this early hour.

In one corner, however, is stillness.

A young girl, her eyes underlined by black smudges of weary, stares entranced at a simple large screen. I turn to see what is so fascinating. On the screen are rows and rows of different colored rectangles, stacked and arranged in a complicated pattern. I'm drawn to stand and watch, despite the cramps of hunger paining my gut and the woozy sensation in my head that makes the room sway.

The girl remains unmoving while a large clock in the corner

of the screen counts inexorably down. Closer and closer it gets to zero. Ten seconds, nine, eight…I find myself holding my breath, sucked in by the girl's concentration.

She leans forward, as though in slow motion.

Two seconds…one second to go.

And touches a single green rectangle.

Nothing happens, and then the rectangles began to tumble, each one loudly smashing into pieces when it hits the bottom of the screen and then disappearing. Until there are only four remaining, each one isolated on the screen. Two purple rectangles, one green and one yellow. A message flashes in neon white across the screen, 'Sorry, not a winner.' The girl walks away, her shoulders sagged, her toe kicking the leg of a chair, and leaves the bar.

"Want to play a game, friend?" A gravelly smoke-filled voice jars me from my game-induced trance.

I turn toward the man behind the bar. He's big, hairy, and looking at me. I shrug, trying to hide just how much I want to play, and shove my hands deep in my pockets. "I have no money."

The man's voice warms, becomes almost seductive. "We also deal in credit sticks. My name's Gan, and this is my place."

If he's sensing a sale he needs to work on his victim. "I have no identification on me, Gan."

Not to mention no idea of whether I've ever had money. From the ease with which I went into the fight earlier, I suspect I'm not pampered.

"You have DNA, don't you?" He jerks his head toward the small screen on the bar.

I edge closer. ID SCANNER it says in large print across the top. Surely my identity won't be answered this easily, but it's worth a try.

My calf muscles cramp in protest when I finally take a seat at the small terminal. The tension of possible answers tightens every muscle. I exhale and deliberately relax each one. If nothing else, I'm safe from the green robes while in the bar and have a chance to rest my feet.

I breathe in deeply and almost taste the different foods being carried to waiting customers. Salty, sweet, and spicy. It all smells great to me. I sniff again. There's something close. Less than an arm's reach away, there's a brown, ribbon-like, fried snack dusted with salt in a small white bowl.

My hand shoots out before my brain finishes registering the food's proximity. It hovers over the bowl. I look to Gan, silently asking permission.

"Potato skins are complimentary for valued customers," he explains, baring his teeth in what might be a smile.

"And water?" I ask casually, eyeing the slightly murky liquid in a jug.

He pours me a glass. My hands don't betray the shakiness inside as I pick it up. I sip slowly. The bitter liquid wets my tongue and slides a relieving trail down my throat. I close my eyes to savor it. And then remember my audience. I take a gulp and slide the glass away. Only someone desperate would drink any more.

Now for food. With my mouth watering, I take a potato skin, place it in my mouth, and chew slowly. The greasy flavor makes my stomach heave but I manage to swallow it. Food at last.

With my hunger stoked, I follow the barman's direction and place my hand, palm down, on a plastic pad connected to the terminal. I press the 'sample' button, and feel a strangely familiar scrape across my little finger.

I don't even have time to hold my breath. A face appears on the screen. My face, but not the one I saw in the water's reflection. This boy looks younger than the one I saw earlier. His hair is longer, the brown strands spiking up at odd angles and his cheeks a little more plump. He's not smiling, I guess he's suffering through the picture, but there's a carefree shine to his brown eyes.

White-hot envy snakes through my chest. Who was that boy? What happened to me?

The hunger to know engulfs my physical need for sustenance. I search for more on the screen. A name. Something to answer the questions that have been building in my mind. Where the name should be is blank.

"Blank, eh?" says Gan with a smirk. "Catchy name."

"It's the one my dear mother gave me," I retort. "It's been in our family for generations." I skim the rest of the ID report. I'm seventeen years old and the medical scan pronounces me free of disease.

The last known address is as blank as my name. Only one other field has an entry. Where my credit history should be, there's only one deposit listed. A large one. I have no real feel for what the number means, but I'm guessing from the way Gan is looking at me like we're long lost friends that I can afford a game or two. I act unsurprised.

His hand comes down on my shoulder. "We print credit sticks here, Blank my friend, but there's a small fee. And of course I ask no questions."

Small? He names a figure and I half-heartedly haggle him down, assuming he's trying to rip me off. His lack of surprise at my lack of information is, in itself, telling.

I clear my throat. "What about the authorities?"

He glances around. "People without a history would be wise not to attract attention. The people in charge around here don't take much convincing to match a stranger with a crime, if you know what I mean." He turns away to deal with another customer.

He might be biased but what he said goes with my gut: I have to find answers myself.

I stare at the boy on the screen while the credit stick is processed. I'm looking for any details in his face and the edge of black t-shirt he wears that might help me work out who I am.

There's nothing.

"Blank," Gan calls from behind the bar.

I look up. He's sniggering to himself. I'm glad my name amuses somebody. "What?"

"Your credit stick's ready."

"Thanks." I take it from his pudgy fingers, tugging a little to get it free.

"Now, what can I get you? Food, games, accommodation." His voice drops to creepy. "Drugs, girls." As he speaks, he flicks off the terminal screen, taking away any hope of spotting something useful.

"Food and drink, first." I choose a hearty-looking meat and vegetable stew and bottled water from the menu, and then wander back toward the rectangle game while I wait for my food to be served.

No one's playing and it's only ten credits.

I glance back toward the bar, but my order isn't ready. One game. I'll play one game. It will use up time and give me a break from all the unknowns begging for attention in my head. Ten credits will hardly make a dent in my credit stick. I swipe it in the slot and authorize the purchase.

I take a moment to scan the instructions. As suspected, the aim is to smash all of the colored rectangles, referred to as bricks, by removing just one and triggering a chain reaction. The first level holds six bricks and takes less than six seconds to solve.

As I progress through the levels it becomes increasingly difficult. If I ignore the clock and concentrate, I discover a pattern in the apparently random bricks. From there it's easy to solve. While I think back over what I could have done in level seventeen before starting another game, I realize my order's sitting on the low table next to me. The bottled water tastes a million times better than the free stuff and the meat, smothered in the stew's rich gravy, is so tender I barely have to chew.

It's only lukewarm and I shovel it into my mouth, ready for the next game.

I look up again and the big clock over the bar tells me over an hour has passed, but I'm at the level that stumped the young girl when I first walked in. I could play out my options in my mind, but time's running down. I let my eyes lose focus. Attempting to see the pattern and not the bricks.

There.

That one.

I press, and hear someone gasp behind me. I turn, my hand drops to the weapon in my jacket. I'm ready to defend myself. What the hell have I been doing playing a stupid game when there might be people looking for me?

But the gasp comes from a girl. Or woman. I can't quite pin her age. She isn't wearing a green robe; actually she isn't wearing anything much at all. My skin shrinks to uncomfortable and heat burns my ears.

She's hot.

Her cutoffs and black tank top leave a whole lot of smooth brown skin exposed. The sides of her head are shaved and the long, purple strands left on top fall over the side of her heart-shaped face. Her lips look soft and her lilac eyes are laughing. At me.

I drag my gaze away, hoping I've managed not to drool.

"Your game's finished," she says.

Her voice is fresh and clear like my first taste of clean water.

Promise me.

It's the softest of feminine whispers in my mind. Almost… almost…Nope. Gone. Was it a memory from my missing past? Have I left someone behind?

I try to remember more, but the walls there are as strong as before. I imagined the voice. Or my embarrassment is trying to save me from making an even bigger fool of myself.

Back to the present. The girl said the game was finished, that's right. The screen flashes my victory in neon green, 'Winner'. I nailed it. I allow myself a mental fist pump and can't help a grin. I nailed it, and the girl was watching.

I aim for casual when I turn back around, but she's gone. A scan of the room shows her hips swaying through a door marked 'Staff Only.' Great, here I was thinking she was watching me and she was just doing her job.

And I'm not exactly dressed to impress.

My ears heat up all over again. It's probably for the best. Speaking to hot girls won't get me answers. Neither will playing games. But while I played, I could forget all the questions I need to answer. I was just a guy, playing a game. Reality won't stay at bay forever.

First, I need a place to stay. Despite gnawing guilt from the phantom girl's voice in my head, half my attention is on the 'staff only' door the whole time I'm negotiating room rates with Gan, but the hot girl doesn't reappear. With a place to sleep sorted, I head back to the market and pick up some necessities.

I don't know whether it's because of the game I've been playing, but this time I notice a pattern in the movements of those in green robes. Five of them pass through the market in a way that seems structured. A patrol. My stomach tightens. Are they looking for me?

Once I see the pattern, it's easy enough to avoid them and I make my purchases fast. I'm drawn to the brightly colored fruit stands. I could buy a whole meal for the cost of a single piece, but I spoil myself with two apples and an orange. With a bag of clothes, shoes and some bleach to disguise the stubble on my head, I return to the bar. I tell myself I'm not really interested, but I'm aware the girl isn't anywhere to be seen as I make my way through the crowd to the steps at the back.

At the door I have to key in a code Gan provided. The room's simple. There's a mattress on the floor and stuck to the wall are directions to the shared bathroom. Metal bars cover the tiny mottled-glass window. Everything reeks of deep-fry from the kitchen below and there are two dark stains on the timber floor, but otherwise it seems clean.

The showers are right across the hall. Before long my scalp burns from the bleach. While I wait for it to work, I munch on a green apple. It's tart, sweet, and juicy, and I wish I'd bought more. Then I ease my aching muscles under the shower's hot spray. A few minutes later, I'm clean and dry with orange fuzz for hair. I drag on the black jeans I bought, glad to have my ankles covered at last, and add a secondhand gray t-shirt.

I check my reflection in the cracked mirror on the back of the door. It will do. I dump the dead boy's pants on the way back to my room. As glad as I am, it's kind of strange to get rid of them. I've had them almost as long as I can remember.

Now what?

I sit on the edge of the mattress to think. It's softer than it looks. Almost comfortable. I lie back, better to think that way. Tension seeps out of my aching muscles and I stare up at a ceiling speckled with yellow and brown grease stains. There must be some way to find out who I am. Someone might have reported me missing, but finding out involves speaking to authorities. I yawn. Some instinct holds me back. The dull ache behind my eyes ramps up to throbbing. I close my eyes for just a second.

And sleep.

I wake to the sound of a hundred people in the hallway outside my door. Blinking, I jump to my feet, weapon in hand. My sleep-addled brain takes a second to revise the noise outside to one person. In a hurry.

Still half asleep, I key in the code and the door slides open. It's the girl from the bar and she's headed this way down the hall. I'm starting to think there's something familiar about her, but I can't trust the emptiness in my brain. I fumble with the door, not wanting to be caught gawking.

My hope of remaining unseen ends when the toe of a heavy black combat boot jams my door. Purple painted fingernails drag the door open. Her lips curve. "Just so you know, these doors aren't exactly secure."

"Um, yeah, I see that." I'm talking like my mouth is full of sand. Probably because I've been asleep. Asleep. Hell, I hope my breath isn't too bad.

Her eyes, now green instead of lilac, study me. Amusement crinkles their corners like she hears the thoughts tumbling through my brain. Did I speak aloud?

She steps back, allowing me to appreciate that she's changed her shorts for some tight camo pants to go with the high black boots. "Talkative, aren't ya, Blank?"

"Who told you my name?" I blurt the question and feel heat rush to my ears. At least the new orange of my hair might help disguise them.

"I overheard it," she replies.

"Oh." The strange guilt of being near her sits heavy in my gut. But I want to keep her in the hallway. *Think. Think.* The noise of her heavy boots at high speed woke me; she was in a hurry. "Going somewhere?"

Good one, remind the hot girl she has somewhere to be.

A challenging grin lights up her face. "Why? Do you want to play with the big boys?"

The question hangs in the dingy hallway, keeping the cobwebs and peeling paint company. Before I ask her what or whom she's talking about, she executes a graceful turn and heads toward the stairs.

"Is that an invitation?" I call after her.

But she's out of sight.

Chapter Five

[Asher]

Lady has a surprise? For me? Shock leaves me speechless. Fishies do *not* give their servants anything but weary muscles and gossip to share below. Her frown indicates she's waiting for some kind of response. I cough to clear my throat. "Um…okay."

Smooth Asher.

I rise and cross to where she stands in the middle of a yellow and white striped rug. The softness beneath my feet is unbalancing after the hard floors I'm used to, but not so much as this woman.

Her hand reaches out and clutches my sleeve. The long nails remind me of bird talons in the history recordings of Earth I watched as a child. "I'm so excited," she says in a breathy voice. "I just know you'll love it."

With Lady's hand tugging my arm, I stumble alongside her through a door and into a little hallway. Three identical doors lead off it. She steers us through the middle one. A strange mixture of fear and excitement pounds just behind my eyes. I don't dare blink in case I miss something.

This is my chance to get inside knowledge on the layout of their quarters. Selfishly, I want to know about the surprise too.

I try to keep my bearings in relation to the level below. We turn into another small hallway. Here, there are three doors again, but these are not identical. The surface of the one furthest left is freshly painted. It's the same bright yellow as the entry room.

Her hand reaches out. Her pudgy fingers close around the silver handle. I hold my breath as her knuckles whiten on the handle and she begins turning.

Then she freezes and her head twitches like she's shaking an annoying bug off her face. Her hand drops to her side, and she steps away. "Afternoon tea first, don't you think?"

"Afternoon tea?" I repeat dumbly, following behind. I glance back over my shoulder at the mysterious door. If I was curious before, I'm now desperate to know what's behind it, but I have no choice but to follow Lady, for this is my role.

"Yes. That would be lovely." She returns to the first hallway. "You don't mind having it in the kitchen do you?" she asks over her plump shoulder.

"No."

Maybe I was too quick to be glad Davyd left. Nerves settle in my belly. If I do the wrong thing while serving her tea, I will be sent away and lose this opportunity.

But when we enter the kitchen she gestures for me to take a place at the intimate real wood table. I hesitate. Lifers do not sit for afternoon tea. Certainly not with Fishies.

Nobody seems to have told Lady that.

"Sit."

I obey. The muted color of the walls echoes the browns from the outer hallway. A framed picture of an Earth sunset claims pride of place on the wall. Everything is clean, fresh and warm. No scratches on anything, no stains, no arguments drifting from other families sharing too small a space. This is what I imagined when I pictured Samuai's life away from me.

Lady places a covered tray in the center of the table on a white cloth and lifts the lid. Inside is a perfectly round cake.

My mouth waters and my stomach growls in a most uncivilized manner. Fluffy white icing tops a pale yellow sponge. I've seen such items being prepared in the Lifer's kitchen for those on the upper levels but never had the chance to taste. Our food is plain, filling fare. All the better for hard work.

"Would you like some cake?" Lady asks.

I can hardly say no, but I'm not sure whether I should.

She smiles and takes the decision out of my hands, cutting us each a small piece. "Enjoy," she says. She speaks like we're friends. Equals.

"Thank you."

The way my stomach is churning, I'm more likely to chuck the cake back up than enjoy it. I use the small fork provided and break off a portion. With her watching me, I place it between my lips and the whole thing dissolves in my mouth with a burst of sweetness. "It's amazing."

Lady's brown eyes twinkle. "You know," she begins conversationally as she stands and fills a small pot with boiling water from the tap over the sink. "You look just like your mother."

The next bite of cake turns to sand in my mouth. I cough, sending small crumbs flying into the small cloth I grab off the table. I mop up the mess and meet her gaze, trying to act like I didn't just choke.

I do look like Mother. I've heard it said before, but I didn't expect a Fishie to have noticed. I didn't think she'd know who my mother is and I nearly ask, before remembering Davyd's warning. I have too many reasons not to talk about Mother here.

Lady doesn't seem to expect a reply, sitting again and biting into her cake. Lucky, because I have no idea what to say.

We share the rest of afternoon tea in silence. Finally, the last crumb has been eaten and the last liquid sipped. "Would you like me to wash the dishes?" I ask.

Lady shakes her head. "Of course not. We'll send the dishes to the kitchen below."

Her kitchen is a place to eat and serve food only. Copying her actions, I place my cup and plate in a large drawer next the sink. She closes it, presses the button marked 'kitchen' and there is a soft thud. I assume it's on its way down to where Lifers like me will add it to one of the compact dishwashing machines.

I grip my hands together and wait for orders.

Clearly, Lady is not an invalid, and she doesn't want me to cook or clean. What am I here for?

The question bounces around my head and I have to press my lips together to stop it bursting free. It's like I can hear Davyd's deep tones in my head. *"Do whatever she wants. No questions."*

But I don't know what to expect.

"Ready now?" An excited grin accompanies Lady's question. Her eyes glitter beneath the bright downlights. Shining with joy or madness.

She has to be talking about the surprise. I'm only here at all because she's ordered it. I want to be here for answers about Samuai and Zed, for myself, and information for the rebellion, but part of me is just a little bit excited. I've never been given a present. The only special occasions marked below are when the screen showing the time to destination ticks down another year. Even then it's not like the big annual ball they have on the upper levels.

"Yes, ma'am," I say.

The change in Lady is instant. Her eyes narrow. Deep lines appear on her brow and color blooms in angry slashes above her cheekbones.

"I. Told. You. To. Call. Me. Lady." Fine drops of saliva spray from her mouth with each word. They hit my face. Slide in a trail of disgust down my cheek.

I step back. Automatically, I lift my hands to prepare for the blow that must, must, must accompany such fury.

A heartbeat passes. A heavy thud rocks my chest and leaves my knees weak. Then the wildness leaves her face and again she's the warm, friendly woman who served me afternoon tea.

But I can't forget so easily. I breathe in soft pants as I lower my hands back to my sides. My mother's warnings make sense now. This woman is more than grieving; she's downright crazy. But it doesn't alter my desperation to see what's in that room.

I swallow the fear, fighting the urge to wipe my face. No amount of time in the training room could've prepared me for this kind of danger. "I'm ready whenever you are, Lady."

"Come, my dear."

This time I know where we're going. Again she reaches out and rests her hand on the silver handle of the yellow door.

My stomach flutters like it's become home to a nest of ship moths, the tiny flying creatures that hover close to the vents late at night. I take a shaky breath. The door swings wide.

It's dark inside. I don't know what I expect. More yellow certainly, but beyond that?

Lady reaches inside and the room lights up.

Hot tears sting my eyes. My throat swells. I blink. Blink again, and my nails dig into my palms. Behind the yellow door is a shrine to the boy I loved.

"Samuai." I breathe his name on a sigh of longing. I have no ability to filter my words for the company I keep.

Every surface is adorned with images of Samuai. Some recent, still more showing a smiling chubby baby, a dark-haired boy with a mischievous smile, a young man on the brink of adolescence, all awkward shyness.

My hungry gaze flicks from picture to beautiful picture.

How I've missed you.

My cry goes unspoken. Somehow I pick up the strands of my composure and pull them back in, wrap them around myself, trying not to let my insides spill out onto the black, shining floor.

"You like it." Lady breaks my stunned silence. "I knew you would." Her whole body vibrates in a jig of excitement.

"It's—"

Wonderful. Horrible. Heartbreaking. Agonizing. A million inappropriate words spring to mind and I discard all of them.

"Nice," I settle on eventually.

She leans in close and her floral scent fills my lungs. The sweetness is now cloying. Suffocating me. I have to force my feet not to run for the lower levels.

Instead of arching away as I long to do, I hold myself on the threshold and hope my smile doesn't look more like a grimace.

"His loss was a tragedy," she says.

She says it like he was the only one. Part of me wants to shout my brother's name to force her to acknowledge his existence, but as far as she's concerned, he didn't exist. I bite down on the words, offering silent sympathy instead.

She rewards me by cupping her hands around my ears, peering into the room and then back along the hallway. Her breath tickles.

"I know something secret about how he died."

"How did Samuai die?"

The question spills from my mouth. It hangs there for a long moment. Her eyes, almost the same shade of brown as her lost son's, regard me with a triumphant expression.

"Yes, Mother. What's your latest theory to explain the tragedy of Wonder-Boy?"

Davyd's velvet-on-metal voice has us both spinning to face him.

He stands at the end of the hallway, only a few feet away.

His gaze rests on Lady, but I know he didn't miss my question. Exactly as he told me not to. My hand rises to my chest to calm my thumping heart.

The light flicks off behind me, and the yellow door slams shut.

"I've told you before," Lady says. "What's in here is none of your business." Her back is pressed against the door and her arms are wide. She's gripping the doorframe like she's preparing to be pried away. Her eyes dart from Davyd to me like either of us could pounce at any second. I drop my gaze to the floor, aiming to project the image of an obedient servant.

The way Davyd's arms are folded show defined muscle from the training rooms. He could get past her if he wanted to use force. Now that I've seen them together I couldn't imagine him trying.

"Don't worry, I'm not interested in the shrine," he says. "I was requested to check on the suitability of the new servant." He speaks as though she's standing normally and waves a hand in my direction.

The tactic kind of works. She straightens and shoots me a surprised look.

"Asher is not my servant," Lady proclaims. "She's my friend."

His jaw locks. "Have you taken your medicine?"

"I'm not sick."

He takes a step toward her, his hands clenched at his sides. "You promised you'd take it if you were permitted to have Asher here."

His lowered voice carries clearly in the small hallway. From the tense line of his shoulders, it's obvious he hates to have to say it in front of me.

Now I know the reason Davyd came for me personally. He wants his mother well. For the first time I understand a small part of what drives him. And there's an echo inside me.

I would do the same thing for my mother. Lady slumps to the floor. Her knees buckle and her head hits the doorframe as I turn. Brown eyes roll back in their sockets before she crumples to the ground. There, her mouth hangs open and her pink tongue flops about inside as a seizure wracks her body.

Is she breathing? I don't think she's breathing. There's a speck of dirt on her cheek. She hasn't told me what she knows.

Why am I thinking inane thoughts when I should do something? I must do something. I will my legs to move, but it's all happening so fast.

Davyd isn't frozen. His confident hands turn Lady onto her side and make sure her airway is unobstructed. He clears the surroundings, I guess in case of another seizure. I move closer to be of assistance but he's so in control and assured. There's nothing for me to do but rock back on my heels and try not to get in the way.

When his hands take mine I gasp. Electricity sizzles across my skin, but he's not even looking my way. He places them carefully on Lady's crossed arms.

"Hold her still."

"Okay." I blurt out agreement.

He strides to the kitchen and pulls a small jar from a shelf. From inside the jar he selects a pink tablet.

I'm thankful he warned me; because when she begins to shake again it takes all my strength to keep her arms from flying free and injuring us both. Then he's back and kneeling beside me.

When she stills at last, his gentle but firm fingers open her jaw, unavoidably smearing the cherry red lipstick onto her cheeks. He presses the tablet against her tongue and gently closes her mouth.

"It will dissolve," he explains.

I nod.

Movement of the sagging skin at Lady's throat suggests she swallows. Her chest heaves and she's breathing again. Rasping, angry breaths.

Davyd's smile for her is genuine

Relief washes over me. I'm sure he's just saved his mother's life.

"Maybe you're not all bad," I whisper. I don't mean to speak aloud.

His hand grips my wrist before I see him move. His fingers are strong, just this side of painful.

"I'm bad. As far as you're concerned. Never confuse me with your dead boyfriend." He jerks his head toward Lady, his usually expressionless, gray eyes burning with emotion. "*She* is my mother. *You* are a servant."

I would not have done this for you.

The words he doesn't say shouldn't hurt. I won't let them. "I could never confuse you with Samuai," I say softly. It's meant to hurt, but he doesn't show he's heard.

He drops my wrist and I rub at the red marks he's left behind. I am not afraid.

"What did you mean?" I ask the question that's been nagging at me since he gave me my new orders and ridiculed my ritual.

"What did I tell you about asking questions?"

His jaw's set and good sense would tell me to shut the hell up. He's a Fishie, or close enough to one, and it's not my place. But having seen him care for his mother it's not that simple, no matter what he said.

"You told me not to ask your mother questions."

We're close enough that I feel the rumble of amusement in him. It makes me brave. Or maybe today's been so strange I'm thinking it could be a dream, and if it's a dream I'm going to wake up soon, and if I wake up without asking him, it will haunt me. "Why wasn't Samuai worth mourning?"

"I don't want to speak ill of the departed."

"Since when?"

He shakes his head. "Trust me, you don't want to know."

"I do."

My voice rises and Lady stirs at the noise. Davyd moves quickly to his mother's side and my opportunity passes. Together we carry Lady to the sofa in the big yellow room. I'm careful to make sure our hands don't touch. Davyd's always made me feel uncomfortable and uncertain. Spending time in his home seems to have amplified my reaction. I don't like it.

Reacting to Davyd is a distraction I don't need.

He stops me edging away with a hand on my shoulder. "If details of her illness become public, I will know who spoke out of turn."

"Yes, sir."

The words are empty because there's nothing about the upper levels we don't share. From Ms. Brella-May needing clothes made in a bigger size than anyone else on board, to Mr. Fitz preferring his bathroom attendant to be young. Talking about our masters is a favorite pastime.

Lady spends the rest of the afternoon reclining with her eyes closed. I do what I can, get her water, offer her food, but she doesn't want anything. Thankfully the pink tablet has stopped her fits, and I manage not to beg Davyd to stay when he explains he's going out.

He doesn't even look my way. "I will return in time for dinner. The order has been put through to the kitchen already."

"What should I do?" I hate the tentative note in my voice.

Annoyance ripples across his usually emotionless features and he tugs a hand through his messy blond hair. "Your job. Care for my mother."

I stand from my seat next to where Lady rests and cross the room. He can be annoyed all he wants, but I will not let him treat me a dumb slave. I have a brain, I have valid concerns, and I matter. Our eyes are almost level and I tilt my chin to make up the difference. "What if she collapses again?" I ask.

"She won't."

"Ever? What if you aren't here the next time? Should I leave her to die?"

The pulse throbbing in his throat is the only sign my words have made a point. It's enough.

"Here." He presses a slightly discolored patch on the wall next to the sliding door. A panel opens and inside is some kind of intercom system. It involves small screens with each of the family's names below, as well as other key places on the ship. "Press Davyd and it will put you through to me." He taps a black unit at his waist.

I nod, but am trying to memorize as much about the intercom's layout as possible. There are more than the names, including a button with 'alarm eighteen' marked on it, and something about air purity. We knew the units the Fishies and Nauts wear and knew about the room-to-room communication system, but I didn't realize the two were linked. If we could get our hands on one of those units we could use it to see into the Control Room and affect all the ships' systems.

One screen's name is taped over. It takes me a moment to process the reason. Samuai. Then I can't think of anything else. What would happen if I pressed it now?

I shake the fanciful thought free. On a ship where everything is recycled, people are the only exception. It's tradition to cremate the bodies of those who die and release the ashes into space.

He's somewhere out there in the darkness. I can't call a star.

Davyd slams the panel shut. "Use it only for an emergency."

I nod my obedience. "What's wrong with her?"

His gray gaze fixes on me. "Grief." He shrugs. "It's only happened these last few weeks. Hopefully over time it will get better." His lips press together like he's already told me too much, shown he cares.

He strides from the room and I'm alone again with Lady. Time ticks by slowly on an antique clock brought from Earth that sits on the bookshelf in the corner. Tick. Tick. Tick. The only other sound is Lady's deep, regular breathing.

I have nothing to do but sit. The plush armchair is like a big squishy cuddle and I settle back into it. Zed would never sit still. I used to tease him that he had ship motes in his uniform and he'd wriggle even more, his pretend slaps at the non-existent bugs invariably making me smile. Now the thought of him makes me ache.

Rarely do Lifers get the chance to relax. I move the pillows and manage to find a comfortable position where I can watch Lady for signs of her waking and needing me. I'm bored in about five minutes.

The shrine in the room with the yellow door tugs at the empty places inside me where my forbidden love used to be. I long to see Samuai's face again. The quick look I got before Lady's collapse wasn't enough.

I could investigate the intercom system. Then I would have better information to report to Mother when I finish my shift. But Lady could wake at any moment. Or Davyd might return. I drum my fingers against the armrest. I stand and check Lady's water is filled. I count the number of rooms I've seen and make a mental map of the space.

My hands clench into fists. "Launch it."

Launch it, the Lifer's curse, is far from the worst language I've heard in the lower levels, but it's the one that's full of all the anger of our grandparents' agreement to serve life on the spaceship.

I'll check out the panel under the pretense of being worried Lady's slept too long. I can't sit here and do nothing.

"Did you say something?" Lady's voice is bleary with sleep.

There goes that plan. "Sorry, Lady, just talking to myself."

I wait for Lady's orders. I've seen her collapse once; the last thing I want to do is trigger another seizure.

"Come with me."

I'm not surprised when she leads me back to what I'm guessing was once Samuai's room, leaning heavily on my arm. I hover at the doorway. If I breathe deeply enough, maybe I'll catch a hint of Samuai's cinnamon scent. I try but it's useless. The ship's air conditioning is too good not to have aired this room thoroughly in the weeks since he died.

Lady stands by the wall. It slides back, revealing a small cupboard filled with clothes. Samuai's clothes. Three sets of the black pants and white t-shirt he wore almost all the time and, at the end, two of the black tanks he liked to wear in the training rooms.

My fingers twitch with a need to touch the cloth, to press it up against my face. I miss him.

Nothing is simple. Beneath the pain of missing Samuai is envy of his family. My mother and I were given nothing belonging to my brother. After he passed, his bed was cleaned down and his uniforms put back into the store. His space will soon be taken by one of the children graduating from the care center.

All we have left is our memories. The same happened with my father when the Fishies executed him for attempted rebellion. I don't wish this shrine, these pictures or Samuai's clothes away from Lady, but I hate the injustice.

"Here," says Lady.

She presses something into my hands. The soft, black material is warm and I imagine it's from lingering body heat. I shake out his tank top and the memories flick across my brain. Samuai training, smiling when announced the winner, locked in vicious combat with his brother. He'll never train again.

He'll never smile again.

I attempt to give it back to her with trembling hands, but she shakes her head. "He would have wanted you to have it."

"I can't." I gesture down at my clothes. "I must wear the uniform."

Instead of trying to argue she tugs open a desk drawer and pulls out some scissors. "You can wear it underneath."

We are allowed to wear underclothes, although the color is mandatory navy. Breaking the rules to have Samuai's clothes against my body doesn't take a thought. We trim the stretchy fabric and I pull it on over my bra. It clings to my skin. Soft. Now I catch a hint of Samuai in the air.

It takes me back to the first time I asked him about the tangy sweet scent. He laughed, throwing his head back and exposing the smooth skin of his throat. "It's cinnamon from apple pie, my favorite dessert." His grin turned cheeky. "My mother orders it for me most days."

I'd still been confused. The Lifers had fruit and berries from the modified plants in the farm but I'd never seen it in pie. My mouth had actually watered when he described the short, buttery pastry and the spice—incredibly valuable aboard a generation ship—used to top the filling.

He'd promised me a taste one day but never got around to it. We thought we had our whole lives ahead of us.

"Thank you," I whisper.

My words hover in the silence. A silence that allows the swish of the front doors opening and heavy footfalls to carry to where we stand.

Lady's eyes widen. "Davyd."

I too recognize his stride and try not to think about how aware I am of Samuai's little brother. I follow her out into the hall as Davyd reaches the end of it. His eyes don't even dart to the closed yellow doors behind us.

"Ready for dinner?" he asks his mother.

"Yes. Asher will join us. We'll eat in the kitchen"

Davyd shakes his head. "It is time for her to return to her quarters. The maximum shift length is eight hours."

His words appear to show sympathy toward me but I know he's not worried about my welfare. He only brought me here at his mother's demand and now he's using the first excuse to get rid of me.

I don't mind. My whole body aches with the stress of being on my guard around the unpredictable Lady. My small sleeping cot and the simple stew we're usually served for dinner have never been so appealing. Lady looks from Davyd to me. Her eyes have that wide-eyed desperation I've seen more than once today. "You don't want to go, do you?"

Davyd's gray gaze joins his mother's. As a Lifer I learned to lie young and well.

"It's been a lovely day."

The slight arch of Davyd's eyebrow tells me he doesn't believe a word, but *he* doesn't need to.

Lady's mouth spreads into a happy, hopeful grin. "So, you'll stay?"

Chapter Six

[Blank]

Still trying to shake off the bleariness of sleep, I grope for the sneakers I bought at the market and drag them on. My credit stick is already in my new jeans' inner pocket. When I shrug on my jacket with the weapon inside it, I'm wearing all of my worldly possessions.

I'm thankful there's nothing to steal as I key the door closed, after seeing how easily the hot girl opened it. Following her is a no brainer. Answers can wait until morning and making contacts in this city might help me work out where to start looking, since the authorities don't seem to be an option.

I jog down the hall and take the steps two at a time. I weave through the crowd in the gaming bar without seeing the girl. My heart drums a crazy beat as I hit the street.

She's not here.

My chest constricts. But then, there, between two stalls, is a flash of shining purple hair. I make my way through the nighttime crowd, still wary of those wearing green robes. My stomach rumbles as I pass a vendor roasting something on a spit. I realize I have no idea how long I slept.

The square is well lit, although smog hangs outside the glow of the lamps. If anything, there are more people shopping now than this morning. Vendors call out cheerful greetings and families smile back. If I wasn't so intent on catching up with the girl I would be tempted to sit at one of the big tables and sample some of the food.

I catch up to her on the other side of the market, near the alleyway I came out of this morning, and she throws me a smile over her shoulder without breaking stride.

"Decided to follow/join me?"

I fall into step beside her, still not sure I'm doing the right thing. With my memory gone, I can't let any possible clue go unchecked. "Where are we going? Why the rush?"

"I can't tell you and no one gets in after eleven."

It's later than I thought, but the sleep refreshed me. And being around this girl gets my blood pumping.

"You might as well tell me where it is. I'm going to know in a few minutes." What I don't say is that directions and locations aren't going to mean anything to me anyway.

She smiles that teasing smile and keeps walking.

Leaving the market place signals new territory for me. As I walk, up and down hills, I make sure to keep my bearings so I can get back to my room later. There's little light away from the bustling market and the wind blows icy through ruins and abandoned buildings. Faint moonlight shining between scattered clouds allows me to pick my way along the road. The sight of stars stops me for a second but I shake the wonder free. I must have seen stars a million times before.

It takes serious concentration to keep up with the girl and not sprain an ankle in any of the cracks or potholes, or slip down one of the hills.

"What's your name?" I ask, happy I'm not sounding puffed despite the swift pace she's set.

"Megs."

It suits her, short and no fuss, but cool. Very cool.

She halts at an intersection on the edge of a deep pothole. She unthreads something from the belt loops of her pants. I've never seen anything sexier. My mouth dries. She reveals a piece of black material. There's a challenge in the tilt of her chin. "If you want to go any further you'll have to wear this."

"A belt?" I ask, to buy some time before having to decide whether I trust her. I don't know who I am and I hardly know her. She could be leading me into a trap.

"Smart guy, aren't ya, Blank? Around your eyes."

She closes the distance between us with a graceful leap over the hole in the ground. I look way down to meet her challenging gaze. The green in her eyes is dark and glittering in the moonlight. Logic should send me back to my room, but only Megs seems to exist. Every step I take with her feels in my gut like it's in the right direction. Toward answers.

She reaches up to blindfold me. Her fingers brush my skin as she places the black cloth over my eyes. I angle my head to see beneath the edge but she's smarter than that. Unable to see anything now, I inhale her scent, fresh with a hint of apple like those I bought from the market. The belt's warm from its close contact with her body.

She tugs at the material and it forces me to bend lower. The blindfold tightens around my head.

"Now what?" My voice comes out all throaty.

"Now I lead you."

Her hand is small but strong in mine. I tread carefully alongside her, trying not to stumble. The last thing I want is to fall on my face in front of this girl. With my sight neutralized, my hearing takes over. Gravel crunches under our feet. A vehicle growls in the distance. Wind whines through nearby ruined buildings.

Whatever this city is, there aren't many people around, at least away from the market. The busy stalls patrolled by the green robes seem to be a center for trade. Surrounding buildings are mostly rundown and abandoned.

I am certain I am not from around here.

The lack of familiarity could be a result of my memory loss, but my speech doesn't carry the twang of every person I've heard since I woke in the garden. I've seen a range of skin colors here, but none the exact same caramel as mine. While I know about credit sticks and am able to name most things I see, it feels learnt somehow, like I haven't experienced it firsthand before now. The answers are in my head, I'm sure of it, but when I try to access them I get nothing.

Earlier, being around Megs triggered my memory of another girl. Something else that draws me to her. She could be the key to getting myself back.

She stops me with a gentle pressure on my chest and my hand lifts to remove the blindfold. Megs catches my wrist and holds both my hands in one of hers. I sense her standing in front of me, close, and I tilt my head down toward her, like I would if I could see. Her hand grips mine tight. She's stronger than she looks, but I'm confident I could shake free if I wanted. I don't.

"You're a trusting guy." Her voice teases, challenges, hints at a darkness blacker than the one created by the blindfold. "For all you know I could have lured you here to—" Her fingernail presses into the sensitive skin beneath my ear and trails, in a slicing motion, across my throat.

Fine bumps spread out across my skin and I shiver. She feels it and laughs. Her breath is warm on my face. I notice a heavy beat and it isn't my heart. Or hers.

And I can see. First Megs. Wide green eyes looking at me, her incredible mouth in a half smile. I swallow and drag my gaze away to check out the surroundings. We're in another small alleyway, different to the one from this morning. Here it's all redbrick walls and there's no market buzzing at the end of the street, just darkness in either direction and a thumping I feel deep in my gut.

The clouds gathered overhead while we walked. They make the distant darkness seem impenetrable. I follow Megs through a rusted gate. Beyond is a large tin warehouse. The noise is clearer here. It's some kind of music.

There's a big guy at the door, his arms are folded and he's got piercings in every available skin surface but that's not what freezes me to the spot. The big guy is wearing a long green robe.

Crap.

All my efforts to avoid them and I'm about to walk into some kind of green robe party.

Megs notices my hesitation. She grabs my hand. "Come on, Shamus won't bite."

I laugh. If only my worry was simply about the guy's size. He's watching me now and running would only draw more attention. Maybe a tussle with a kid in an alleyway isn't big news to whoever the green robes are. Here would be the last place they'd expect me to come if they are looking out.

I lean over and fumble with my shoe. "Stone or something," I say loud enough to carry to the guy by the door. As we approach, his three-ringed eyebrow lifts. "Bringing a stray?" he says to Megs.

She laughs. "Keane always says to bring any likely gamers. I reckon Blank here," she jerks her head toward me, "has potential."

Keane? That was the name of the leader the kid was reporting to. It's all I can do not to heave the stew I had for lunch on the security guy's rubber boots.

I hope the turmoil I feel inside isn't playing out on my face. The security guy looks me up and down. This close I appreciate that I'm actually taller than him. Maybe he won't snap me in half with one hand.

"Playing or watching?" he growls.

I look to Megs. Time for a guess. "Playing, same as her."

She flashes me a grin. I suppress a wince when the guy swipes a ridiculous sum off my credit stick and snaps an orange bracelet around my wrist.

Inside, the music is painfully loud. It's a sea of green, with people either wearing the robes or hanging them off the back of their seats. I've landed in a bigger mess than I thought. If I manage to get out of here, I'll think twice before trusting my instinct. I want to blend, but I tower over everyone and people are looking at me.

"We don't get too many strangers to the games," Megs says. I more read her lips than hear her, but I nod to show I understand. The warehouse is bigger than I thought and it takes a few minutes to wind our way through the throbbing, sweaty mass of people to get to the bar.

There are games everywhere. It's similar to the place where I'm staying, but more and bigger. "Why am I paying two grand for this?"

Megs hears over the crowd. "Trust me." Like I have a choice.

She orders us two drinks each and pays for everything. "Since you're so worried about the cost," she teases.

"I'll get the next round."

"Whatever."

We're stopped five times by people who want to talk to Megs before we reach an empty table.

"You're a popular girl," I say loudly. If the tables weren't so small she probably wouldn't be able to hear me. Most of the people who stopped Megs were male. Most wore green robes and the looks they gave me were less than friendly. So far no one has been introduced as the mysterious Keane and the kid hasn't turned up either. Maybe this won't be the disaster I'm expecting.

She shrugs. "They're probably wondering where I found such an overgrown guy."

"I didn't know you were a comedienne."

Her eyes narrow. "You don't know me at all."

She's right. But I like her. I like her attitude and her strength and her hot body. I like her in a way that has guilt lurking in the back of my brain. *She's not the girl for you.*

I ignore it. I'm still working out what the big deal is with this place. Past the games machines, the room disappears into darkness that not even the laser light near the DJs penetrates.

Megs slides one of the bottles across the table. I unscrew the lid and the whole thing warms up. It's green and thick and it's bubbling. I sniff it. The sour fumes make my eyes begin to tear up. "What is it?"

"*Focus'n.* You'll want some to concentrate."

I hesitate.

She turns the bottle, where I read the 'All natural' label. I'm not convinced but all the ingredients are plants or herbs. Megs drains hers in one long swallow and raises her eyebrows. She leans across and takes a sip out of mine. "So you know it's safe." She wipes her mouth, eyes sparkling. "Trust me."

Now there's a challenge. I take a swig. It burns my throat on the way down and leaves me gasping.

Megs hands me another bottle. "Water to wash away the taste."

I want the water but I don't want to look weak. So I take a quick breath and choke the disgusting liquid down. The water that follows is clean and clear and cold in comparison. Delicious.

"Have you eaten?" Megs shouts across the table.

"Not recently."

"Good. Less mess for later."

"Later?"

"Motion sickness is pretty common."

I swear the green drink is still bubbling in my gut. Great to know there's something more sick-inducing ahead. I crowd watch, losing my thoughts in the persistent throb of the music.

Every time someone in green robes moves close to our table I feign extreme interest in the other direction. No one pays me any attention. Maybe coming here wasn't so stupid. This Keane might be able to help me. This way I'll get the lay of the land without having to reveal myself and my strange memory loss.

I look back at Megs and meet her green-eyed gaze. I'm captivated. Despite the dim light and flashing lasers I'm able to discern flecks of gray in the green, green depths of her eyes. Not just gray but shades of brown too. Is she wearing some kind of contact to make the color so brilliant? Everything around me disappears to nothing. I'm lost in those eyes, counting colors.

I lean across the table to get closer. There's a darker ring of color dividing the green from the whites of her eyes but I can't pinpoint the exact shade. Dark green? Brown?

Megs blinks and the spell breaks.

She laughs. "Eyes, huh? Just relax, you'll get used to it in a minute."

It's the drink, not the girl. Or at least, it's mostly the drink, because I was pretty fascinated with her before I choked it down. I lower my gaze and try to resist the urge to count the fine dark hairs on the back of my hands. She's right. I begin to employ my enhanced focus without getting lost in the details.

I'm not sure which happens first but I notice the music has stopped and the lights at the other end of the warehouse are on. Like everyone else, I turn toward a huge room divided from the rest of the warehouse by a glass-like partition.

The darkness conceals the ceiling, if there is one. Inside there are huge boulders and scrap metal pieces drifting on unseen currents. On the floor, five small spaceships are scattered with their hatches open. The whole setup looks familiar somehow, like I've seen a game like this before. I blink and the hope of a memory fades.

The game resembles the graphics in so many of the games I saw at the bar, clunky games where players control spaceships and fire unreal-looking rockets to create low FX explosions in waves of descending aliens.

Without the music, the announcer's voice carries easily over the crowd. "Could all green players report in. Game starts in ten minutes."

Megs points to our orange wristbands. Not our turn yet. Good, I'll have the chance to watch at least one game before having to play. The games machines around this end of the warehouse are warm-ups for the main event. I don't bother with them. Pressing a few buttons and watching a screen won't get me prepped for whatever controls are inside the plastic and metal vehicles.

The music starts up again, providing a soundtrack for the players to make their way to the game entrance and then follow an organizer to their ship and get strapped in. We're not close enough here for me to see everything.

I glance at Megs and she seems to read my question. We weave through the crowd once again and nab a spot close to the glass. The partition is thicker than it seems, making the people moving on the other side a silent movie. Each ship's about the height of me standing and wider around and has a number sprayed on its hull. What was cool from a distance is less impressive up close. None are exactly the same, and I'd bet they've been recently welded together from pieces of junk metal and plastic.

"Are these things taped together?"

Her chuckle bumps her arm against mine. "Pretty much, but the games are rough."

Now, her comments about motion sickness make sense.

One by one the assistants slam and seal the hatches by smearing some kind of black jelly on the join. There's a hum and the glass in front of me vibrates. Nothing happens with the ships.

"Do they manage to get off the ground?"

Megs nudges me with her shoulder. "Wait a second."

The lights around us switch off and the playing arena lights up. Moments later the little ships rise off the ground in jerky movements. They dodge and dart through the crowded space, avoiding rocks and floating debris by a finger's width. And each other. The ships seem to be steering clear of each other by mutual agreement. The tubes protruding from the body of the ship that I assumed were weapons systems aren't being used.

I lean down toward Megs' ear, trying not to get sidetracked studying the shining purple of her hair. "What's the point? Are they trying to out-fly each other?"

She shakes her head and a strand of silky hair brushes against my lips with a hint of apple scent. "Gamers get five minutes warm-up with the vehicles."

"What if you fire early?"

"Life ban."

"Happen much?"

"Never."

The lights flash off and signal the start. Ship One fires, hitting Five, and hits another from behind. Flames erupt along the jelly seal. It looks real. Hot, burning, real.

"It is real," Megs says.

I glance down at her but she's watching the game. Am I so easy to read?

The ships don't get much of a chance to fire on each other before a line of green objects appear above them and move down in a regular pattern. The 'aliens' of the game. These fire in a regular pattern and are quickly dispatched but cause an engine to fail when they collide with a ship.

There's a lull between the first and second wave of descending aliens. I picture LEVEL ONE COMPLETE flashing up on a screen. Ship Three takes the opportunity to strike at Ship Four. An explosion in the smaller craft's right wing sends it ricocheting off a large rock. It smashes into the ground, causing an appreciative 'oh' to ripple through the crowd. This isn't a game for teamwork. I don't need Megs to spell out there will be only one winner.

I point to the still-burning craft. "What if the guy in there is hurt?"

"There's an emergency lever inside, but if the player uses it they can't play again for a month."

After the next wave of aliens is dealt with, only ships One and Three remain and they've both taken hits. They circle each other, using the debris for cover. Three scores a good hit, and One crashes to the ground.

As the lights come back on people hurry out to attend to the other ships. The winner's lifted on her friends' shoulders and three others are able to hobble out. A small crowd gathers around Ship One. A couple of assistants have a stretcher ready. It takes two others to get the girl out of the ship's harness. Her chin rests on her chest. Blood runs down the side of her face and seeps into her white t-shirt. She's placed on the stretcher and carried out another exit. Even with my enhanced focusing ability she doesn't move. At all.

I can't help but wonder whether she landed like that or wanted to play again so desperately that she chose not to signal for help. It looks like fun, sure, but that good? Maybe there's a decent prize.

"What does the winner get?"

"The player chooses before the start of the game." She shrugs. "Money usually. Information sometimes." Her eyes narrow. "Sometimes people have stuff they want to know."

I moisten dry lips. I guess I haven't hidden that I'm a stranger and she's a smart girl. My gaze returns to the place the girl was carried out, my breath fogging the glass. "The loser, what's in it for them? Injury? Death?"

"They get to play the game. A game isn't worth playing unless the stakes are high. It's simple, don't lose, and don't get hit. Play to win."

Unexpected anticipation zings through my veins. For all my questions, I want to play. I want to play desperately, now that I know winning could help me get information. The draw of the game comes from deep within me. Have I played it before?

Megs prods me in the arm. "We're up."

We expose our wristbands and the crowd parts to let us through. I follow Megs' lead and remove my jacket at the entry. I'm careful to tuck the weapon I stole this morning out of sight in the inside pocket, roll it up and leave it on a bench. I didn't realize how much I appreciated having it within easy reach until I have nothing.

We draw lots for the ships. It's a fresh set as the ones from the first match are in pieces. Now I get why they looked patched together. I'm in Ship Four, Megs is in One. A blond older woman and a guy about my age are the other players.

I head toward my ship with what I hope is a confident stride. It all comes to a halt when I can't even work out how to open the hatch. The ship's mostly a metallic gray and there are no obvious buttons or levers. There's a welded together crack down the middle. The lumps and bumps give a little beneath my fingertips as I run my hand over the join.

"Newbie?" a young tech guy asks.

I must look as out of place as I feel. There's no point denying it. "Yeah."

He flashes a grin. "I'll be gentle."

I glance over toward Megs. She slides into her craft while a girl tech assistant readies the harness. An excited energy gives her a kind of glow. She catches me looking and winks.

"Ready, bro?" The tech guy's waiting with the hatch open. I was too busy looking at Megs to see how he did it. I slip off my shoes. The plastic crate I stand on to get in cracks beneath my weight but holds steady long enough that I perch over the opening.

It's pretty dark inside. I hesitate and the assistant notices.

"Slide into the central cavity and then slip an arm into each of the side pockets. It's like a huge great suit of armor." The tech guy chuckles at his own description. "Except it flies. And you'd be screwed if you tried to ride a horse wearing it."

The guy might as well be speaking a different language. I understand enough to position my bare feet over the middle of the opening and drop, or more accurately, fall in. The squishy insides of the machine mold to my body on contact. When I slide my arms into the slots the guy points out, it feels like a big glove.

"I'm in. I think."

"Cool. Can you feel the different levers in the hand compartments?"

I stretch my hands, getting a feel for all the buttons and levers inside. "Yes."

"Make a fist with either hand and punch three times to trigger the emergency."

The anticipation in my stomach ramps up to nerves. I nod.

"When I lower the hatch you'll see the other emergency

trigger button. Just smash your head against that one." He laughs. "The whole thing is pretty well insulated. We haven't lost a player permanently yet."

The safety talk takes a while. All my competitors have their hatches lowered already. Hopefully it's just because I'm new, not that I look like I'm going to need it.

He lowers the hatch. It's black inside. My heart thuds and I resist the urge to stretch. There's a beep from somewhere above my right ear and a display appears in front of my eyes.

Megs was right. One of the prizes is 'archive access', whatever that means. I choose it with a flick of my wrist.

The controls are self-explanatory. There are levers for up and down, forward, and back, as well as several fire buttons. Movement of the hands, head, and feet control them. A countdown timer tells me I have ten seconds to lift off. When the engine kicks on, it vibrates through my whole body. The other ships around me rise into the game space and I lose sight of which one is Megs.

I need to work this out fast. The boring warm-up time when I was watching is slipping away too fast now I need to work out how to fly this thing. The controls fit into my hands like they belong and I feel the extra levers at my feet. No wonder I needed to lose my shoes. The display is down to four minutes by the time I rise with a flex of my arm muscles, jerking up into the air. There's none of the smooth ascension of the other ships.

Bang.

I duck and send the ship into a roll. My head slams into the brace on my right, and pain radiates from the contact. What the hell was that?

A scan of the display shows a radar screen with the obstacles and the other ships. I was so busy being impressed with getting off the ground I flew straight into a rock. It hurt. This might be a game but there's nothing virtual about it.

I force myself to concentrate. When I use the enhanced focus from the drink, time slows. When I think a little less, I find the mechanism for controlling the ship is intuitive. Before long I have the ship dancing under my control.

The display flashes. The ship shudders. Game on.

Chapter Seven

[Asher]

Stay? Here with Lady? With Davyd? The neutral brown walls of the small hallway close in around me. I imagine a terrified expression on my face in the distorted reflection on the shiny floor.

I feel like the flowers on the table I liked so much earlier. Forced into a narrow-necked vase with no hope of stretching out or escaping. My stomach flips.

"She can't." Davyd is the first to find words for the situation. He's strong and sure as always.

Relief gives me breathing room again. Of course I can't. I'm a Lifer. I live and sleep two levels below the Fishie quarters. My mother's there, and Kaih, and my other friends. It's where I belong.

That's why you spent so much time with Samuai? Because you belong to the Lifer world?

"I don't belong here," I say aloud, ignoring my traitorous thoughts, but no one's listening to me.

Lady folds her arms, glares at Davyd. "What if I need help during the night?"

"Mother, I'll be here."

"I want Asher to stay." Her voice rises on a petulant note.

The tight band around my chest returns. I've only been here for a day but already I sense that this woman rarely fails to get what she wants. For some reason she wants me. I don't dare ask why but it adds to the questions clamoring in my head.

"We'll get someone else," Davyd suggests.

"No." Her lip juts out. "Only Asher."

The Fishies aren't even looking my way, so intent are they on deciding what should be done with me. I know I'm a servant, but their arrogance makes my teeth grind together.

The faint sound must draw Davyd's attention. He moves to stand next to me. "She's a person, not a plaything. You can't expect her to wait outside your bedroom door in case you want her on a whim."

It's too smooth, too practiced and too different to everything he's ever said. I don't buy it for a second. But my jaw relaxes a fraction and a different kind of warmth spreads through me. And this is much more dangerous than my temper.

"She's a person, you say?" Lady asks.

Davyd jerks his head in the affirmative.

"Then you'll have no problem with me asking her." The full focus of Lady's madness descends on me. "What do you want, my dear?"

This is my moment. While I don't really have a choice, I could sway the decision. If I speak up now about Lifer roles and side with Davyd, I sense he'll convince his mother of the folly of her idea. If I don't, I have to stay.

Here, I have access to Fishie secrets that might help my mother and the Lifer rebellion my little brother believed in so fiercely. Here, I have hope of solving the mystery surrounding Samuai and Zed's deaths.

But the other servant never returned.

So be it. My arms wrap around my waist and the hidden tank

top, so intimate against my skin. There is no going back.

I ignore the united front Davyd is trying to present by standing at my side and take a step toward Lady. "If you need me, I want to be here."

The smile she shoots her son is triumphant. "See?"

He exhales a huff of frustration. "Where's she going to sleep? She can't be on call all night."

I know the answer even as Lady says the words. "Samuai's room."

"Lovely," I say, before Davyd offers another argument.

The evening passes in a blur. A blur of Lady's chatter and Davyd's glares. I don't taste the food I retrieved from the serving drawer for everyone. All I can think about is the night ahead. Alone in Samuai's room.

I'll be fine. I have to be.

When Lady retires for the evening, we part in the hallway. "The bed is made up fresh."

I'm not her guest; I am her servant. "I will be alert for your call."

"Sleep well, Asher."

When she closes her door, two down from the yellow one, I linger in the hallway. This is what I wanted, a chance to explore Samuai's room, but now that I'm here I find a million different reasons why I should wait out in the hallway alone.

"Scared are you?"

My head jerks around. Davyd leans against the wall behind me. "Sneaky, aren't you?"

"Watch your tone."

"Or what?" Lady wants me here and if I've learned nothing else today I know that within these quarters Davyd's not master. I'm weary, desperately weary, of the games and the undercurrents. An argument with Davyd holds a weird kind of appeal. At least I know he thinks I'm scum.

He straightens, all rippling, angry muscle, and closes the distance between us. "I don't want you here."

"Really?" I refuse to take a step back.

"I have better things to do than babysit a Lifer."

I recall Lady's earlier taunts. "Like following Maston around?"

He bristles, his gray eyes narrow. "You don't know what you're talking about, little girl."

Little? Mere months separate our birthdays and I'm not far from looking him in the eye. It's a diversion I'm supposed to snap at. He's pissed. The bunched muscles in his shoulders, the hard line of his jaw, the barely sheathed anger. "It seems I've hit a sore spot," I muse aloud. "The boy wants to grow up to be an astronaut."

The irony. He might have all the luxuries a Lifer could dream of but he's just as trapped by his birth as I am. I don't stop the giggle from escaping. It's hilarious.

Upsetting Davyd won't help my cause but I can't stop. Today's been all about biting my tongue and thinking before I speak and all fake. This is real. Now, with my heart pounding hard, I'm alive in a way I haven't been since Samuai died.

He moves closer. His hands hit the wall behind my head and despite my desire to stand my ground, I've edged back so that I'm pressed against the wall.

But he doesn't touch me. Davyd's all about control.

"I never saw what kept my brother so interested in the forbidden romance thing. You're pretty enough, but it's not like you were putting out." His gray gaze sweeps a lazy path over my body, lingering on the swell of my chest and fixing on my mouth. "If you even have the right equipment. Our women at least dress like women."

I should be afraid. I've always thought Davyd was just this

side of human, and having spent time with his mother I know there's crazy in his blood. But there's something in his eyes beyond anger. An echo of the hateful warmth in my body.

"Samuai loved me."

Davyd laughs and the dangerous moment passes. "Then why isn't he here?"

That's what I need to find out. I stay silent. Defiant. He drops his hands and waves toward the yellow door. "Sweet dreams."

I slip inside without looking back at Davyd although I'm aware he hasn't moved.

"I'll be right next door if you need me." His taunt follows as I close the door.

My legs shake and my pulse hasn't quite settled down. I breathe his scent, like I imagine a forest would have smelled before the Upheaval. I slump against the door and replay the conversation with Davyd in my mind. It seemed so momentous but it was nothing. He's nothing.

As my body calms down I allow myself to look around the room, to drink in the images of the boy I loved. I whisper again the words I said to his brother.

"Samuai loved me."

Samuai smiles back at me from a hundred different moments of his life. His brown eyes are warm as always but I can't quite meet them. My body reacted to Davyd out there in the hallway. How could I have let myself feel anything for someone else when my love has only been dead for days?

It won't happen again. I'll solve the mystery surrounding Zed and Samuai and make my mother proud. It'll be enough to make me feel alive again. I close my eyes and see my brother's face. Zed was so young and full of life. Too young to fight Samuai, even in practice. I open my eyes to the pictures of the person I trusted with my brother's life.

"What were you doing with Zed that night?" I whisper to the faces on the wall.

There's no answer from the images and the weariness of the day catches up. I slip between Samuai's crisp white sheets and lay my head on his soft pillow. I sleep.

***

"Asher."

A woman's voice. Mother? I fight my way to consciousness from a dream where Zed and I were children again, playing hide-and-seek. I couldn't find him. I never found him.

"Asher," the voice whispers. Not Mother, but familiar.

A weight settles on the side of the bed. Samuai's bed. My eyes fly open. It's Lady.

My hands grip the blanket as I make sense of what she's doing here in the middle of the night. She's wearing a thin, silky cream gown that hugs every plump curve. She holds a wax blob with a flame dancing on the end, spilling soft light. I've only seen such a thing on the Earth recordings. My brain searches for the word. A candle.

"Do you need me for something?"

When Lady looks at me over the flickering candlelight, it's like a veil's lifted from her eyes. The clearness of her gaze takes my breath away.

"I miss him. Every day. And the pain of it—" Her voice breaks and it takes a moment for her to regain control. "You see what it's done to me. A mother should not have to out-live her son."

She's right. Neither she, nor my mother, deserves what's happened. I'm reminded of the tears and mourning after the

Upheaval that we learn about in our history sessions. I know from the recordings that unfriendly alien explorers caused worldwide earthquakes and tsunamis. The threat led to the surviving rulers sending out a colony ship with us on board. Whole cities and states were buried, flooded. Islands disappeared. Everywhere people died, and the pain brought a planet to its knees. "I'm sorry."

She takes my hand gently, motheringly. "You know what it's like to mourn him, don't you?"

Unable to choose the right words, I nod.

My silent agreement's enough for Lady. "He spoke of you."

"Really?" All my secret hopes and dreams for our future are exposed in that one word. If he spoke of me to his mother, then maybe I wasn't the only one dreaming.

"Not often enough to make his father suspicious, but I knew from the way he said your name you had something special."

I want to open up to her but the madness of the day lingers. Just because she seems so normal now, it doesn't mean she won't use my words against me later. With one word she has the power to add years to my sentence.

So I say nothing, although I ache to be loud and proud of my love for Samuai.

She nods. Maybe my thoughts have played out across my face.

"You don't need to say anything. I know how difficult forbidden love can be." Her voice drops, filled with the pain of regret. "Believe me I know. Of course it never would have lasted. My son was meant for bigger things than a dalliance with a servant."

My jaw locks. "Why am I here?"

Lady looks at me with Samuai's eyes. "My husband informed me of my son's death. He said it was a terrible accident in the training rooms." Her gaze fixes on one of the pictures above my head and locks there.

I keep the strength of my interest from showing on my face. I don't want to do anything to disturb her tale.

She sighs. "And your brother was killed too. Ironic that Elex's and my boy should pass together."

Why? Why is it ironic? The questions I'm not asking crowd my brain, and I squeeze my eyes closed to keep them in.

"I was heartbroken. Unbelieving my baby could be gone. I begged to see his body so I could hold him one last time," she continues. "But my husband refused. I was told he'd already been cremated because the injuries were so horrific." She pins me with her gaze and there's an intensity about her that's all Davyd. "There wasn't time."

"What do you mean?" The question slips out and I bite my tongue. So much for letting her speak.

Please let me not have messed this up.

My interruption doesn't seem to have bothered Lady. She places the candle on the bedside table and clasps her hands together in her lap. "There wasn't enough time between the accident and the cremation sequence. It takes at least an hour to complete the protocols. I don't know why my husband lied, but I'm sure there's something he's hiding about how Samuai died." Her hands cup my face. "I want you to find out what really happened."

This woman has access to the whole ship. How will I succeed where she's failed?

"Where are the time logs kept?"

Her hands drop to her sides. "The Control Room. You'll have to go there."

Go to the home of the Remote Device that can end any of us in an instant? It's suicide. And the only place on the ship where you can see the stars.

"Why me?" I ask softly in case it makes her turn.

Her smile trembles and a tear falls. "You're the only one who cared for Samuai as much as me."

"What about—" I hesitate to say his name; like it will betray the strange affect he's had on me. "Davyd?" I manage.

She shakes her head. "No." Her face is hard. "He's too much his father's son."

I don't understand, but with Lady so odd I don't dare question further. I shove aside doubts and fears.

"I'll do it." It's easy to promise when it's the same goal that keeps me going.

She stands and looks down at me, the imperious Lady. "Do whatever it takes."

I lie awake for hours after she pads across the room, exits and clicks the yellow door closed behind her.

Getting inside the Control Room could mean so much to the rebellion. Ship legend says that there's a second Remote Device like the one the Nauts used to switch off my father. Maston carries one; locating the other would alone be worth the risk of getting there.

Excitement mixes with fear and I shift in the far too-comfortable bed. Lady's visit leaves me with more questions than answers.

What really happened to Zed and Samuai?

Why would the head Fishie lie about it?

What does Lady think a slave can do what she can't?

Fear settles in my belly like a stone. Heavy and hard. I am not going to be able to work out any of this without help. All my allies are in the lower levels of the ship. While I think Lady is on my side, the madness could return at any moment. My only option is Davyd.

Davyd, who—even as he saved his mother—said he wouldn't help me. Davyd, whose touch skitters awareness across my skin. Davyd, who I argue with every time we speak. Somehow, without letting him know my true purpose, I'll need to ask for help.

I have no reason to trust Davyd, not personally, but he's not hiding how important his mother is to him. And she asked me to find out about Samuai. Maybe if her questions are answered she'll be able to grieve properly, and then the clear-eyed woman who visited me in the night will return and stay.

I don't care about Lady. Not really.

Samuai, Zed, the rebellion. For them I'll get to the Control Room. Whatever it takes.

***

Sitting in Samuai's room, it's hard to escape the fact that he's gone, but I dreamed of Zed. A simple memory of playing hide-and-seek when we were children. Waking to the knowledge I'll never see him smile or hear his too-loud laughter again made my eyes sting and heart ache, but I have to be strong.

There's a knock on the door.

"Come to breakfast." It's Davyd.

My already stretched nerves wind up to a breaking point. "Coming."

I open the door with a thumping heart, but the small hallway is empty.

I'm supposed to be here. I'm invited.

No matter what Lady says, I'm a trespasser here. I'll never belong. A sharp tug of longing for my life and family below digs beneath my ribcage. When will I get to see them again?

My hand shakes on the kitchen door handle. I push it open. My heart stops. Davyd and Lady aren't alone. The head Fishie has joined us for breakfast.

"Come in," he says. His puffy face wobbles in what I guess is a jovial smile. His hair looks like a furry animal was laid to rest on his scalp. This man has the power to order all my friends and family cremated on a whim. He executed my father for mutiny.

I bow my head in obedience. "Sir."

His laugh is like slime dribbling down my spine. "Call me Huckle."

I hope the sound I manage is taken for agreement. Does no one here remember the generations of class divide? I step forward. One step, two. And I sit on the chair he indicates.

Do I act like servant or guest? I clear my throat that panic seems to have swollen shut. "How can I help?"

Lady raises her hand to stop me before anyone else speaks. "You're our guest."

My Lifer uniform makes a joke of her assertion, but I don't dare argue. I should have prepared for the head Fishie's presence, but I forgot about him amid the drama of Lady's collapse and late night visit.

I eat the food put before me. Part of my brain registers it's delicious but mostly I'm preparing for what my breakfast companions will do next.

Lady's back to happy crazy. Light and airy, she twitters about nothing to fill in the silence. Davyd's silent. His glare rests equally on me along with the others and I wonder what new thing I've done to annoy His Royal Fishie-ness. But the person I'm most aware of is Huckle. He's studying me like one of the samples from a new crop down on the farm being tested by the workers.

At the end of the meal, I'm permitted to help clear the table and load the dishes into the chute for the kitchen.

"Leave us now." Huckle's command cuts through the silence. I head for the door, but his hand comes down heavy on my shoulder. "Not you."

I freeze.

Lady is gone in a blink but Davyd takes his time. The look he shoots me is full of something. There's the usual disdain for my station, the sullenness of earlier, and there, just before the door closes, a flash of sympathy.

My nerves solidify to dread.

"Sit."

I do as ordered. At the same time, I try to read his face. His is a face that has nothing of Davyd or Samuai. The bloated cheeks, fat lips and upturned nose remind me of the pigs from the Earth recordings, animals that died out before one generation had passed on board. Is he angry?

He sits next to me. The expression 'too close for comfort' suddenly makes a whole lot of sense—and that's from someone raised in the cramped Lifer quarters where physical privacy is only a dream.

I resist edging away.

He leans in close. There's a sour note to his breath. "I know about the new rebellion."

Somehow I don't choke or cry out or faint or react at all. On the outside anyway. "What rebellion?"

His clenched fist slams into the warm wood of the tabletop. "Don't play games with me, little girly. You know what happened the last time your people tried to take control of the ship."

I try not to flinch. What would my mother do in this situation? She'd be silent, stoic, never break. As sure as I know this, I feel that Huckle would hate her for it. And because he'd hate her, she'd find out nothing.

I need him to keep talking. He doesn't have to sit me at his kitchen table with his family to punish me. So he must want something else. I mentally cross my fingers and do what I haven't dared to since mother informed me of Zed and Samuai's passing. I cry.

Once I start it's easy to let the hot, salty tears flow. I taste my grief on my lips and pray that wherever they are, the dead boys will understand my show of emotion. I keep it to gentle sobs, like I'm trying to be strong.

It works. Huckle's chest puffs and he sits straighter. There's a satisfied slant to his mouth. "Get control of yourself," he says with scorn.

I hiccup and fake bringing the tears under control. "Sorry, Sir."

His waved hand dismisses my words. "Of course we have spies planted in the lower levels, but you are uniquely placed to give us information."

Spies? How could a Lifer betray the rest of us? Who? More importantly, what have they told the Fishies?

If our masters know about the rebellion, then as leader, my mother's in terrible danger. My heart squeezes at the thought. I will not lose someone else.

My brain races with a million terrified questions before I remember my act. "I just don't want anyone else to get hurt." I make sure there's a tremble in my voice.

He nods as though he expects my answer. "Weak. I thought so. Your avoidance of the training rooms told us you'd be the right person for this important job. We know Neale was groomed to take over from your father."

Neale?

"How did you know?" I don't have to fake shock. Whoever's reporting to the Fishies is deliberately misleading them. Mother's the leader. Our staff captain's more like an old woman than a rebel. He's more concerned with us servants fulfilling our duties in the traditional fashion than inciting change.

Mother's role has not been compromised.

"We have sources," Huckle continues. "This is what you'll do. Under the pretext of visiting your mother, you'll plant a listening device under Neale's bed."

Now I understand what he meant by me being well-placed. Neale's bed's only one over from mine. I guess the cameras set above the screens in the Lifer quarters could monitor activity. They've been in disrepair for years but no one's bothered to use the limited supplies to repair them. It's only this generation that there's been a plotted rebellion.

"I'm scared," I say softly.

This time the pat on my shoulder is more of a rub. The hint of dampness from his clammy hands through my thin top makes it hard to keep down the small amount I managed for breakfast.

"If you fail, or the intelligence we receive from the device suggests you warned them, we'll kill your mother."

He speaks so matter-of-fact that it takes a few seconds for my brain to process the threat. My relief that they don't know Mother is leader of the rebellion evaporates. In its place bubbles blind panic.

If I don't deliver the device she'll be killed. But Neale isn't leader. Even with a hundred listening devices planted on Neale, they will learn nothing.

And she'll die.

I don't exaggerate the heaviness of the burden he's given me. My head drops to the smooth surface of the table and rests there. Maybe if I move quickly when I plant the device I'll have time to warn Mother.

I look up but don't dare to meet his blue eyes in case he sees the fight in mine. "I-I'll do it."

He stands and slides a small clip across the table. "I've arranged with Lady for you to be released from her duties this afternoon. To make sure you comply with my orders, Davyd will accompany you."

Huckle leaves but I don't see him go. I'm too busy rubbing at the pain building in my neck. Tension makes the muscles so tight I'm afraid I'll snap. With Davyd for company there's no way to warn Mother.

And I need to get his help in order to keep my promise to Lady and fulfill the task I set myself when Samuai and Zed died—find out the truth.

Now I have two missions. Either one could get me or people I care about killed.

Chapter Eight

[Blank]

The game's speed is insane, even with my enhanced focus. The ship's an extension of my body. I fly and evade and fire and dodge and don't have time to think.

There's a lull in the aliens and I circle up high, using some metal debris as cover. A ship moves into range. I fire, squeezing with my left hand.

"Yes!"

Direct hit.

I must have hit a weak spot, or maybe it was already wounded, but the side of the ship splits open, exposing bare, vulnerable feet. The ship free falls, bouncing off rocks and debris on its way to the ground. My mouth dries. Were they Megs' feet?

I've been so caught up in the game that I didn't think about Megs being my competitor.

I pass low over the shattered ship. There's a three on the hull. Not Megs. But the next one might be. I rise back into the main game space with some of the joy missing. *Everyone here chose to play.* But the thought doesn't wipe away my fears of being responsible for hurting someone else. For fun.

The next wave of aliens stops my musings. In between, I fly mainly to avoid. Hanging back lets me observe. Megs isn't merely good, she kicks ass. Every time she has a chance to take a clean shot she nails it and her flying of the clunky ship is damn near graceful.

After the third wave of aliens it's just the two of us left in the air.

Can I take her down to win?

An image springs to mind. Megs on the stretcher. Bleeding because of me. The second of distraction leaves me open and Megs takes the shot. I jerk my knees up and chest down to roll but it's not enough. I'm hit. Pain shoots from a cut above my eyes and I blink away blood. The seal I noticed when I was getting in is skimmed and catches alight. The flames distort my readouts and I'm flying half blind.

My legs are warm. Then hot. Then holy crap the fire's through. Pain. White-hot and tear-inducing, it bites into my right knee. I smell meat cooking. Me. My stomach revolts but part of me manages to keep flying. Anything not to get hit again. I fire indiscriminately while I scan the half-lit display. I saw something. Where was it? Where. Was. It?

There.

Slamming my head back releases a fluid through the ship. I groan aloud when it reaches my leg and brings instant relief. The pain isn't gone but it's not spreading. I grit my teeth and drag my mind back into the game. Get it finished, then get some treatment.

I could give up. Land. Pretend I'm too injured to continue. My brain rejects the notion. It's one thing to lose but I can't give up. I won't. The solution is simple. I must win.

The ship's less responsive than before and it takes me a few seconds to locate Megs. She's up high, almost hiding. Maybe I was lucky enough to hit her. Good. The better to end this thing.

I head up. The relief from the fluid's short lived. It stopped the fire but sweat from the pain dribbles down the side of my face and I blink it from my eyes. I can't afford to muck around with tactics. I fly straight for Megs. All guns firing. The plan is straightforward. I'll hit her before she hits me. It works.

I land a few seconds after her and have to wait a frustratingly long time to check she's not hurt. The damage to my ship means it takes a few minutes for the tech guy to cut me out.

The hatch cracks open and his grinning head fills the space in front of me. "You won, bro," he shouts. "You didn't just win but you beat Megs."

Is that awe in his voice? A flush of triumph dulls my pain. "Is she okay?"

He chuckles. "She wishes she didn't bring you along." He finishes undoing the harness and hooks a hand under either shoulder, then hesitates. "Any injuries?"

There's a stab of pain in my leg like the question reminded it to hurt. "A burn."

He jumps off the ship, inspects, and then comes back up. "That's a good one. Nothing for it but to rip you out. I'll make it quick." He gives me what looks like a sweet. I place it in my mouth and feel a pleasant numbness flow through my body. "One. Two."

There's no three. Just the agony of tearing my thigh from where it has melted and fused with the interior of the splintered ship.

With the tech's help I manage to get to the ground and then use the side of the ship to support my weight. My unburned leg shakes and the burned one…The material of my jeans is mixed with bubbling flesh, blistering before my eyes. I swallow hard to keep the liquid I drank earlier in my gut and look away fast.

"You missed three," I growl.

"Better to get it over, bro."

He's probably right but that doesn't make me any less pissed.

Or steadier on my feet.

"Nice win, need a bucket?" It's Megs and she's grinning.

I fight to keep my upset stomach under control. She wasn't kidding about the motion sickness. "I'll be fine. Great game."

She shrugs. "Haven't lost one in a while. I'll be wanting a re-match." There's challenge in her words.

"Must have been beginners luck. How come you can walk so easy?"

"Experience." Her gaze sweeps over my leg. "Better get you cleaned up before you meet your new fans."

I take up Megs' offer of a shoulder to lean on after I put on my shoes and jacket and we hobble over to the medic station. Maybe I drag my feet a little more than necessary to have the excuse to hold Megs close for a few extra seconds.

"This is Blank." Megs introduces me and the illusion of being at home here vanishes. I need to remember I'm here for answers.

It doesn't take long for the medics to clean up my burn. They apply a balm and I walk pretty well on it straight away. Someone tosses me a tube of the stuff. "Three times a day."

"Thanks."

Megs is right about the fans. People who glared at me before the game gather around to talk to me about it afterwards. Everyone wants to go back over the best moves of the contest. I'm not sure how to explain what I did. Most of the time I wasn't thinking much at all. But that sounds pretty lame.

"Are you sure you haven't played this before?" The teasing question comes from Megs, who's stayed by my side and taken the teasing about losing top spot with good grace.

"I—"

A loud bang shakes the building.

"It's a raid!"

I don't see who yells, but panic grips those around me.

The lights flicker off and a wave of night sweeps the room. People cry out in fear. There's the sound of ripping, tearing metal, and a man screams in pain.

What the hell?

A familiar, small hand grabs mine. Megs. Her body presses against my side and her breath teases my ear. "We have to get out of here. Now."

The green robes who run the warehouse are obviously prepared, because dozens of doors swing open to the street and patrons disperse before the first officer enters. The officers conducting the raid wear helmets and are dressed just like the woman I saw at the markets.

The officer uses a weapon like the one I pulled from my jacket to line up a young green-robed boy from behind.

"Watch out kid," I yell, but my warning's caught in the rush and he doesn't hear.

The officer raises her weapon and fires. The boy in the green robe crumples mid-stride and the officer turns her attention to her next victim.

"My brother," Megs mouths, looking up at me. "He's not supposed to be here. I didn't know."

I don't stop to think.

The extra focus from the drink courses in my bloodstream and everything around me moves like it's in slow motion. I easily dislodge Megs' grip on my hand. Once free, I push against the mass of bodies fleeing the building. Their wide-eyed, panicked faces tell the story. You'd have to be crazy to head back toward the officers. Maybe I am.

My height gives me an advantage. I don't lose sight of the boy despite the crowd between us. It's probably a lost cause. I might not have a memory with details of my own life but I know people don't fall like that and get up and walk away. But the image of the dead boy from this morning won't let me give up.

I thought I'd lost Megs in my concern for her brother, but she's by his side before me. She's on her knees in the dirt and tears leave a shining trail on her cheeks.

Megs' hands fumble in the shadows at his neck. Looking for a pulse I guess. She gulps. "He's alive."

Another girl…another brother…I almost… The faint memory's gone before it solidifies in my brain.

There's no time to check whether moving the kid's a good idea. Either way I can't leave him here at the mercy of those who hurt him. With Megs' help, I slide one arm under his knees and the other under his shoulders and haul him into my arms.

A convulsion of pain arches his body and he screams, deep in his throat. It's not loud but it rips through me. Again, a half memory of another boy crying weakens my knees and I almost land us both face first on the floor.

The memory happens in a heartbeat.

I pull myself into the present. He's lighter than he looks. I stand. He arches again. His dark green hood falls back. It's the boy from the alleyway. "Hello again, buddy."

It shouldn't surprise me to find him here. This rundown city doesn't seem big. The fact he's Megs' brother explains why she seemed familiar when I first saw her in the bar.

"Buddy?" Megs asks. "His name's Janic."

There's no time for introductions. "Later."

We move with the crowd now. Megs tries to clear a path in the mass of panicked people. Through the doors and out onto the street. We're on the opposite side of the warehouse, where we arrived. I think. I'm lost. I have to hope Megs knows somewhere safe to go.

"Hey. Hey you. Stop there," a deep male voice shouts behind us.

It's an officer. I glance behind and he's a dozen feet away, weapon in hand. Playing a hunch from the morning, I move my body between Megs and the officer. A faint tickle tells me he fired.

But I'm not hurt. It doesn't bring me down the way it did the boy. I was right. Whatever the weapon is, it doesn't affect me. I file the information away for later when hopefully I'll have time to think.

Then we're through a gap in the fence and away into the night. Heavy footfalls echo off the walls of the empty buildings around us but I don't see another soul.

We're on the street and a block away before we settle back to a fast walk. Megs obviously knows her way around, taking short cuts through abandoned buildings with confidence.

"Who were those people?" I ask without slowing. "Who would shoot a boy in the back?"

She kicks at a loose stone on the path. "Officers of the Company."

"Who are the Company?" I manage in between trying to drag oxygen into my lungs.

I picture her shaking her head from the movement in her shoulders. "You really aren't from around here are ya, Blank?"

We support Janic between us when the path's more difficult. Thankfully he's passed out from the pain, because here any cries could carry through the night to wherever the officers are searching and give away our location.

When we reach an intersection I recognize the crumbling orange wall from earlier in the night. It rained while we were inside the warehouse and the potholes are filled with murky water. The smog's washed clean, but the layer of dirt on the road turned to slippery mud. Every step is laced with the possibility of ending up on my face.

From here it's straight ahead to the market and the gaming bar. Megs moves left.

I don't follow. "Where are we going?"

"Janic needs help. There are medics at the station."

"The station?"

"It's our city headquarters."

"Who is 'our'?"

She runs her hand through her purple hair. The white lines around her mouth give away her frustration. "Forget it. I'll take him myself." Her slender hands grip the boy's shoulders and she strains to drag his limp body from my arms.

"Don't be ridiculous. You won't get five feet."

"I don't have time for twenty questions." Her voice breaks. "Janic doesn't have time."

The boy's breathing is shallow. I can't leave her to deal with him, but I have no idea what I'm walking into.

"I'll come with you, and carry your brother to the help he needs, on one condition."

"Anything."

"I leave whenever I want."

She hesitates. Then brushes a lock of her brother's hair from his pale forehead. When she looks up at me her eyes shine with unshed tears. "Fine."

"Lead on."

She does. We cut through a ruin, and it takes the both of us to maneuver Janic over the rubble. There's not an ounce of fat on his skinny frame, but he's heavier with every passing minute. My arms ache, but I ignore the shooting pains and adjust the boy over my shoulder.

A damp patch in my jeans spreads above my right knee. The burn beneath has long since stopped hurting. My injury is minor compared to the boy in my arms. I grit my teeth and tell myself it's only splashed water off the road.

"Nearly there," Megs assures me.

We enter another warehouse. There are no windows. When she drags the door shut behind us it's black. I blink and make out a narrow path between stacked crates.

I keep up with Megs and I wish there was some way I could take back my questions about the Company people. If I didn't already look different and sound different I've just put a neon sign on my head and it's flashing 'No Idea.'

I don't notice the sentry until we reach the final door. He's old, like really old, with white bushy hair and a matted beard. He's wearing a faded green robe with a hole over the left knee.

"Janic's hurt," Megs calls out.

The guy slouching against the wall is on his feet and by our side in an instant. "What happened?"

"Raid at the game."

He curses in a language I don't recognize but with clear intent. "No one else has returned."

I don't know these people but I get the implication. With the extra burden of an unconscious Janic, we weren't moving at top speed. Someone should have made it back before us.

Megs presses her fists into her eyes. Her shoulders shake. Is she crying? I've only known her for a short time but I'd bet it's not something she does often. I stand there silently holding Janic, wishing I could do more to take her pain.

Megs drops her hands and she's pulled herself together. "We need a medic."

The sentry leads the way through the door. It opens out onto another courtyard, graveled and encircled by high brick walls. I'm reminded a little of the garden I woke in. Was that only this morning? It feels like a lifetime ago.

It's empty except for stacked piles of rubbish either side of the far door. The walls have high windows. It's incredibly defendable. Are they at war?

No one challenges us but I see faces in the windows. Watching. The further we get into the compound, the more exposed I feel. I have Megs' word that I can leave when I want but she doesn't speak for everyone.

We're only halfway across the courtyard when the far door busts open. It smashes against the wall behind. A man and two women come through at a run. One of the women goes past us, to take the sentry's post I assume.

"Keane," Meg cries.

Keane, the leader I've heard so much about. He's surprisingly ordinary. He has shaggy black hair atop a big square head. He's solid but not as powerfully built as the security guy at the warehouse. He doesn't wear a robe over his jeans and white t-shirt. I'd built him up in my head to be a man mountain. I exhale and relax a fraction.

Then he speaks with all the command I would expect, "Was it a Q?"

"I don't know." She points to me. "Blank saw it."

Keane's black eyes focus on me and I get a glimpse of his power. "Was it a Q?"

I don't know.

"I…" Dust coats my dry mouth and my arms are aching. I don't want to reveal my ignorance about the weapons, about everything, so I change the subject. "I can't hold him any longer."

Keane jerks his head and two more men come running from the building. Between them they carry a makeshift stretcher. When Janic's eased onto it and carried away and Megs stays by his side, I feel even more out of place. But no one's firing at me indiscriminately so I'm one step ahead of being caught by the Company officers.

Keane gives the sentry a look and the old man crosses to my side. "Toby, look after our guest."

I fight a laugh. Look after? More like guard. I keep my mouth shut on the semantics. There will be time to ask questions when Janic's stable. It's not like I can do anything more to help him or Megs. I realize I'm starving.

"Does this looking after include food?"

Keane nods. The old man leads me into the building proper and down a long hallway with at least a dozen shut doors. Toby walks with a slight limp but his bare arms are still wiry with muscle.

"You carried him all the way from the game?"

"Yeah."

"It's a fair way." There's a trace of respect in his voice.

"Yeah."

The kitchen's at the end of a long hallway. It's on a platform in the middle of what looks like two old train tunnels. The station. I get it now. Long tables surround a work area lit from above by lights suspended from a ceiling I can't see in the shadows. It reeks of damp mold and burnt wood.

Toby slices some crusty brown bread and then grabs butter and meat from a huge, well-stocked refrigerator. He sees me looking.

"Some nights there are lots of mouths to feed here."

I can imagine. I estimate there were more than eighty green robes at the warehouse and that doesn't include those at the markets or the faces watching from the windows when we came in. A chill breeze whistles through the tunnels and I shiver.

Toby slides a sandwich across the bench, and I suspect there's a grin hidden beneath that beard. "It's warmer when the ovens are going."

"Thanks." I take a bite. The bread's fresh and soft, the meat and butter rich. "S'good," I mumble, my mouth half full.

"Blank, hey? Nice name."

"It's the only one I've got."

For now.

I'm swallowing my last mouthful of the sandwich when Keane joins us. He strides into the kitchen and owns the space.

"Janic should be okay."

"Good news." Toby claps me hard across the shoulder. "Thanks to you. You're a hero."

Keane turns his full focus on me. It's hard not to back away from the force of him. I stick to wiping crumbs from my mouth and sitting a bit straighter. I hope my cheeks aren't as red as they feel after Toby's enthusiastic praise.

"Well done."

I shrug. "I couldn't leave him there, he's just a kid."

"You could have, but you didn't. There's always a choice."

His words nag at me; they speak of something I can't quite remember. "Whatever. I'm glad he's okay." I want to ask about Megs but I don't want to show how much a girl I hardly know matters to me.

Keane's gaze drops to the exposed burn on my leg. "Do you need medical attention?"

"No." I show him the tube of ointment I got at the game. "This seems to be helping."

"Get the kid some new jeans from the store," Keane barks at Toby without his gaze leaving my face. "It's the least we can do for him."

Toby's exit leaves Keane and me alone. He straddles a chair opposite. "You're the stranger Janic reported this morning."

I nod.

"You must have something that belongs to us then."

He's talking about the weapon. I resist patting my pocket where it's stored. "I was thinking finders keepers."

"Finders?"

So it might be a twist on disarming Janic and taking it, but I sense that backing down to Keane won't win me any respect. He's in charge here and while he might not be able to solve who the hell I am, he'll be able to tell me what officer versus green robes war I've stumbled into.

If the officer who shot at me and Megs outside the warehouse realizes I took the hit but wasn't hurt like Janic, then 'the tall guy who doesn't go down under Q assault' would have to be in his report. Then they'll be looking for me too.

"Who sends a kid out armed with a weapon?"

I'm disadvantaged here as it is, in their stronghold with no idea of who I am. I don't play all my cards at once.

Keane is silent for so long I don't think he's going to answer, but then he sighs, and the leader is just a man.

"He wasn't sent out. He shouldn't have had access to the weapons."

No wonder Janic was so nervous and so easily disarmed. He stole it to play with the big boys.

"So I can keep it?"

"For now. But I want some answers. Who are you?"

"I could ask you the same thing."

He stands, knocking the chair so it smashes against a bench, shattering one of the plastic legs. His hands are fists. My heart thumps. "This isn't a game."

I rise to my feet, ignoring the stab of pain in my leg. There's only a foot separating us but thanks to my height he looks up to meet my gaze. If I want answers I'm going to have to give something in return, but when I say the words aloud it's harder than I thought.

Just get it over.

"I'm Blank. It's my name and it's who I am. I woke up yesterday morning with no self. I function, mostly, but I don't know this place and I have no memory of my life or where I've come from."

Keane blinks but other than that doesn't show any surprise. "Then you probably really need sleep."

"No, my turn. Why the raid?"

Keane considers. "Because the game's our freedom. They don't control it and they don't like it."

"So they want to control everyone?"

"You've had your question. Rest now. As interesting as you are, we have people out there missing and I'm needed to help."

The exhaustion comes over me in a wave so sudden I fear they've drugged my food.

But the nap I took hours ago at the gaming bar's only a blip in a grueling day. "Why should I trust you enough to stay here?" My words slur.

"I'm not sure you have a choice." When I fold my arms and say nothing he adds, "There are Company people out on the streets. There's no way you'll be getting back to the gaming bar anytime soon."

"Sleep doesn't give me any answers."

"You'll get some answers after you rest. I'll have Toby show you to a bunk."

"But—"

"You have my word."

There's no arguing with that, even if I thought I could stay awake to do so.

Like he's beckoned by some pre-arranged signal, Toby appears in the doorway with some fresh jeans. They match the ones I'm wearing. It reinforces my suspicion that the green robes and the market are somehow connected. The station's an oasis of life in what looked like a pretty rundown, deserted place when I walked through it with Megs.

"Thanks," I say. I go to follow Toby, but stumble and have to fight the need to vomit.

He's stronger than he looks and props me up with one arm as we walk. "The game and *Focus'n* does this to some people. Sleep and you'll be fine."

I've lost all ability to argue. He opens the third door, revealing a plain room with a single bed against the far wall and a set of drawers beside it. There's no window but thanks to a skylight I know it's still dark outside. "You'll find a blanket in the top drawer. There's a bathroom across the hall."

"Looks good." With the weight of the escape through strange streets, combined with the comedown from the game, it does look good. I can't wait to take the weight off my aching legs and close my gritty eyes.

But I have a question Toby might be able to answer first. "Has anyone else returned?" I think of the girl victorious in the game before mine, of all those people who spoke to Megs before we played, of the guy I beat.

"Not enough."

"I'm sorry."

Toby hesitates in the doorway. "We appreciate what you did for Janic, but if you're found anywhere in the station other than here or the bathroom, you'll be shot." He offers me an apologetic smile and closes the door.

Before settling on the bed, I retrieve the blanket from where Toby said it would be. I don't change my jeans, unwilling to risk opening the wound by putting material over the top of it. I do reapply the balm, exhaling in pleasure when it completely numbs the area. Logic tells me that sleeping here and leaving myself unguarded is insane, but I'm too weary to stay awake a minute longer.

I settle back into the bed's soft embrace and close my eyes, making sure the weapon lies within easy reach. All I can rely on here is my instincts. My instincts tell me Keane, while ruthless and maybe deadly, won't break his word. So far he seems like my best hope for answers and that's worth the risk.

Besides, what could they do to me in sleep that they couldn't do while I'm awake?

Chapter Nine

[Asher]

"I'm sure you have better things to do than come with me," I say to Davyd as we wait for the elevator to the lower levels. "You could take me down and come back in say, half an hour."

He shakes his head. "Father might believe the sweet little innocent act but I know better."

"Oh."

There's not much else to say. I plan to wait for the right time to ask him for help getting to the Control Room and the logs. The tightness of his jaw and stiff shoulders suggests now isn't a good time to ask for a favor.

A soft ding indicates the elevator's arrival. We step inside, Davyd never more than an arm's length from me. He takes his role as guard very seriously. We reach to press the button for the training level at the same time. My hand slides over his.

He jerks away like I have razor blades hidden in my fingertips. His gaze fixes on the doors. Anywhere but at me.

I think back to the moment of heat between us in the hallway last night. Maybe Davyd wasn't as in control as I thought. Could he hate me less than he seems? Something like anticipation skitters up my spine even as I reject the notion.

Then the doors slide open and I don't have time to think. My fellow Lifers look at me as I walk through the hallway toward the sleeping quarters. Davyd's a glowering shadow behind me but the stir of interest is muted. Fishies don't come down here, but questioning one isn't worth the risk.

I ignore them all. The listening device in my palm's tiny. It couldn't possibly weigh as much as it feels like.

We pass Kaih near the doorway. She offers me a tentative smile, flashing white teeth. Still here for me if I need her despite my brushing her off so many times the last few weeks. The device in my hand grows heavier.

Back when my whole world was wrapped up in Samuai and our secret romance, I'd be late all the time or forget to meet her. As bad as I feel about it, I don't regret those captured moments now that Samuai's gone, but she deserves a better friend. One not carrying in her hand the possible destruction of everything she holds dear.

I send her a message with my eyes and my attempt at a smile. *I'm sorry.* But I don't say the words aloud. Not with Davyd here. I walk past her without a word and fail my oldest friend again.

Think Asher. There has to be some way to warn everyone.

I duck to enter the sleeping room. And gag. Lingering body odor mixes with musty damp since the air circulation isn't at its best down here. Why didn't I ever notice the smell in here before? The day I've spent in the clean, fresh air of the upper level's made the dank, cramped quarters down here even more depressing.

I look for Mother. Did she worry when I didn't return last night?

There's no sign of her tall, svelte shape among the Lifers gathered at the sinks or in the one or two small groups talking quietly on the beds. My search becomes more frantic. If she's in the training rooms or swapped shifts with someone, I'll have no hope of giving her a message.

I'm deliberately clumsy as I walk the route between the beds to Neale's area, glad he's nowhere to be seen to earn me a lecture about proper behavior around my betters. I gain a few more seconds to think, or more accurately panic.

"Get your things, inform your mother, and get a move on," Davyd says a pace behind me.

I reach my area and fumble for a bag or something to put my clothes in. I try to draw it out, but the task is over far too quickly. I rise to my feet. "Mother's not here."

Davyd grunts. "Too bad."

I know what he's thinking: his task was to chaperone me down here and ensure I plant the device for his father. It doesn't matter to any of them whether I actually get a chance to speak to my mother and let her know I won't be back for the foreseeable future. It was only ever a cover story. But it matters to me.

"Kaih," I call. Davyd steps close behind me so that I feel his breath on the back of my scalp. A prickle spreads across my skin. It's a warning. A reminder he's here.

My oldest friend's at my side in a moment, eyeing Davyd with suspicion. "What's up?"

I hoped she might see me with Davyd, worry, and linger nearby just in case I needed her, but the actuality of it makes my tongue thick with emotion. "Where's Mother?"

A perfectly valid question.

Kaih frowns. "Elex should be back by now."

I've delayed all I can. I offer Kaih a tight smile. "Thanks."

She gets my conversation-over tone and walks away but not before I've seen the concern she can't hide in her eyes.

Davyd's hand grips my elbow, firm but not hard enough to hurt. He forces me to face him. "Get it done."

I nod. Like I have a choice. He releases me and I move toward the end of my bed. I fake a stumble. My momentum lands me in

Neale's space where I use his bed frame to drag myself up. And leave the device behind.

I close my eyes for a second. There's no going back now.

"Asher?" My mother's voice, but warped almost unrecognizably high-pitched it carries out across the sleeping quarters. "Is that you, darling?"

Darling? That's a new one. Must be for our visitor. "It is me, Mother."

She hurries between the beds and I move to meet her halfway, feeling Davyd follow. I need to get away from the device and think of a way to warn Mother. It's going to be pretty difficult with Davyd close enough to hear every word.

When she embraces me I notice dampness on her back and strain in each breath. Kaih must have run to find her while I planted the device. Mother presses me close and her heart races against my own chest.

I open my mouth to tell her and feel Davyd's hand on my back. He's too close.

"I've been asked to stay on the upper levels with Lady," I explain loudly.

Her eyes narrow at the woman's title but she manages to keep her response to the expected worries of a parent. "For how long? Will you be allowed to visit? I'll miss you."

"I'm not sure." I glance over my shoulder at Davyd but he shrugs. I guess the whims of his mother are as mysterious to him as they are to me.

My mother asks some more questions I don't have enough answers to and lectures me on good behavior. None of my words are the warning I need to give her. I'm hoping we get a little time before Davyd escorts me back to the upper levels since the whole pretext of our trip was seeing my mother.

As I listen, I'm thinking. How do I get Davyd far enough

away from us to be able to speak to Mother undetected? It's not like I've ever been able to vomit on command and I saw how he was with his mother, a fake collapse wouldn't bother him at all.

What bothers Davyd?

I flash back to the elevator when I touched him unexpectedly. *I* trouble Davyd sometimes. There's a connection between us that he likes about as much as I do. And he's always strange when I remind him of my relationship with Samuai.

It's the barest glimmer of a plan, but launch it, I have to try something.

Sorry Samuai.

With perfect timing Mother, perhaps recognizing I need a delay, goes on about how I must always present myself in neat and clean attire when dealing with the Fishies.

I clap my hand over my mouth. "Oh my, you're right."

"I am?" Mother sounds a little surprised.

"I wore this top to sleep in last night. I should change it." I immediately start to dig in my bag for a replacement.

"Lifer." Davyd's voice holds a warning.

As though I'm unaware of his tone I turn so I'm facing him. His arms are folded across his chest and there's tension in the veins in his shoulders revealed by his tight black training tank top, a match for the one of Samuai's I'm wearing.

"It won't take long," I promise, allowing a small, embarrassed smile to play on my lips.

My fingers grip the lower hem of my top and the tank beneath. I meet and hold Davyd's gaze. His gray eyes appear black in the shadows but they're fixed on me. The room around us fades. The tug of awareness zaps between us. Usually, I'd look away to hide from the intensity of him, but not this time.

The flesh of my lower lip is tender under the onslaught of nervous teeth. The pain gives me courage. Focus. Down here there is no privacy and no point in attempting to change anywhere but in the open.

I lift my left hand a little first, then my right. A slow reveal of the bare flesh of my midriff. Davyd's gaze drops to my skin and then returns to mine. Hot. Challenging. I lick at dry lips. I lift my hands higher still.

He doesn't look away. Heaven help me. Is that appreciation in his eyes?

I'm holding my breath, trying to remember the point of what I'm doing. Distracting Davyd, driving him away. That's right. The future of everyone I care about depends on this working.

I lift my hands high enough to reveal a hint of bra. A curve of breast. His smile is satisfied. All male.

Not for long, I hope. I let the soft material of Samuai's tank top slip from my grasp.

It takes less than a second for Davyd to notice the black undergarment. His jaw tightens and I imagine his teeth grind together. He spins away and stalks toward the doorway. "Time to go."

It worked. Is there hurt in the too-straight line of his back? Not Davyd.

I'll only have a moment before he'll come looking for me. *Please let it be long enough.* Mother closes the gap between us even as I'm tugging the new top over my head. "Nice performance," she whispers.

It's either censure or pride in her voice and I don't have time to think about it. Under the cover of a final mother-daughter embrace I warn her.

"There's a listening device hidden beneath Neale's bed frame. They think he's the rebel leader."

She nods and I hope she'll connect the dots on everything I don't have time to say. Then I'm following Davyd back to the upper levels.

He's silent until we reach the training levels. "Mother doesn't expect you to return until dinner. You're under my supervision until then."

Is this where I get payback for downstairs? "Don't you have work to do?"

Young Fishies don't work shifts like us but they're given junior roles in the system. From what I heard yesterday, Davyd's somehow been allowed some Naut work too.

His slow headshake borders on menacing. "I finished up before babysitting duty." He stretches his thick-muscled arms above his head. "I could use a work out."

"There's probably someone free."

His jaw sets. "You."

"No. No way." He must know I avoid the training rooms other than the minimum required for fitness aboard the ship. After what happened to Zed and Samuai, I taste bile at the mere thought of going in there.

"Yes way. Unless you want to refuse a direct order?" His sigh is long and exaggerated. "Won't look too good on your sentencing report."

Davyd's father already noticed me more than I'd like. I don't need any more red flags if I hope to find out anything more about Samuai and Zed. I need Davyd's help and I don't want to piss him off any more than I have already.

But fighting?

My hesitation seems to improve Davyd's mood. He's smiling and against my will I notice again just how good-looking he is. I drag my gaze away. I have too much to lose by refusing and he knows it. I swallow nausea. "Fine."

There's a free room set up with a variety of suspended rock-like obstacles. They allow the full area to be used with fighters able to leap from one to another. Falls are rarely serious thanks to the protective mats on the floor. Directed lights create bright areas and deep, dark shadows. The winner is decided when the other player cries for mercy or when the wrist straps we collect by the door detect serious injury.

We both remove our shoes. It's strange to be in here. I haven't entered a training room since Zed and Samuai died in one.

Davyd seals the room, and flicks the switch to reduce gravity. The familiar hum vibrates through my body and I make a show of limbering up a little and familiarizing myself with the layout.

"Ready?" he asks.

Despite having already decided to lose, I can't help the lick of nerves beneath my skin. He won't be gentle. Not after what happened in the sleeping quarters. I tighten the wrist straps and feel the nano-probes nestle into my skin. I breathe in the scent of past fights—sweat and fear, adrenaline and triumph.

My mouth's too dry for words. I nod and slap my wrists together, the start signal. Davyd does the same. We begin.

He saunters toward me, his muscles rippling with every step. "You're pale." He arches a brow. "Scared?"

I jump lightly onto a rock behind me. It gives slightly beneath my weight. Now I'm looking down on him. "Are you?"

"Of you? Never." He follows me with a bound, but doesn't move to strike.

I wait for the attack. I've seen him in the training rooms, he'll act first. Patient, but deadly, and he wants to win. Sick of the tension, I jump higher and feel him on my trail, but still not closing to make contact.

Just fight already.

I stop on the highest obstacle. Under the direct beam of a white, bright light. Nowhere to hide. It's a long way down from here and being around Davyd gives my usually steady legs the shakes. Questions battle in my head. Was Zed this high when he took his last breath? Did Samuai die first? The waiting feels like one of the kitchen graters slicing across my nerves.

Enough. I launch a half-hearted kick at his groin. His left wrist swings down to deflect and his right follows up with a punch to my solar plexus. I huff and automatically block a kick while I catching my breath.

My hand rubs the spot I know will bruise in the morning. A leap to a lower rock seeped in shadows gives me a second to recover. Davyd's there a moment later. It's easy to drop to my haunches in pain.

"Mercy," I say, exaggerating my gasp for air.

His brows come together. "You're not this weak."

"It was a good punch."

"Fight properly or don't fight at all," he growls.

I shrug. "I tried that option. You weren't interested."

His annoyance adds gravity to a place where I should be light on my feet. He stares down at me. "What will it take, Asher?"

"To fight you? Why does it matter?"

One fist pounds into his palm in obvious frustration. "Everyone else on board lives for the training rooms, whatever level they were born to. Lifer, Fishie, Naut. Not you. What makes you think you're better than everyone else?"

The question hangs there. Hovering in the low gravity.

"I don't."

Is that how I come across? Does Mother think that? Did Samuai and Zed? I clamp my mouth shut to stop from defending myself further and giving weight to the accusation.

And then his words sink in. He's noticed. He's been watching me. For how long? I try to read his shadowed face for answers but the flat line of his mouth says nothing more than I've pissed him off again.

He glares. "Then compete for once."

He doesn't even hide how much he wants this.

I could use him. He wants me to fight and I need his help to get a look at the cremation logs. My distaste for pointless fighting must be secondary to getting the answers I need. I rise to my feet in an easy movement. "You want me to fight?"

"Yes."

I settle my hands on my hips. "I'll fight you on one condition."

"You're not in any position to be asking for favors."

"Whatever." A flip puts me on a lower rock and I swing to the ground, leaving him behind.

There's a long silence. "What do you want?"

"If I win, I want access to cremation logs. I promised your mother." I hold my breath.

"You want me to get you into the Control Room? You know it's forbidden."

"Yes."

A long pause and then a shrug. "Okay."

"I want your word you'll help me."

"My word?" He laughs. "You think that's worth anything when given to someone like you?"

Like me, a Lifer. Less than human. "Give me your word. Or I walk away."

"Fine. You have my word I'll help you get to the Control Room."

I slap my wrists together. "Let's get this over."

He gives the signal and we begin again. This time I move warily. I don't have the training room experience to trouble someone like Davyd but I suspect he'll know if I don't try. He's balanced, his weight distributed on both feet, the consummate fighter.

He holds his hands high. "Free hit to get you started."

I know he expects me to argue. Instead I step close. Punch him hard, aiming for the kidneys. My fist hits a wall of muscle and I cover a wince, but he couldn't hide his surprise.

"I said hit, not tickle."

"Now you're making me wish I'd gone for your face."

His chuckle brings an answering smile to my lips despite my determination to hate this. To hate him. Then he closes in. Swinging. One. Two. Three. My ribs are on fire and I can't breathe. I manage to block the next one and I swing as hard as I can for his head but he dodges out of my reach.

Can't breathe, can't move. That hurt. That really hurt.

I retreat to the rock, blocking his blows and attempts to follow me as I go higher and higher. Twice I land a good kick but my foot bounces off his muscled thighs. By the time I reach the top I have a bruised calf and my ribs still burn.

Davyd looks at me from the rock below. "Nowhere else to go, baby."

"There are always choices."

"Not for us."

He leaps and I attack before he lands. Left. Right. I punch with everything I've got. Then he's closer and there's amusement in his eyes. I'm scratching, clawing at his throat. There's a rush of adrenaline through me but it's gone as fast as it arrives. My blows have no effect. I can't hurt him. I can't stop him.

He grabs first my right wrist and then my left, holding them easily in one hand. I kick out, slam my forehead into his grinning mouth but he's too strong.

"See? Nowhere to go." His hand closes around my throat, but doesn't squeeze. "Nice that you put up a bit more effort though."

I glance at the ground a long way down. Launch it. "Always… choices."

I throw all my weight forward, knocking him off balance.

His hand tightens at my throat and then releases as we both go over the edge of the rock.

It is a long way down. Long enough for me to have time to regret my impulsive action. I might not like the fighting in the training rooms, but it doesn't mean I like to lose.

We land in a painful tangle of legs. I can't breathe and my body refuses to respond to the orders I'm sending.

Move Asher.

Then I'm scrambling to get away but Davyd's faster. He straddles me, holding me down with superior strength and weight. He presses me back against the smooth surface of the ground mats. Everything about him, from his cocky grin to his puffed out chest, screams victory. He leans close.

"You never fought against Samuai." His low voice caresses. His breath is warm and sweet on my mouth. "So nice to have something special, just between us." His finger trails down my cheek. "Then again, my brother was always pretty soft."

He's gone too far. "You think this makes you special?"

His smirk is answer enough.

With an arch of my back, I bring my body flush against his, forcing him upwards and follow through with a knee to the groin. I put everything I've been through since my brother and my love died into the blow.

Flesh crumples under my knee. Davyd's eyes bug and breath explodes. He doubles over.

I manage to stand. He's distracted, open for the finishing blow. I jab at the side of his knee with the ball of my foot. Hard. He topples over, his hands still covering his private parts, the color missing from his face. I crouch over him so my knee presses against the side of his neck. "Say it."

"What?" He barely squeaks the word.

The pressure of my knee increases just enough to make sure

he knows I'm serious. His brow arches. He's amused, I've just kneed him in the balls and could cut off his breath in a heartbeat and he's amused.

My breath hisses through my nose because my teeth are clamped shut. "Say it."

He hesitates long enough that I think I'm going to need to suffocate the bastard before he'll give in. "Mercy," he says loudly.

The game's over, but with the amusement in his eyes as he climbs to his feet, I'm not sure who won.

"What a little surprise package you're turning out to be." His gaze sweeps me from head to toe. "You're not as piss weak as you look."

I don't like that he knows how to get under my skin. I should've lay down and lost. Hand-to-hand fighting isn't the answer. The big battles are won with words, not losses of temper and lashing out. But I'm never going to convince him.

"The Control Room," I say simply. Time to remind him of his promise. Funny that for all my dislike of Davyd I have no doubt he'll work out a way to get me there. Oh, I fully expect him to twist his obligation, but he won't break his word.

Not even to me.

Chapter Ten

[Blank]

*B*reathe. *I can't breathe.*
     Something soft is across my face. Smothering. Soaked in a chemical that coats my throat and makes my mind wander. My hands scrabble for purchase on the slippery material.

Is it a pillow? It must be a pillow.

My nails find skin. Someone's hands hold the pillow down. Tiny, wrinkled hands. I should be able to dislodge them but the heavy weight on my chest crushes every other thought.

"Get off me." I waste precious air trying to yell but the material muffles the sound.

Bucking and writhing, I fight to get free. I fight to keep conscious. I fight to win. I know with a sudden certainty that if I lose this fight I'm dead.

The liquid on the pillow makes it hard to focus, makes me think how easy it would be to slip away to the fuzzy place in my thoughts.

"Why isn't this working?" my assailant mutters.

A woman's voice, old and stretched with time. I should overpower the owner of such a voice. I attempt to throw her off me, but I'm strapped to the bed with ties across my chest, stomach and hips. My legs are free and I kick out at the voice while my hands search for the skin on the pillow.

I'm not getting anywhere.

Think.

First I need air, and then I'll worry about escape.

I go still. Completely. Drop my hands. Relax my legs. Freeze the thrashing of my head. My lungs scream for oxygen. My thoughts blur. Black teases the edge of my mind. Despite it all, I play dead. I feel it. A slight movement of the pillow. She thinks she's won.

My hand snakes out, finds a wrist. I pull down hard, twisting her back and with my last ounce of strength and bring my knees up. Crack. The happy sound of kneecap finding bone is followed by a woman's cry of pain.

Yes.

The pillow lifts a little and I suck in air, scratching at the material to get it off my face. Then I'm free and gasping. Above me, the skylight's a black shadow in the darkness. I haven't been asleep for long. The horrible chemical that almost knocked me out lingers in my mouth. Sweet, sickly and gut-churning.

I fight nausea down and look around. A faint light shines around the door seal but there's no sign of my assailant. She must be on the floor. I blink, trying to adjust my sight and see deeper into the shadows, while my hands tug uselessly at the straps holding me down.

Scrape. It comes from the floor. The unmistakable sound of someone gathering themselves to stand.

Damn. I hoped I'd hit something vital. Any moment she'll return, and I'm lying here like dessert on a platter. The straps are tied too well and too tight for me to get up. The weapon I kept by my side is gone. I have to do something

"Megs!" I yell as loud as my aching lungs will let me. "Toby!"

My only hope is that the woman who attacked me works

alone. I have to believe that Megs, Keane and Toby had plenty of opportunity to take me down without resorting to sneaking in the night.

"Keane!" I shout again straining my chemically abused vocal chords.

A black shape blocks the light from the doorframe and my gut contracts. She's up on her feet. What the hell have I done to make this woman want me dead?

There's the click of the weapon that was within my reach a few hours ago. She swears again. "Why won't this work?"

I stretch out in the direction of her voice, but she doesn't move close enough for me to reach. Distance equals time. The more I delay her, the more chance someone will come to check on me. I clear my aching throat. "It's never going to work."

She says nothing, but I hear more clicking.

"I said," I speak louder this time, "the Q is never going to work. Any minute someone will come and you'll be discovered. Better make a run for it now." I inject my words with a confidence I don't feel.

"Better for you, maybe." There's frustration in every angry syllable. Frustration I don't mind. If we're talking, I'm not dead.

"The weapon's broken," I say conversationally. While I speak I'm listening for noise from outside the small room.

"They can't both be broken."

So she's got another Q. It's a hell of a way to have my immunity to the Q weapon confirmed. "Bad luck. Might as well cut your losses. Even tied down, I'm stronger than you and if I'm not asleep you won't get close enough with that chemical to knock me out."

As I speak, I'm picking at the edge of the straps. Somewhere there's a weakness.

More clicking is her only answer.

"Why the attack anyway? I don't even know you." In the silence after I say the words, I hear a familiar step in the hallway outside the room. The drag of the slightest of limps. "Toby!" I scream.

The woman comes at me in a rush. She uses the weapon as a baton, striking over and over again at my head while dodging my attempts to grab hold. I'm hit square on the nose and my eyes tear up. So it's with blurred vision that I see the door swing open and the light come on.

Toby's jaw actually drops. "Eliza, what are you doing?"

The woman spins to face the doorway, hunching over. To appear small and weak, I guess. "He attacked me," she says with a quaver in her voice.

Toby's gaze swings from me tied up on the bed to the weapon in the older woman's hand. "Keane will have to sort this out." He unhooks a device from his belt and waits before speaking into it. "Problems with our guest."

With me? More like problems with a crazy old woman on the loose. I'm in no position to defend myself. "Can you at least untie me?"

Toby shakes his head but there's sympathy in his gaze. "Keane won't be long."

When I wipe my watering eyes, my hand comes away bloody. One of the woman's blows must have opened the cut above my eye from the game. I move to get comfortable and a stab of pain from my leg reminds me of the burn. Once I notice, it's all I focus on.

I force myself to breathe slow and deep. My teeth come together and my jaw locks. Showing these people my agony isn't an option.

Don't think about the pain.

I switch my focus to my attacker. The old woman, Toby called her Eliza, is lean and fit despite her deeply-lined skin and her attempts at frailty. Black pants and a black sweater combine with a tight black beanie over fine white hair. She's dressed for the shadows and armed with both a Q and the chemically drenched pillow. Whatever this attack on me was, she planned it carefully.

Why? Did I do something before I was Blank, in the time before I remember? I try to catch her gaze but she stares at the door, arms folded, preparing her story for Keane I bet. It better be a good one. He's not stupid. It's clear who initiated this. The wait drags on until the tension holding Toby stiff in the doorway relaxes. Keane walks through the door a second later.

He takes in the situation at a glance.

I open my mouth but he silences me with a raised hand. Then he turns to the older woman. "Eliza, explain what happened here tonight."

"Oh, Keane, I'm so glad you're here. He attacked me. I was checking on him like you requested and he lashed out. What could I do but defend myself?" As she speaks her hands wrap around each other. Over and around. Over and around. They whisper a sound like two pieces of paper rubbing together.

Keane says nothing, just watches her steadily. Seconds pass and become a minute.

His silence bothers Eliza. The movement of her hands becomes feverish. Her eyes dart from Keane to me and back and her wrinkled cheeks flush. When she shrinks before my eyes it's no act. Her mouth opens and closes but no sounds come out.

Still, Keane waits.

I shift on the bed, to avoid the straps cutting into me. It would be nice if someone would set me free, but I sense Keane's making a point about exactly who the victim is here. And the demonstration isn't aimed at me.

"You don't know anything about this stranger," Eliza says eventually.

Keane nods. "Do you?"

"I know he doesn't belong here."

"The solution was to drug him in his sleep, tie him up, and Q him."

"But—"

Keane steps toward her. "Blank's here as my guest."

Her head drops, but not before I see anger blazing in her pale blue eyes. "You're going to take his word over mine?"

"I'm looking at the evidence." He picks up the pillow, sniffs. "You came in here with a chloroform-soaked pillow and a weapon. I didn't request you check on him. Every word you've said is a lie. Blank didn't attack you. What I want to know is why you attacked him?"

The glare she gives me is deadly and I see the other side of her face. A purple bruise forms just beneath her ear from the contact with my knee. She sighs. "He's a spy for the Company."

Keane looks to me. "Are you?"

It's a good question. I can't ignore the possibility that I was sent here to cause trouble. Not when my past is a mystery. "I don't know."

He flashes a smile. "At least you're honest." Then he turns to Toby. "Take Eliza to the holding cells. She can't be trusted."

"No," she cries. She fumbles for the weapon and aims it at Toby while stepping sideways toward the door. "You won't take me anywhere."

"It's broken, remember?" I pipe up in the hope she won't test it on the old sentry. At my reminder, she glances down at the black shape in her hands.

Toby lashes out with a roundhouse kick. Surprisingly fluid considering his limp. The weapon falls to the floor. In one movement he grabs her and twists her arm up behind her back until she moans. With her neutralized, he removes the second weapon and marches her out the door, throwing me a grateful grin on his way out. Then I'm left alone with Keane.

He picks up the Q from where it fell on the floor, looks at it a moment, and then throws it to land next to me on the bed. "It's not broken is it?"

I become very aware I'm still tied down. My original relief at being believed evaporates as fast as the sweat forms at my temples. "No, it's not."

"That fits with Megs' report of you taking a hit at the warehouse and Janic's earlier story."

He draws another Q from his pocket and flicks the safety off. "I need to be sure."

"You're going to shoot me?"

"Yes." In three steps he's standing over me on the bed. "I'll aim for your hand though. I'm not inhuman."

"And the straps?"

"It'd be a shame to waste Eliza's effort. This way you won't move and cause me to miss the target."

I nod but my mouth dries. Despite my experience so far of being safe from the weapon, it's not easy to be told someone intends to shoot you point-blank.

Keane holds my wrist down on the bed, firm but not painful. With the Q positioned over the palm of my hand he meets my gaze. "Ready."

I catch myself from another nod. It takes all my will to keep my hand steady and speak at the same time. "Yes."

Without hesitation he presses the small button. I feel the familiar tickle on my skin but no pain. A faint, round, green discoloration forms on my palm's surface.

He shakes his head slowly. "That didn't hurt?"

"Not at all."

Stubby fingers press at the mark. "Do you know how it works?"

"No."

"The technology for the Q apparently came from the Upheaval itself. Alien technology." He says it with a sneer. "Tell me everything you know about the Upheaval."

I search my memories of the worldwide disaster. "Depending on whom you believe, the earthquakes and tsunamis were a result of a terrible, natural chain reaction or alien intervention."

"What do you think?"

I catch myself from saying I don't know. I dig through the memories I've been left with. "My memory says aliens." I hear the surprise in my voice. I take a guess, "You don't think the aliens are real?"

"I think humans have done plenty to cause nature to reach a breaking point." He shrugs. "There are no aliens here now."

I have enough problems in my own head to worry about aliens. Like these learned memories someone or something put in my brain. "Does the government say they're coming back?"

"It's one of the Company's lines. Anyway." he gestures to the weapon. "Using laser-like theory, it's been tuned to the wavelength of the vibrations of the molecules it targets. Bone, skin, blood whatever. The breaking of those bonds in isolation is incredibly painful. And selective." Keane runs a hand through his hair. "Why not you?"

"I don't know. Can you release me now?"

He reaches beneath the bed and the straps across my chest loosen. "Here." He drags a rag from his pocket and throws it at me. "For your head."

My muscles protest the movement as I ease to a sit, slumping against the wall. The cloth comes away bloody when I wipe my brow.

Megs taps on the open door still wearing the clothes from the warehouse. "Did I miss the party?"

I'm stupidly happy to see her but play it cool. "Seems killing the stranger is the fun thing to do."

"Sorry I wasn't here."

"Me too."

Keane clears his throat. Funny, I'd almost forgotten he was here. "We were just testing to see whether the weapon works on Blank."

Meg crosses to stand next to Keane. "Does it?"

I hold up my hand for her to see. The green mark hasn't faded. When I lift my top there's a similar mark on my side where Janic aimed yesterday. Megs prods at the mark, her touch sends a whole other kind of tingle through my skin. The muscles in my belly tighten and she lingers a second before removing her hand. "It really doesn't hurt?"

"Really," I squeak, sliding my top back down and adjusting the way I sit. My ears are burning and I don't meet Megs' or Keane's gaze. "What now?"

"We need some answers. First, why do you think Eliza attacked you?"

"I don't—"

"Think."

My heart rate is slowly returning to normal and with the fumes from the pillow dispersing through the open door, I'm thinking a little clearer. An image springs to my mind. Not Eliza all in black and on a murderous mission but something else. Sometime else.

"I've seen her before. I'm sure of it," I say slowly. Keane waits as I mentally scan back through the events of the day before. It's not like I have a heap of memories to go through.

She wasn't at the warehouse or the gaming bar. Was it the market? There were dozens of people there and I'm sure the green robes are associated with the market but…No.

It hits me.

"She was in the garden when I woke yesterday morning. My earliest memory."

"What garden?" asks Megs.

I describe the slice of green in what's otherwise been a mass of broken concrete, dirt and mud. "I was naked and the old woman, Eliza, looked horrified. I ran for cover, assuming she was passing through, but what if she had something to do with the wiping of my memories?"

"Eliza," repeats Keane. He doesn't discard the possibility out of hand. A frown marks his brow and I imagine he's turning the idea over in his mind with what he knows of Eliza. "Maybe."

Now that I've started thinking I can't stop, the words tumble out. "It would make sense. She wouldn't want to be discovered, and it might lead to an unprovoked attack when word spread through the station that a stranger had arrived."

"She's been a bit secretive lately," adds Megs.

"Maybe," says Keane. "I've known Eliza for a long time."

It's a warning. I wouldn't want to make accusations without proof. "I need my memories."

"Yes." He stands and looks down at me as though he's come to a decision. "I think I can help you out."

It can't be that simple. "But?"

"I've heard of the process where the 'me' is taken out of people's memories. We've suspected it's been happening to green robes who've gone into the Company's New City and never returned."

"Can you reverse it?"

His mouth curves but it's more of a grimace than a smile. "We've been working on something, but it's hard to find a willing test subject."

Me. He's talking about me trying some untested theoretical process. What do I have to lose? My life. Two days of memories.

My gaze goes to Megs. I don't want to lose her. I've known her for only hours but the thought of wiping from my mind this time with her, the game, even the dash through the streets is scary. Almost sad. It's all I know.

Finding the answers was never going to be easy. "What are the risks?"

Keane's arms cross. "Brain damage. Death."

No.

The instant denial in my brain is all about self-preservation. My head drops into my hands. It's heavier than ever with the weight of the decision I have to make. Either I hope that I somehow remember on my own, or risk everything to find answers. The pounding in my head makes logic painful.

"I need to think," I say.

Keane nods. "What do you remember apart from Company propaganda about aliens? The garden where you woke and first saw Eliza, that was just before Janic confronted you?"

"A few minutes."

"Then what?"

"The game bar, where I met Megs."

She looks up at last. "Blank was a natural. When I bumped into him after my shift I suggested he come to the warehouse." Her nose wrinkles. "He thanked me by kicking my butt."

Keane's expression doesn't change. Maybe he's heard this from someone else who was there. "Then after the raid you brought Janic here."

"Yes." But there's something he doesn't know. "I wasn't alone when I woke in the garden. I found a dead boy in the pond." The nagging guilt expands in my belly.

"Dead by your hand?" Keane barks the question.

"No. I don't know."

A pulse ticks in his jaw. "That seems to be your answer for

everything."

I rub at the pounding in my temples. "What do you want me to say?"

"I want you to say you'll let us do the procedure." He exhales through gritted teeth. "But I won't force you. Before you decide you need to see the world you've woken into." Keane points to the skylight. "But that won't happen until morning."

"Finally some answers." Answers, not about me, but the green robes and the Company. I'm too amped up to sleep but at the same time I'm weary. The aftermath of the adrenaline rush from the fight I guess. While my mind's racing, my body's glad for the prospect of a few hours rest. "The last time I tried sleeping in this place I nearly died."

Keane rubs at his jaw. "You have a point."

"I'll stay with him," Megs says.

"Does that work for you?" he asks me.

Does it ever. "Yes."

He stands. "That's that then. See you in the morning."

When the door closes behind Keane I'm not sure where to look. I sneak a glance Megs' way and the full intensity of her gaze is on me. When she focuses on me, it's like I'm the only one in her world. It's a strangely familiar feeling and the nagging guilt makes me shift on the bed. "You don't have to stay."

"I want to." She pauses, twirls a lock of long purple hair between slender fingers. "I promised you'd be safe here."

I catch her fingers and still them, reveling in the spark it starts beneath my skin. "It's not your fault."

"But—"

The brush of my fingers on her soft lips cuts off whatever she was about to say. "You can't take the blame for the actions of some crazy woman."

She exhales in a long sigh and then flashes a cheeky grin.

"Okay, but your leg must be burning."

"It is."

In a graceful movement she rises and crosses the room to pick up the small tube I left on the table. "This the stuff?"

"Yeah, but I could've got it."

She returns and kneels beside me on the bed. "Let me."

I nod and settle back on the bed, bracing myself for contact. Dread of any touch on my burn wars with me wanting her closer. The wanting wins. My eyes close.

Careful fingers move the edges of the material away from the wound. "Wait."

I stifle a groan. My eyes fly open. Does she know what she's doing to me? I'm sure that's a smirk on those pink lips. "Why?"

She points at my leg. "It needs to be cleaned first." She picks up a towel and a bottle of water. "You might want to move off the bed."

"What about my jeans?"

"You should probably remove them."

"What if I'm not wearing anything underneath?"

She shoves the water at me and turns her back. "Be quick about it."

I'm quick, but I grin at her uniquely-Megs mixture of daring and shyness. The water on my wound's icy and burning all at the same time and not as bad as I expected. It's begun to heal already, thanks to the balm. When my jeans are back on and I'm sitting once more, I put her out of her misery. "I'm decent."

She settles again beside me and opens the tube. Waiting for her touch is delicious torture. Most of all I'm hoping I don't show any pain. I tense, waiting for contact. It comes with instant cool relief. I stifle a moan of pleasure as her fingers rub the cream into the wound in firm, confident circles. The sparks from her touch make my every nerve-ending leap to attention.

She shows no sign touching me has any effect on her. Her eyes are lowered, her lashes dark against her pale skin. Her lips are pressed together in concentration.

The pain's forgotten. All I think about are those lips leaning close, making contact. The need to know if she kisses with the skill that she flies and the spark when she speaks. It's like a game I can't resist playing.

She looks up, catching me staring.

I don't look away.

"How does it feel?" she whispers.

"Good"

I guess whether she wants to kiss me too but I wait too long. She stands, shaking her head. "I don't even know you." The words are softly spoken but I get the message loud and clear. I should have just kissed her.

She turns off the overhead light, leaving us in almost total darkness. My pulse's accelerated but in a different way from the last time a female silhouette approached the bed. She pauses at the edge, suddenly awkward after the intimacy of before. "Sleep time, I guess."

I wriggle sideways in case she's about to suggest one of us spends the last few hours of the night on the floor.

"There's plenty of room for two." She doesn't move. "You're safe with me."

Unfortunately. Because I'm too dopey to make a move.

There's a flash of white teeth as she smiles. She sits beside me and leans back against the wall so that our shoulders are almost touching. "I think I could kick your butt if needed."

"Like in the warehouse?"

She chuckles. "Beginner's luck."

We share a blanket and the warmth from her body wraps around me in a poor imitation of the embrace I crave. I settle back against the pillow, the wall hard and unforgiving against my spine. It's worth it not to be alone. In the morning Keane will want my decision.

I'm not sure I really have a choice.

There is always a choice.

The memory of a girl's voice trickles into my brain. It disappears before I lock it down.

"What do you think I should do?" I murmur the question to Megs, unsure whether she's still awake.

She turns to face me in the dark. Our breaths mingle. My eyes have adjusted to the darkness and I see the lines on her brow. She bites at her lower lip. "I don't think I'm the one you should be asking."

Her voice lowers, the rage in it snakes between us. "Answers about what happened to you might help in our fight against the Company. And might help me get revenge for what they've done to my brother and my parents."

Insane that I didn't think she had parents. Maybe I have parents and other family who want to avenge me with the passion in this girl's voice. I feel no sympathy for these people I don't remember and it's easier to feel for Megs. "What happened to them?"

"Killed by a Q." Her head bows to touch her knees. "The Company of course. Toby says they looked into joining the rebellion because a friend of theirs disappeared mysteriously. They were killed before they could decide. I was only five and Janic wasn't even walking. Someone left us at the door of the old headquarters and we've been with the rebellion ever since."

Where I expect to hear pain, her voice lacks any emotion. She could be talking about the weather. But her shoulders? Her shoulders shake with tiny, jerky movements. This time I don't think. I reach out and slide my arm around her, pulling her close to my side. I ignore the flash of guilt in my mind. I'm not thinking about kissing Megs, I just want to take some of her pain away.

She holds herself stiff. The knowledge I could be a Company spy rears between us. Without my memory I can make no promises, but I know one thing.

"I don't *want* to be Company."

She relaxes and leans into my side.

Chapter Eleven

[Asher]

The next two days pass in a haze of waiting. Waiting for Davyd to take me to the Control Room. Waiting for Huckle to say something about the listening device. Waiting for Lady's next mad idea.

For a whole morning I paint a strip of green along the bottom of the wall to 'make it more meadow-like.' The work's hard but rewarding and I make good progress until she changes her mind on the color. I'm not even halfway through.

Each night, under Samuai's watchful, dead gaze, I hardly sleep. When I do, it's broken with nightmares of him and Zed being cremated alive.

Serving Lady is lonely. It involves long stretches of boredom while she thinks, plans, or sits for hours staring at the pictures of her dead son. She collapses again and I note how the panel intercom works when I use it to contact Davyd. The pink pill does its trick before he arrives. Afterwards it's like the fit never happened.

While I wait for something to do, I think. Where do the pills come from? How are the flowers fresh every day? What is happening in the levels below? When will I get to see the Control Room?

On the third day, Huckle's waiting when I enter the kitchen. Usually it's just Lady and me because Davyd's avoided me since our fight in the training rooms. I don't know where Huckle usually eats. His sticky, expectant grin when I push open the door turns my anticipation at the sweet scent of pancakes to faint nausea.

He leans toward me. "You'll visit your mother on the Farm level today."

Good morning to you too.

"Yes, sir." The reason behind the visit dampens my happiness at the prospect of seeing Mother. It's only been two days but I miss her more than I imagined. Her strength is contagious. Despite not always agreeing with my decisions, she's always been a wonderful sounding board to help reach them. She asks the right questions.

The patience I've required in the last few days has been good for something. It helps me keep all my curious questions unasked in front of the head Fishie. I perch on the edge of my seat—strange that I think of it as mine so quickly—and wait for Huckle to tell me more.

Lady bustles around the kitchen, stopping to pour her tea just so, bringing stacks of pancakes to the table from the food drawer. She allows me to clean up but insists serving the food is part of her role as hostess. Who am I to argue?

But we're not usually observed "May I help you Lady?" I put deference in my tone.

Out of the corner of my eye, Huckle nods approvingly.

Lady's smile is warm. "By eating a decent amount. I don't want you fading away." She piles a huge serving on my plate.

"Thank you."

Under Huckle's watchful gaze, I force myself to eat. The Lifers on the levels below would enjoy the light, sweet, and delicious fare in front of me instead of the slop we get at breakfast. Zed would've loved even a single bite. Today, it might as well be made of shavings from the wooden table.

While I chew, Huckle scratches his nose.

I'm nearly done when he speaks again. "They're worried by your absence. Neale has delayed further rebellion meetings until they ascertain whether you are well."

I don't show my relief. Mother understood everything I attempted to tell her. That she convinced Neale to be distracted from his duties long enough to play the part of leader is a small miracle in itself. They deliberately planned this to force the Fishies to let me visit. "Of course I'm well."

He pats my leg. "I know."

Does his hand linger? I fight a shudder, scoff the last bite, and jump to my feet to clear dishes. I feel rather than see his slimy presence cross to the door. "Remember what will happen if you tell anyone about the device."

How could I forget? Lives depend on it.

He leaves the room. A light hand rests on my shoulder. Lady's painted fingers dig in to just this side of painful. "Be careful."

I'm not sure whether she's warning me about her husband's wandering hands, the trip to the lower levels, or finding out about Samuai and Zed. Really, it doesn't matter.

"I will."

***

The day drags, but finally Davyd calls for me to accompany him to the first of the lower levels. I wait for him in the entry room. The bright yellow of the walls no longer hurts my brain, and I still love the flowers.

Lady's in her private suite and Davyd's nowhere to be seen. My feet take me toward the table and the vase. The yellow petals are so vibrant and the smell so sweet. All day I've been thinking about my old life and old friends. Kaih would love these and I owe her so much.

I don't stop to think. As soon as I take one I regret it. If I'm caught...Davyd strides in before I put it back.

"Ready?" he snarls.

I nod, hoping my nervous sweat isn't visible.

We walk together. He won't allow me out of Lady's quarters without him scanning me out. Sometimes it's like an inescapable straightjacket of luxury, but I picture my brother and Samuai and it's bearable.

The elevator doors slide open on the shared level. "I'll meet you here. Be on time," he says.

"You don't want to come?" I ask sweetly. He doesn't, it's all over his face. The smells, the heat, the damp of the Farm level are so far removed from his pristine existence. When I planted the listening device, he had to be glued to my side. Now, he escorts me as far as the elevator.

"I have better things to do." His gaze flicks to the training room.

Memories of our fight make my heart drum a faster beat. I don't think I gasp or hesitate but the way he grins I think he knows the anger he brought out in me, the way he drove me to lose control and fight to win.

I smile. "Looking for someone who'll go easier on you?"

"I don't need to hear my opponent cry mercy to know when I've won."

Being the one to look away first feels like losing, but I can't stand the knowledge in his gaze. My clasped hands make a good focus, and when the elevator opens, I get in.

"Thirty minutes," he calls out. "Don't be late."

I hold my head a little higher when the elevator's doors close and I'm finally alone. The isolation of sleeping in Samuai's bed is different. Made worse by being surrounded by his family. At least on the Lifer levels my thoughts are my own as long as I'm not working. Thirty whole minutes of freedom before I have to meet Davyd and return to the upper level. I'm going to use them.

The Farm level's two floors below.

The door opens on a small hallway. The solid white walls here were built only two years ago when those above complained the smell drifted to the upper levels through the elevator shaft. It required the destruction of two farm buildings but the Fishies didn't care.

Following protocol, I wait for the doors to close before sliding open the first and then the second heavy door leading to the farm.

Animal poop, fertilizer, and beneath it all, one of my favorite smells—soil—hits me first. Father always said Zed and I were made to be farmers. From the time we could talk we'd beg to leave the care center where an older Lifer looked after the ship's children and go with our parents to the farm.

Here, there's warmth, damp, and relaxed activity. Nothing happens quickly. The timescale of crop production and animal maturity are lightning compared to back on Earth, but still happen over weeks and months. While the components of the Pelican were being built and sent into space to be put together in pieces like a massive 3D puzzle, scientists designed a self-sufficient farming system to feed the travelers in the available cramped space.

To get to the tanks where Mother works her shift, I need to cross the wheat belt. It was one of my favorite parts of Farm visits when I was a child. The compact fields perch on a huge conveyer belt at about head height, moving the crop through the conditions required for optimum growth and eventually through the stationary harvester.

Paths across the moving belt divide the fields to allow access to the rest of the farm. It only takes a few minutes to go around but Zed and I used to cut across. Now, I walk along the edge of the belt to a set of stationary stairs. At the top, I wait for the belt of wheat to move past, the golden plants wobbling gently. A path approaches. When it aligns, I take a breath and step on. The belt moves slowly but enough to make the ground unstable beneath my feet. With the memory of my brother's dares, I run along the path, determined to get to the other side before it aligns with a matching set of stairs on the other side.

Each slap of my slippers on the path echoes through the huge space, the biggest open area on board. Warmth from the lights above play the part of the sun and heats my skin. The spray of water from the spring that lies ahead hits my skin. An older Lifer looks up from her work at the laden fruit vines growing along the side of the belt and flashes a grin.

I leap off the other side, beating the stairs by less than a foot, and roll to avoid slamming into one of the rabbit pens on the other side.

"Still playing that game, are you?" It's Mother. If I didn't know better I would swear there's a sheen in her eyes.

"Zed loved the belt run," I say.

"He landed a little better, I think."

I laugh. "You weren't here the time he snapped one of the pen railings with his butt."

She joins me in laughter but it quickly fades. There's a lump in my throat and the pain of loss makes it hard to remember the joy with which Zed embraced everything he did. I squeeze my aching eyes shut. A Lifer stays in control; it's one of our few defenses. When a Fishie can switch you off at will, it's better to be able to keep your temper.

Mother's strong arms encircle me and she pulls me against her chest. I allow my head to rest on her shoulder.

"He'd be proud," she whispers, her hand brushing over my short hair and rubbing my back. She's talking about my part in warning the rebellion and gathering information, but I want to believe she means finding the strength to run across the wheat belt like my brother loved.

My control returns when I force myself to pull away. I glance around the farm area but the other Lifers are deliberately looking the away. A sixteen-year-old getting a hug from her mother isn't normal in the Lifer world, but neither are the losses our family's had to bear. Mother's respected and they allow us space.

We walk together to the tanks. She checks the temperature gauge and prepares the feeding pellets. I watch the plump catfish swim around and around and around.

"Is everything okay on the Fishie level?" she asks.

Her intense look implies caution. We know they've planted one listening device. There could be more. I nod.

"Can you help with the feed?" Mother asks.

The food pellet ricochet down into the catfish tanks gives us a few precious seconds of cover.

"We've been using the listening devices," she whispers. "Playing with false information and observing their response."

"So you haven't missed me?" I go for light but there's hurt underlying everything.

Mother's hand shoots out and cups my cheek. "I've missed you," she says with a fierceness that takes my breath. "Never doubt it."

"Yes Mother," I say with a mock salute, but the silliness keeps me from breaking down here where anyone could see me.

I relay what I can about the intercom system and the general layout above. The panel by each door sparks her interest, but I want to get to the decision that's kept me awake at night. "I'm going for the Control Room," I say finally.

"Why?"

Lady's suspicions about Samuai's and Zed's deaths are too painful to explain right now. "To get the Remote." Getting hold of that which could kill any of us in a heartbeat would change everything.

Mother's brows meet in the center of a forehead with more lines than I remember. "You'll be killed."

"I have a plan."

"What?"

"Lady is helping me."

The feed chutes jerk under her hands. "Don't trust her."

Does she think I'm stupid? Probably. Sometimes I fear I'll always be five in my mother's eyes, the age I first questioned the point of the training rooms. All the other kids in the care center couldn't wait to be old enough to get in there.

"I wouldn't tell her about the rebellion." I keep my frustration from my voice.

"Don't talk to her at all."

I say nothing. We both know in my position that's impossible.

Mother gracefully backs down, eventually meeting my gaze. "I'm sorry, Asher. She brings out the worst in me."

"Why?"

Mother finishes the first tank and we move together to the second. A flick of her wrist opens the chute to drop pellets into the tank. In the water below, large whiskered fish circle hungrily.

She sighs. "Fishie and Lifer kids have always trained together. Lady and I both excelled."

I'm not surprised about Mother. She's steely. I wouldn't mess with her, but Lady? "She's soft."

"Don't let appearances fool you. There's a fighter in there."

My Mother's strong and competitive. She wouldn't have liked being beaten by a Fishie, particularly not one like Lady. "You were enemies."

She sighs and shakes her head slowly. "No. Best friends."

This is like one of the puzzles Zed and I had in the care center when we were little, where you shake the board and a different picture comes out every time.

"Best friends?" I repeat.

"Inseparable."

Mother and Lady? I picture the two of them together and the image hurts my brain. "What happened?"

Mother's smile is tight. "What always happens between girls? A boy."

"Father?"

"No."

My head snaps around. "*Huckle?*"

She shudders. "God, no."

I'm relieved. It's odd enough thinking about Mother being interested in someone other than Father without it being someone so creepy. Mentally I flick through the similarly-aged men on board. They're limited but I come up blank. I can't imagine Mother in love with any of them.

"Who?"

"It doesn't matter." She concentrates hard on checking the temperature and fish numbers in the next tank. I swear her cheeks are pinker than usual. "Lady might have talked about equality and eternal friendship, but we're Fishie and Lifer. Something was always going to come between us."

No. My heart cries out in denial. The situation sounds all too familiar. No wonder Mother never approved of my friendship with Samuai. But Samuai wasn't Lady and I'm not my mother.

"We would have made it."

Mother doesn't argue, but she doesn't agree. "The woman has no love in her for us or ours. Be very careful."

"Is there any other way to be?"

We finish the chore in silence and my visiting time passes far too fast. I touch her arm. "I'd better go."

"My shift's finished. I'll go with you as far as the training level, if you like."

"Please."

I'm happy to have a few more minutes with her. Unspoken between us is the danger of the upper levels. I don't know when I'll attempt the Control Room. Despite Davyd's promise of aid, there's the chance I'll be discovered there and killed. Could Mother survive another loss? It's a question I never want to find out the answer to. I shut the lid on the pellet store. "Let's go."

"I need to scan out first."

"I'll meet you at the doors."

As I walk past one of the pens for the giant rabbits, a pink nose pokes over the top of the waist-high fence. I absently brush the animal's warm head as it nuzzles my thigh through the wire. When he was seven, Zed became convinced he'd tamed one of the babies and it would let him ride on its back. When he tried to show Mother, the mischievous rabbit dumped him in the water trough.

It's hard being down here without thinking of Zed.

His mysterious death shadows the happy memories. What's a training accident, anyway? The report Mother stole stated that something went wrong with the oxygen, then the gravity, and both boys were crushed. But what were they doing there together? Samuai didn't seek extra fights, and he would never fight someone so much smaller. Would he?

My heart isn't up to a dash across the wheat belt this time. Like the boring grownups Zed scorned and will never become, I wait for the path to align with a set of stairs and step off. I stand at the doors, waiting while Mother crosses.

The present I stole for Kaih weighs down my pocket. If she's not in the training rooms when I pass, I'll miss my opportunity. If I'm caught in the Control Room I might never have another.

I use the time I'm waiting to scan the whole of the Farm, but no bright splash of yellow breaks the monotony. The area's designed so that the animal pens are grouped together and the sheds ring the walls. A bright yellow crop of flowers would be impossible to hide.

Maybe Mother can answer where Lady gets getting them.

"Are there any flowers grown down here?" I ask while we're waiting for the elevator, my hand strays to my pocket and what I've hidden there.

"Why?"

"No reason."

She doesn't buy my attempt at casual, but she doesn't press. I hope she trusts that when I have something worth sharing I will. Her hand waves toward the area set aside for the specially engineered fruit plants. "There's blossom on the apple bushes."

"Nice."

The elevator arrives and prevents further questions.

I hate keeping secrets from Mother, but I'm doing the best I can for Zed, the rebellion, and of course Samuai.

We reach the training levels far too quickly. A part of me wants to cling to Mother and beg her to take some of the burden, but she's taught me too well. As we move through the hallway, our progress slows and I wonder whether I'm the only one in no hurry to part. It can't be easy for Mother all alone trying to lead a rebellion.

I spot Kaih coming out of the training rooms. Sweat shines on her face beneath the lights and her cheeks are flushed from exertion. Her smile widens when she sees me. "Asher." Her pace picks up to a run.

She embraces me, sweat and all. And I cling on. Happy, easy to understand Kaih, who I've brushed off whenever she's tried to talk. Until now. Another Lifer stops Mother to chat and Davyd isn't by the lifts yet.

I grab Kaih's slender hand and tug her closer to the wall. "I brought you a present," I whisper. With a glance around to make sure no one's paying us attention, I reach into my pocket and pull out the yellow blob of sunshine.

"A flower?" Her eyes widen and light up.

"From Lady. Keep it hidden."

She pushes it back into my hands. "If you're caught you'll get in trouble."

"No one will notice." I hope.

Kaih traces each petal with the most reverent of touches. "It's so soft." There's awe in her voice.

Kaih's delight makes stealing the flower worth it. It warms the inside of my heart where the darkness has lingered these past few weeks.

"Asher." Davyd's commanding voice carries along the hallway.

"Time to go," I say to Kaih.

She nods, tucking the flower into her pocket, holding the treasure I gave her close.

Mother catches my hand as I pass her on my way to where Davyd waits. The squeeze she gives me says everything. I want another hug but I refuse to show such weakness here. "Bye Mother." I squeeze back and then let go.

"Take care," she says to my back. Two simple words but I hear so much more.

Be safe. You don't need to risk the Control Room. I'm proud of you. I love you.

Davyd's silent in the elevator. I expected some caustic comment on my friend or family and when it doesn't happen, I study his face for a reason. He seems distracted, but beyond that I have no idea.

Just before we enter his family's quarters, he stops me with a touch on my shoulder, but stares ahead at the door. "If you're staying up here for a while, you will need to familiarize yourself with the clean room next to the kitchen."

"Clean room?" Is this a cover story to get me to the Control Room? Except he means inside the apartment.

His nose crinkles and he clears his throat. "Standards are different up here."

I copy him, sniffing and get a whiff of the terrible smell in the Lifer quarters. "I get it," I mutter. Davyd's trying to tell me I reek and he's almost being diplomatic about it. Somehow it makes the whole thing worse.

I don't care what he thinks, I don't. But I avoid his stare. My cheeks warm.

I lift my arms a little and inhale. It's awful. Down in the Lifer quarters we clean with a sponge irregularly at the troughs but mostly count on the UV shower to kill anything.

Obviously the Fishies expect more.

The heat in my cheeks burns. Did Samuai think I smelled too? Maybe he did but he was too much a gentleman to say anything. I hate that Davyd constantly makes me reassess my relationship with Samuai. Davyd's words twist and change things and Samuai isn't here to reassure me.

We go inside and Davyd disappears in the direction of the kitchen. I should be hungry too but embarrassment combined with my own stench is an appetite killer. I offer my services to

Lady but she declines, waving me away. It gives me some free time to use the clean room but I hesitate to ask. "Um…"

"What Dear?" asks Lady with a smile.

Her eyes are bright today and as far as I know she hasn't had a single episode. Maybe knowing I've taken up her challenge to check the cremation logs helps.

It's hard to spit out the words when she's sitting there so elegantly, so classy, so clean.

"I, ah, should probably use the Clean Room." I look at my toes making swirling patterns in the rug. They remind me of my unfinished memorial for Samuai. The ache of not finishing is sharpened by the realization I'd forgotten about it. For days.

A chill sweeps over me like one of the water condensers above has burst. How could I have forgotten? There's no way I can finish the ritual here. It will have to wait, but this time I won't forget. I won't.

Lady looks up at me, sniffs delicately and wrinkles her nose. "Is that horrible stench you, dear?"

I nod.

"You really should do something about it. I thought one of the ship rats had died in the wall somewhere." She points me to the clean room and leaves me at the white door in peace.

The handle is smooth and cool beneath my fingers but I hesitate. What if Davyd's in there already? The reality of our living situation makes him hard to escape.

I knock but there's no sound from inside.

I push open the door, flick on the light and am nearly blinded by the glare reflecting off white tile. It's fresh and sparkling and I step over the threshold quickly, before I decide I'm not clean enough to enter such a space. I lock the door behind me, aware that Davyd suggested I wash.

With him in my mind, stripping doesn't happen easily. A

mirror fills one whole wall and my naked reflection's almost as embarrassed as I am and she doesn't quite meet my gaze. The tile's cool beneath my feet. I step from one foot to the other while I try to figure out the shining metal taps.

I press the button marked 'on' and am rewarded by a burst of oh-crap-that's-cold water. My hand slams on the button and cuts the flow but not before I'm soaked. There has to be a way to adjust temperature. Lady wouldn't stand under this.

At last I find it. With the temperature control adjusted I push the button again. My teeth chatter loudly in the moments before the flow begins. Then the water hits me. Hot and fragrant with soap. Spraying down from four angled metal heads dousing every inch of me. A massage of water droplets caresses my skin.

I groan. It's so good. I arch under the spray, scrubbing the grime from my skin and my scalp.

Too soon the reality of my place in the household forces my hand toward the 'dry' button. It hesitates there, while I enjoy the water for a few extra seconds. How much would my mother enjoy this after a long shift working on the farm?

Those Lifers who rebel against the injustice of serving out our ancestors' crimes don't even know what they're missing out on. A stab of fear presses my hand down to stop the flow. For all Mother's planning and insistence on waiting, if those below knew the extent of the lifestyle differences in the upper levels, rebellion would be impossible to stop.

Chapter Twelve

[Blank]

A knock on the door startles me awake. I stretch, the accompanying pain in my leg makes me wince. My movement causes the girl in bed with me to stir.

The girl in bed with me!

Megs' in my arms. The last thing I remember is talking about nothing. Lulled to sleep by her lyrical voice. I don't remember lying down. Or her lying beside me and allowing me to take her in my arms. I will remember this though. Everything about it.

Her scent's sweet but earthy at the same time. Maybe she hasn't washed since the game. Whatever, it makes my whole body tight. On edge. I arch away from the curve of her back so she doesn't notice my response to her closeness. It takes all my control not to press closer to her. Her hair's only an inch away from my face. I lean forward, allow the silky strands to brush my nose.

Guilt and pain from my leg wars with the perfection of the moment.

The knock sounds again, louder this time.

She wakes and sits up. I bite down on a curse. She felt good. Damn good.

"Come in," I call. I cough to clear my throat; thankful the

darkness hides Megs' reaction. She must know the effect she has on me. It's not like I'm doing a brilliant job of hiding it. I have no idea if I'm usually this hopeless with girls. Probably.

The nagging hint of a memory tinkles with another girl's laughter in my brain. It brings a wave of guilt that I'm so into Megs but I tamp it down. If I agree to Keane's plan I'll have my memories back later today. Now belongs to Megs.

The door swings inward without a sound. Light from the hallway outlines Toby's familiar silhouette. "Rise and shine kids."

"Morning already?" asks Megs with a groan as the overhead light flickers on.

I'm concentrating on willing my body back under control. *Think Eliza; think Eliza.* The image of the crusty woman who attempted to kill me cools my blood and I stand without betraying myself.

"Do we have time for a wash?" I ask.

I must smell pretty bad by now and I need some balm for my leg.

"If you're quick." Toby hooks a thumb back over his shoulder. "Across the hall. Keane's waiting."

I cross the hallway and hear light feet following. With my hand on the door to the wash area, I turn. It's Megs, looking rumpled and stunning all at once.

Sweetness fills her shy smile. "I figured the wash was a good idea."

My mouth dries and I can't form words. I didn't imagine her joining me in the bathroom. I'm relieved the cubicles filling the once-white room are private. Mostly, anyway. I duck into the first one. Dark stains mark the corners of the small space but it's clean.

There's a disposable washcloth and I use the small sink, not wasting time on a shower. I'm out before Megs but wish I had clean clothes. Mine reek of adrenaline and fear.

Toby waits for me in the room. He tosses me a black hoodie. "Thought you might need this."

I pull it over my head although it's not particularly cold in here. At least it doesn't reek.

Megs is out in the hall when we return. "Took your time," she teases.

"How did you change?" I'm certain the tight blue jeans, white tank top, and gray jacket she's wearing are different.

"The bathroom links both sides of the station close to my room."

I picture her making the journey through the hallways naked and blush. Time for a change of subject before I make a fool of myself. "Where are we meeting Keane?"

"Out back. I need to check Janic on the way."

"Of course." Again I'm reminded of her personal stake in all of this. I like Megs but no one here belongs to me. That I know.

She leads me through long corridors and down two flights of stairs. Finally we reach an area marked 'Recovery'.

"Janic was in critical care for a few hours but with Q injuries the only thing to do once they're stable is wait," she explains as she pushes the door open.

Antiseptic odors hit us as we enter the long well lit room with maybe ten beds along either wall. Makeshift curtains separate each one. Seven are closed, the scraps of striped, flowered, and patterned material too cheerful for what they conceal. I imagine the patients inside, still and silent like Janic was in my arms, maybe recovering from injuries sustained at the raid.

Megs flashes a smile at the bearded man in the corner who nods in return. I follow behind, hoping no one asks me any questions. Either rumor of the strange guy has spread down here or being with Megs is enough and no one questions my presence.

We move silently toward the last bed on the right. Bright purple stripes cover this curtain. It makes sense for Megs' brother. They know her here.

"Come in," she says when I hesitate. "If it wasn't for you he'd be dead at the warehouse."

Not knowing what to say, I step in behind her, pulling the curtain closed. He lies on the bed, tiny and frail under the white sheet. A drip keeps him hydrated and a screen monitors his vitals but there's no other medical stuff.

Megs must notice my surprise. "There's nothing else we can do once they're in the Q-coma." She perches on the edge of the bed and takes her brother's hand, rubbing it absentmindedly. "Everyone takes turns at the desk out front in case there's a change and our medical staff are on call. But mostly they're needed for more urgent cases."

"How many doctors do you have here?"

"Not enough."

I stand with my hands hanging at my sides. Maybe if I'd blocked the shot earlier. Maybe if I wasn't so caught up in the game. Maybe...

Megs' other hand slips into mine. "Thank you."

"But I should have—"

Her brow arches. She's knows me too well already. "What? Janic shouldn't have been there. Thanks to you we got him back for treatment. Now it's up to him."

She leans forward without releasing my hand and kisses her brother's forehead, whispering something in his ear. Then she stands and tugs me toward the door. "Keane's waiting."

He's at the back of the station in a garage filled with what looks like salvaged vehicles in various states of repair. An older woman in overalls and grease streaks works underneath an old school bus.

"The Company are the only ones with access to new vehicles," Keane explains. He tosses Megs the keys to a dirt bike similar to the one he's leaning against.

"What about me?" I ask.

"Vehicles are valuable," says Keane, pulling on a helmet from the rack.

Megs hands me one. "You're riding with me."

"Put this on." Keane throws me a strip of black cloth and I nearly drop the helmet trying to catch it.

Another blindfold. I should've expected they wouldn't want a possible Company spy knowing the location of the Station. First, I swing one leg over the bike and then tie the blindfold. My fingers fumble with stress. Megs takes the helmet and helps secure the material. So much has happened since the last time she did this. She slides the helmet over my head and I'm in complete darkness. Megs climbs in front and I inhale her fruity scent. It brings back memories of holding her close through the night.

There's a scrape of feet on concrete and a rush of air near my face. The bikes roar to life. I hear a roller door creaking open and we're out in the air. With nothing else to do, I make a mental note of each turn, building up a map in my mind, and trying to fit what I saw when we fled the warehouse.

We've made maybe seven turns when Megs speaks.

I lean closer, so my helmet bumps against hers. "What?"

"You can remove the blindfold."

It's not as easy as it sounds but by flipping the visor I manage to uncover my eyes.

Purple hair fills my vision. The long strands trail under the back of Megs' helmet and blow into my eyes. I brush them aside and the true devastation to the city becomes clear. It's like a giant emerged from the bay flashing in the distance and walked over the hills, randomly crushing whole blocks of buildings and leaving others mostly intact. The earth itself fought back, with gaping holes and cracks as common as towers of rock sticking up out of the ground. Ribbon-like roads twist and buckle.

We ride ever upwards, weaving through the streets and sometimes cutting through tracts of land and rubble where buildings once stood. We cross over huge chasms on the flimsiest of roughly-built wooden bridges. In those places, the earth disappears into darkness and I hope Megs knows how to steer a bike.

When we turn off the road it's into what I'm guessing was once a park. Here are the first trees I've seen since the garden. While many are burned-out trunks, there are some that have grown since the Upheaval. I breathe in deeply, catching their scent over the burned odor blanketing the city. Mostly I smell fuel from the bike beneath me. The ascent starts in earnest and I hold on to Megs a little tighter. Nowhere during the trip do we see people.

Eventually Megs pulls to a stop behind Keane, kills the engine, and we climb off the bike. Pink streaks across the blue sky and the clouds are high and scattered. I'm guessing it'll warm up later.

A strange city's nestled in the valley below. Low-lying pale domes shine in the early morning light, resembling some kind of alien settlement. A fence rings the area. Guards, wearing the same gray uniforms as I saw at the raid, man lookouts at regular intervals.

There is nothing in my general memory that describes this "What is it?"

"New City," says Megs.

Keane gestures back to the bikes. "We need to get out of sight before the guards wake up properly and start doing their jobs. Or we're seen by one of the patrols. The sound of distant machinery helps cover the noise of the bikes."

I stare at the strange sight. Here and there square windows protrude from the curve of the structure, reflecting the warmth of the early morning light. Roads between the buildings are perfectly paved and swept. It's so clean.

There's an order to it that speaks to me in a way the dirty, rundown place I've left doesn't. This place feels a little like home and Keane wants to leave already? "I have questions."

He swings a leg over the dirt bike and it roars to life under his hands. "You'll get your answers but not here."

We clamber back on the bike and I'm careful not to latch onto Megs like a drowning man. I place my hands on her narrow waist and hold on. As she accelerates away I look back at New City and the surroundings. They've picked an area relatively unscathed by the Upheaval. Twin peaks rise in the distance and the ruins of a huge antenna spikes into the sky.

It might be my home.

Instead of heading back down the mountain, we hit the narrow trails and climb higher. The dirt bikes weave beneath a canopy of oak branches and through blackberry bushes. Either the fires from the Upheaval didn't make it up here or it's grown well. Finally it clears ahead and the white tree trunks spread apart to reveal a towering white cross.

Megs stops the bike at its foot and I strain my neck trying to look up to the top. "Does it belong to the Company?"

"No." It's Megs who answers as she lifts her helmet and shakes her hair free. "It survived the Upheaval."

I touch the white surface. Concrete I'm guessing. "I hardly believe it."

Keane leans back against the structure that survived when whole countries didn't. "Did New City look familiar?"

I suppress a reaction. Having seen the Company's base, I

realize Megs and Keane might not be my allies and I need to be on guard. Some of my longing for its order must show in my face and Keane won't miss it. "A little," I admit.

Megs' eyes widen and she backs away from me. "He's Company."

I hold my hands up, palm out. "I'm Blank."

Keane stills Megs with a touch on her wrist. "He's done us no harm…yet."

Everything I don't know does my head in. "What's so bad about the Company?"

"You mean apart from what they've done to my family?" Megs spits the question.

This time Keane only looks her way. She turns on her heel and stalks over to sit on a tree stump, her back to us.

"The Company, led by their CEO, is the one pedaling the alien myth. They're recruiting in preparation of another invasion," Keane explains.

"You think they're lying?"

"I think they're using fear to make people give up their memories and their freedom. They built New City from the ruins of the Upheaval. The more people who go there, the greater their power. Soon they'll have the strength to round up every person left here."

"What do they want?"

"To wipe us all out," Megs calls.

I look to Keane.

"We don't know," he admits.

I rub at my aching head. "If the Company really believes aliens are coming, I would think they'd want to recruit fighters like I saw at the warehouse, not be at war with them."

Keane shakes his head. "Most of the people who go to New City haven't been seen on patrols. It appears they're creating a community, not an army."

It doesn't make sense. "I saw the markets. Green robes walked around without being harmed by the Company officers."

"And you saw the warehouse. There are still enough people undecided that they don't want open warfare on the streets." Keane looks at the sky like asking for an intervention. "Not for much longer. The other night was the first time they've made such a raid. They're not happy with uneasy coexistence anymore. They're making their move to wipe us out."

"What happens then?"

"You were at the raid. You saw what happened to Janic. They have weapons we can't resist. There will be a massacre."

In my mind I picture Megs' brother being shot in the back and my stomach revolts. How could I be part of the Company and not know it? "So you hide in your station waiting for one person to give you away and then let them win?" My raised voice echoes through the trees and a single brown bird launches itself into the sky.

"No." Keane doesn't yell. He doesn't have to.

Megs' on her feet, crossing to stand between me and Keane. "Don't tell him everything," she says with a glance back at me.

I get it. I understand I can't be trusted with their most secret plans, but coming from Megs it makes my hands curl into frustrated fists. "I don't want to betray you."

Keane looks me in the eye. "Then don't."

We spin towards the trees at the snap of a twig. "The bikes!" yells Keane, already moving.

Megs and I grab our bike, slide on our helmets and hit the trails close behind Keane. I hope it was an animal or the wind but then there's a familiar tingle on my spine. "Someone's firing," I shout. I'm afraid my words are lost in the roar of the bikes but Megs tenses in front of me

Keane simply accelerates.

Heading toward the ruined city, we veer off the trail and weave between trees. The dirt and grass beneath our wheels turns to gravel. Tiny rocks scatter and shift with every change of direction. Keane's faster and changes direction easily. Twice we lose him in the trees, but each time he's ahead when we hit a clearing.

A vehicle rumbles behind us through the undergrowth. I hope whatever the Company officers are on it's not as agile as the bikes. I wrap my arms tight around Megs, shielding her with my body. In my mind, it's her instead of Janic on the bed in Recovery.

I hate not being in control of the bike. Megs' driving is awesome, but I feel useless.

"Left." Keane's shout comes to us on the wind.

Megs turns. Hard. Gravel scatters and spews off the ground. We're sliding. And sliding.

Megs attempts to right the bike but the steep slope provides no traction. She's heavy on the brakes. The wheel locks. My kneecap skitters close to the ground.

Then I see why Keane called. A few feet ahead gapes a chasm. It's long and dark and too wide to jump without a ramp or wings.

We're sliding straight toward it. Holy crap, we're going to fall. The black, rocky edge grows and grows until it fills my vision. We won't stop in time. And if we do, we'll be easy targets for the people chasing.

Our only hope is to right the bike and get it back under control. My heart pounding drowns out all other sounds. Megs' body vibrates but I don't know whether she's screaming or praying or trying to give me instructions.

It doesn't matter.

Everything in me is focused on fighting gravity and momentum.

What we're doing isn't working. Try the opposite. "Off the brakes," I shout into her ear.

Her body tenses and I think she's going to ignore me. I don't blame her. I reach around to help but then her hands move and we're accelerating again toward the edge. The bike catches on the grassy edge. She's back in control. We're upright and parallel. Relief drenches my body in sweat.

"Woohooo!" I scream some kind of victory yell to the sky above and glance behind.

I actually see our chasers. A man drives. He's about Keane's age but stockier in build. Behind him sits a dark-skinned girl a couple of years younger than Megs. They're on a motorcycle too, but it's bigger than ours.

There's no sign of weapons and they aren't looking our way. I'm sure their eyes are wide through clear visors, their gazes fixed on the chasm.

We're putting more and more space between us and them. They turn the bike and start sliding. A slide they won't be pulling out of. My stomach twists at the inevitability of it all. The dark-skinned girl leaps for her life, moments before the bike goes over the edge with her bigger partner.

She's going to make it.

The bike disappears and the girl screams, scrabbling at the edge of the cliff. She looks at me. Although she's too far away to hear, I read her lips and her wild, begging eyes. "Help me."

A minute ago the girl fired on us. To wound. Maybe to kill. But letting her fall?

"Stop." I shout the plea in Megs' ear. "Please."

It's crazy but the bike halts beneath me and I'm off it and running through the grass. My gaze fixed on the girl. A stranger. An enemy. A young girl.

"Blank, what are you doing?"

Megs shouts behind me but I don't stop. There's no time, and besides, there's no words to explain what I'm doing. I don't understand it.

I duck under an oak branch and stumble to the cliff's edge. I think she's gone until I see one small hand holding on to the edge. The knuckles are pale and the veins bulge with the strain.

I'm almost there. I can save her. I have to try.

"Hold on," I call.

But the hand slips. There's no scream, only her clattering to a stop a few feet below. "Help me," she cries again.

I lie flat on my belly. A part of me hears the bike approaching through the grass behind me but I don't spare Megs a glance. I wriggle closer to the sharp edge, jagged rock biting into my belly. The helmet's bulky but I don't waste time taking it off. Instead I reach down to the single hand.

It's too far. "Damn it."

I edge out further, and gravel rains down the rock face below. I breathe in dust and cough to clear my throat. Up close, the blackness of the chasm is absolute. Megs stops beside me.

"She's hanging on," I mutter.

I wouldn't blame Megs if she got on the bike and rode away.

"You're crazy," she says, dropping to the ground. "What the hell are you going to do with her if we get her out?"

"I haven't thought that far ahead."

With Megs weighing down my lower body, I manage to touch the hand. The girl's face remains hidden but her sobs echo on the rock walls. "I'm sorry, I'm sorry," she says. "I can't hold on. I'm going to fall."

"Calm down. Take a breath." I wait a heartbeat for her to get herself under control.

The sobs stop but she's breathing heavily. "I'm going to fall."

"Not if we can help it."

I strain out as far as possible. "Can you take my hand?"

"No."

"Try."

Megs grunts as she stops me from sliding down the slippery slope. "Stay with me, Blank."

This is useless. If only we had a rope. "Wait," I call and wriggle back to safer land.

The helmet sticks but I get it over my head, shaking sweat onto the ground. The black hoodie follows. I don't know if the material will hold her weight but it's worth a try.

The ground's hard beneath me as I wind the material over my wrist and drop it down toward the girl. "Grab the hoodie."

Nothing happens.

"Take it."

The girl groans. And leaps. She hangs in the air and then both hands are on the black material.

The sudden weight yanks my arms so the sockets burn. I'm sliding. The black opens up before me. Everything in me says to let go of the material. But now I see her eyes. Dark brown and awash with tears in a young, terrified face.

There's no way I'll let go. We stop falling but we still have to pull her up.

"If it comes to it, let me go," I say to Megs.

She barks a laugh and her grip on my ankles tightens.

The girl looks at us like we've lost our minds. In my case it's probably true. "We'll get you out." I put confidence I don't feel into the words.

She nods, but it's clear she doesn't believe me. Her eyes are still wide, the whites red and bulging as she swings over nothing.

Inch by inch, I pull at the material. Slowly and surely I lift the girl closer to the edge. I'm holding my breath, completely focused on dragging her out. One minute. If I give it everything for sixty seconds I think I'll have her free.

But the earth's damaged from the Upheaval.

It starts with one rock. A piece of gravel tumbles down into the darkness. Then another and another. The girl ducks her head to avoid the rain of dirt and gravel in her face. The ground gives way beneath my chest. There's no time for careful.

My fingers are twisted in the material. I heave on it with everything I have. She rises. Just a fraction. But more and more of the ground crumbles away.

I taste bile. I suck in a breath filled with the scent of sweat. I'm going into the blackness with the girl who tried to kill me.

But letting go and watching her fall?

"Megs," I shout. "Let. Me. Go."

"I won't."

Arching my body makes things worse. Megs' hands don't budge. More guilt settles like a boulder on my back. Unlike me, she has a brother, friends. People who will miss her if she goes off a cliff with me. I close my stinging eyes. We're all going to die.

"Thank you." I look down. The soft, calm voice belongs to the girl hanging on the end of my hoodie. "For trying."

And then, with a final sad smile, she lets go.

Chapter Thirteen

[Asher]

"Ready?" Davyd asks.

I look up from the small pile of mending Lady left me to do while she had her afternoon rest. He's leaning against the doorframe, not looking at the images of his brother that decorate the walls. As usual, Davyd's focus is all on me.

"Ready for what?"

"Me to keep my word."

My head snaps up. I jab the needle into my thumb and muffle a cry of pain.

Davyd laughs. "If it scars, will that be a memorial for me?"

"No."

He places his hand over his heart and adopts a pained expression. "Always second to the wonderful Samuai."

"Yes." What scares me isn't the easy smirk Davyd responds with, it's the way my memories of Samuai are being replaced by the still pictures surrounding me each night. In my efforts to understand how he died, I've become too busy to think of him as much as I should.

In contrast, Zed's memories linger as a blanket of bittersweet, catching me when I least expect it. Zed's still around in the taste of a new delicacy he would've liked and the amusement I know he'd feel whenever I do something foolish. Maybe I shouldn't envy Lady her shrine. Maybe one day it's all she'll have left.

I tidy up as fast as I can, but my brain's going even faster. The Control Room? Now? All my mental planning disappears and I taste my nerves in the dryness of my mouth. I fumble, dropping some of the thread.

Davyd laughs. "Nervous?"

"No." The lie slips out easily. Showing Davyd weakness is like inviting a wild animal for the kill.

"Then why do your hands tremble?"

I curl them into fists and shoot him a glare. "I'm ready."

I have to be.

Davyd turns and strides out the door. I trail behind. I didn't expect us to make an attempt on the Control Room in the middle of the afternoon, without any kind of preparation. I wish I'd eaten something for lunch, but after a few days of rich food my stomach's constantly queasy.

When we reach the hallway I jog to keep up. "What's the plan?"

He gave me his word but I don't want to head into the Nauts' stronghold blind. He halts without warning so I slam into his shoulder. His brow arches in that amusement I despise. "The plan?"

"Yes."

"What plan?" he asks with a smirk. He's messing with me.

But why? He's far too pleased with himself and far too unconcerned about the challenge ahead. Maybe ice does flow in his veins.

"How're we getting to the Control Room?" I whisper.

"The Control Room?" He repeats dumbly.

The words curl around me like a snake, twisting and squeezing so it's hard to breathe. Due to the lack of food, I fight back a dizzy spell. I fold my arms. "Where are we going?"

He reaches out and gently angles my head to lean close to my ear. The fine hairs on my neck rise and I don't dare move so as not to miss a thing. Up close his smooth skin's perfect, his gray eyes full of secrets. I wonder if he thinks I smell better than I did before using the clean room.

He exhales. "Manufacturing." He drops his hand and walks down the hallway, leaving me standing open jawed in his wake.

What the hell?

I'm tempted not to follow. To let him go to Manufacturing, or whatever it is he's doing, alone. Of course that would leave me standing in a hallway on Fishie level, a place I'm not supposed to be unattended.

He doesn't look back.

Damn him, he knows I have to follow. Even if regulations didn't require it, my lost brother's memory does. Feeling more like a servant than I ever did washing dishes or scrubbing floors, I force my feet to move. He doesn't look at me in the elevator or as we walk through the different Manufacturing areas.

Each area's divided by clear partitions to dampen the noise of the machinery inside and contain any fire outbreaks. Food Processing's burnt remains add a trace of smoke to the air. The biggest ship disaster of my childhood was this fire. The Fishies allowed us to refurbish the sprinkler systems afterwards, but it was easier to convert another part of the Manufacturing quarters than try to reclaim anything left from the fire.

The floor vibrates beneath my feet and I taste grease on every breath, making my empty belly churn. The work down here's mostly automated recycling, but Lifers oversee everything under the management of a Fishie.

Davyd stares straight ahead, not sparing the men and women working in the humid, sweaty conditions a glance of sympathy.

I offer those I know a surreptitious wave and understanding grimace. These are some of the least favored posts on the ship.

At Clothing Technology, Davyd activates the scanner and enters between the sliding doors. As I step inside after him, I'm already searching for Kaih. Boring uniform repairs occupy the majority of workers here but a few Lifers work almost exclusively to create the casual wear of the Fishies and Nauts.

Kaih's one. If not for the Upheaval and her great-grandmother's crime, Kaih would've been a designer. Her flair for shapes and colors is unmatched on the ship. With the ball to celebrate the New Year changeover approaching, there are several Fishie females here before us, checking on the progress of their outfits for the biggest social event on the Pelican.

A Fishie girl stands almost naked on a box in the center of the room with her back to us. Her long brown hair trails to her waist over plump curves, a stark contrast to her perfectly white skin. I haven't seen her in over a year but I know it's Tesae.

Tesae's two years older than me and we never mixed as we went through the training rooms. But she's infamous for losing every training room fight and for being the first to the side of any male victor, where she would bat her eyelashes and thrust out her well-developed chest. As the best fighters in our age group, Samuai and Davyd were two of her favorites.

Even if I weren't a Lifer, and therefore beneath her in every way, she would've hated me because Samuai didn't.

She says something in low tones to the Fishie woman who's with her and then turns.

Her eyes narrow and her thin mouth presses to a flat line when she recognizes me. "You."

Then she spots Davyd and her mouth curves into a simpering smile. "Oh, I'm just so embarrassed," she purrs, without making a move to cover any of the flesh exposed by her tiny pink bra and panties. If anything, she arches her back to more prominently display her curves.

Davyd doesn't appear to notice, instead approaching Kaih, who's walking in from the storeroom next door.

I smirk at the dismay on Tesae's face, but fail miserably to hide it.

Kaih frowns at me over Davyd's shoulder, biting on her nails as usual. I attempt to school my features into subservient neutral. But not fast enough. Tesae folds her arms and glares. "I'd like some privacy while I'm being fitted."

Kaih moves to intervene. "You're welcome to return to one of the fitting rooms."

"No," says Tesae. "I want her to leave." She points a silver-painted fingernail at me.

I back away automatically. If a Fishie says go, it's not prudent to wait. I don't even know why I'm here.

Davyd steps between us, facing Tesae. "Use a fitting room."

"But—" begins Tesae.

He takes a single step toward her. "A fitting room."

There's no questioning the authority in his tone. He turns his back on Tesae, dismissing her. Twin spots of angry color appear in her cheeks but she doesn't dare argue, storming toward the rooms in a dramatic huff. Davyd doesn't see because his focus is on Kaih. "You're the best here?"

She hesitates, shooting me a confused glance, before nodding slowly.

"Good. My mother demands we get a dress. You will help us."

We get a dress?

"Why isn't the lady here?" Kaih asks the question I'm thinking.

Davyd looks at me then. He holds my gaze for a long moment

and as usual I struggle to look away. He returns his attention to Kaih, but not before I catch amusement lurking in his eyes. "The dress isn't for my mother."

I go still. I can't let myself believe it.

"For Asher?" Kaih whispers the question.

In the heartbeat it takes for him to answer, I don't even know what I want him to say. I've never wanted to be a girl like Tesae with her long hair and fancy clothes.

Really? Not even when you thought about her and Samuai together at the End of Year ball?

With Samuai gone, nobody's left I want to impress.

"Mother requires our servant to be more suitably dressed," Davyd confirms.

I don't know whether the gasp I hear is mine or Kaih's. It doesn't matter. The blood rushes from my head and the room begins to tilt. It's kind of funny how wide Kaih eyes get and how the green wall behind her begins to go fuzzy.

Concern squiggles across her face and she steps toward me. "Asher, are you okay?"

"I'm fine," I begin. But my knees have other ideas. I sway. Black teases my vision.

Strong hands grip my shoulders. Davyd. He holds me upright when without him I would fall. I pull myself together and shake free of his touch. Hopefully the smile I force onto my face appears less shaky than it feels.

"I'm fine," I repeat.

I resist lifting my hands to where he touched me. Why did he catch me when it would have amused him to let me crumple at his feet?

I read his face but his expression's ice. "The dress must be completed before the ball." He exits without looking back.

Kaih clutches my hands. She's doing a little jig. "You're going to the ball, you're going to the ball!"

"I can't believe it." The ball's the stuff of many whispered stories in the lower levels of the ship. It's the only time anyone sees the Nauts away from their Control Room and their most private quarters on the top level of the ship, where Lifers aren't even allowed to clean.

"It's the ball." She lowers her voice. "You'll be the first Lifer to attend as a guest."

Where someone else might be envious, there's only excitement from Kaih. Something closer to dread churns in my belly. I never wanted to be the first anything and I won't be welcome. The divide on the ship between the Lifers and everyone else has existed for three generations. With our final destination approaching, it's not time to mess with the order of things.

I'm a servant, while Lady has already broken protocol by having me stay in her dead son's room, but having a dress made is a public statement. Of what, I'm not sure.

Most Fishies, like Tesae, plan their outfits for months. I don't know what Lady expects Kaih to create in a few days. Although if anyone can, it's Kaih. She tugs on my hand, dragging me toward the storeroom. "Come with me."

Tesae stalks from one of the fitting rooms as we pass. She's fully clothed now, in a green casual dress that hugs her figure, and she looks pissed.

Seeing me with Kaih, she freezes. "A lesser servant fitted me so you two could gossip? There will be a report with your name on it."

I don't want to get Kaih in trouble. "We're on Lady's orders, miss." I bow my head. "Sorry." I choke out the word.

Some of the stiffness drains from Tesae's shoulders. "I'll check to make sure you're telling the truth. Now do my shoes."

She points her untied lace-up slipper in my direction, daring me to refuse and prove the subservient act is just that. If it weren't for Kaih, if it weren't for the greater goal of Samuai and Zed, if it weren't for the rebellion, I'd tell her where she could stick her slipper.

Instead I drop to my knees and wind the ribbon carefully around her ankle, tying it in the fashion Lady favors. I keep my breathing even and resist tightening the ribbon any more than necessary. Some things are more important than this girl's petty games. But it's Fishies like her who make the rumblings for rebellion grow louder with every passing day.

I finish and stand, keeping my gaze on the floor. Without another word, Tesae leaves the clothing tech room and Kaih exhales in a long sigh. "She's such a bitch."

"Forget her. She was probably pissed because she wanted you to oversee the fitting."

Kaih flashes a smile. "Probably. She wants some terrible red leather number that would look better on a sofa."

Everything's recycled from somewhere. An image of the plush furniture in Lady's apartment springs to mind. "Was it a sofa? Before?"

Kaih giggles, quickly covering her mouth when one of the Fishies across the room looks our way. "Probably."

Salvaged pieces of material fill the storeroom. There are machines to recycle cloth from the thread components but sewing actual scraps is preferred because of the power the machine takes to run.

Kaih's slender hand on my arm stops me inside the door. I back up and nearly bump into a big pile of material.

"Careful," she snaps with more force than I've ever heard from her.

I frown.

"Don't move," she orders.

For so much of our lives I've been the leader, but this is her thing and I do as I'm told.

Kaih stands in the middle of the room. She's perfectly still. Except for her eyes. They dart from me to the material and back. "Have to consider the hair…Narrow…No bust to speak of…" she mutters.

I squirm under her professional eye and I stop myself covering up.

Finally she claps her hands together. "I've got it." She drags a bundle of fabric from the bottom of a towering pile. It's white. Plain, ordinary white. "What do you think?"

"Looks…great?"

Instead of being upset, Kaih laughs. "Wait 'til you see it."

She takes my measurements in a whirl of prodding and poking. When she's done, she rests her hands on her hips. "Do you want input or can I create something that will actually look good?"

"I get to choose?"

"Yup."

I should tell her to design me something to blend in, so no one will notice the Lifer girl in the corner. But that will never happen. An image of Davyd's knowing grin appears in my mind. I imagine blowing him away and putting him off balance for once. "Make me look good, I guess."

I don't wait long before Davyd returns to escort me back to the upper levels. He's silent as we walk together toward the elevators and says nothing as we step inside. He scans his wrist and presses the button for the Fishie apartment level. The doors close.

In two steps he's wrapped his arms around me, pulling me against the length of his body. My breath escapes in a hiss as his hands brace my shoulders. His gaze hooks me and I'm unable to look away. My heart beats like it's trying to get out of my chest, closer to him. "What the hell?" Is what I mean to say, but I make no sound.

He leans in, close to my ear. "Did you choose something pretty for the ball?" He trails a finger down my cheek.

Goosebumps race across my skin from his touch. I arch away, pressing back against the lift wall.

"Don't you like our game?" he whispers.

Game? "Are there microphones or cameras in here?" There's got to be an explanation for the seduction act. Maybe he doesn't want to be overheard. I'm trying to not think about how good his hand feels.

He smiles. "No."

I shove against the hard muscle of his chest with everything I have. He stumbles back, laughing. Rage shakes my body. "Don't mess with me."

"Or what?"

I slam my palm against the wall because it's all I can do. There's nothing to say, no way to win this argument with Davyd. I fold my arms across my chest and stand as far away as possible. We're almost to the upper levels and almost out of time.

"Why the ball?" I ask.

The lift doors open.

"Because when everyone else is celebrating, we're going to the Control Room."

***

I've never looked forward to the end of the year so much. Knowing when it's going to happen makes the wait easier. I'm busy helping

Lady prepare for the big occasion. Her outfit's orange with black bands around the sleeves. "I'm in mourning for Samuai," she explains.

Because Kaih has an extra dress to make, I'm recruited to sew seventeen black Ss around the hem of Lady's dress. As I stitch, I imagine Samuai's smile at his Mother's tribute. I feel closer to him and mostly manage to keep Davyd from my thoughts.

Over the next days I only see him when he's sitting opposite at the dinner table or if I bump into him coming out of the clean room, his hair damp from the water. Just seeing him sends a flush of awareness over my body. But it's nothing I can't handle. He's good looking, so what? He's not decent or kind or even civil most of the time.

My heart's with Samuai and I don't need it back.

The day before the ball, I'm serving Lady a glass of iced water when Davyd enters the yellow living room. His usually smooth features are twisted into a frown.

Lady smiles, oblivious. "There you are darling. You must take Asher for her final fitting."

"She can't take herself?"

"You know she doesn't have access to the upper levels to return," Lady reminds him. "Although I could talk to Huckle about getting that changed."

Davyd holds up his hand to stop her granting me free run of the ship. "I'll take her. Now."

"Yes." Lady turns her crazy smile toward me. "I can't wait to see how lovely you'll look."

"Thank you," I mumble. I wonder if there's talk about Lady including me in the ball. There must be. I bet no one's questioning her directly. She wears her role as the highest ranking female on board with ease.

I say nothing on the journey down to Manufacturing. Davyd

stares at the elevator doors, a faint frown creasing his forehead. It's strange I'm so caught up in the approaching ball—only because of the Control Room attempt—while Lifers on the lower levels continue the Farm work and cleaning and cooking. I flush. I've become about as aware of the ship around me as a Fishie.

The moment we enter the sliding doors, the waiting Fishie girls surround him like disciples.

The air's filled with the sweet perfumes these girls seem to favor, the cloying scent makes it hard to breathe. I edge away, looking for Kaih, but she's busy with all the final alterations.

One of the Fishie girls asks to feel Davyd's bicep and I fight down annoyance. These privileged girls simper like fools. In a few years, he'll choose one of these pretty idiots for a wife.

He looks at me, over their heads, and there's amusement in his eyes. It's like he reads my thoughts. I look away rather than smile back. We're not partners. He might be helping me get to the Control Room but after that I'll be on my own. If there's a way to turn me in without upsetting his mother, I have no doubt he will. He's not Samuai.

Best that I remember that fact.

"Sorry, Asher."

It's Kaih. Her clothes are askew and a smudge of dirt darkens one blond eyebrow. The tablet she records her notes on is covered with sweaty handprints.

"I don't mind waiting."

She shakes her head. "It's not a matter of waiting. I'm not going to get a chance to fit you properly."

My insistence that I don't care about what I wear to the ball disappears under a wave of disappointment. Maybe I was looking forward to seeing what magic Kaih could create more than I wanted to admit.

"I understand."

"I knew you would." She squeezes my upper arm and then drapes a few scraps of old material over my shoulder and around my hips, taking notes as she moves. The muslin feels too tight and it barely covers me at all. A few seconds of pinning and poking and I'm glad she's running late. "That's all I have time for but I'll get it finished and sent up in time. I promise."

"Thanks."

Her fingers on my arm tighten, stopping me. She glances around to see how close any Fishies are. "Your Mother said to tell you to prepare," she adds. There's an excited glint in her eye.

To anyone listening, Kaih would appear to be passing on a message about the ball, but I know better. Mother doesn't care about fancy clothes or fancy food. Her focus is the rebellion.

When? How? A million questions leap to my lips but I don't speak them aloud. I know Davyd's watching me because I feel his gray gaze on my skin.

"Will do. The ball is a big event."

She nods once and picks up a container of pins from the closest table. "Next," she calls.

Not wanting to add to Kaih's stress, I cross the room quickly to Davyd's side. The Fishie girls surrounding him don't spare me a glance. My mind's caught on Kaih's warning. If what she said is true, they'll have to take notice of Lifers soon.

Davyd's different. He welcomes me with exaggerated surprise. "That was fast."

"It's not like she has much to work with." I don't see which of the girls speaks but they all laugh in high-pitched tinkles.

I have more important things on my mind. I simply adopt a demure smile and wait for orders. The image of an obedient servant.

However Davyd isn't buying my act. "Let's get you back to work." He gives the girls a full-watt grin. "Looking forward to seeing you all dressed up."

They sigh as we walk to the doors. Pity mingles with scorn. Can't they hear the sarcasm in his voice?

Maybe you know Davyd better than all of them.

I ignore the voice in my head. All I want is to use Davyd to get to the Control Room. Zed and Samuai are the only boys I care about.

Kaih's message replays in my mind. What did Mother mean by prepare anyway? That I should be ready to fight Davyd and his family when the time comes?

I have no problem turning on Huckle, but the others? No, it won't come to that.

The rebellion's been in the planning stage for so long I can't believe it's nearly here. I wish I knew more of the details. The Fishies won't cede control of the ship without a fight. The prospect of freedom and equality has a bitter edge. I thought Mother would wait for me get to the Control Room and locate the Remote Device rather than push ahead. Like always, she's assuming I don't have the courage to succeed. Or worse.

The thud of the machines around us matches the rhythmic thud of my heart. Maybe it's not too late. I'll get the intelligence she needs tomorrow night at the ball and prove her wrong. Surely the rebellion won't happen before then. With new purpose in my stride I reach the lifts ahead of Davyd.

"Why were you so fast?" he asks again while we wait.

"Not much to work with." I do my best imitation of a Fishie girl.

His gaze flicks over my body. When it meets mine again there's appreciation there that makes me look away. "You're different than of them."

"Really?" The line is smooth and I have to force myself not to roll my eyes.

"You know I don't like soft girls."

"I don't care what kind of girls you like," I say with a sugary smile. But pleasure at his implied compliment spreads through me like the warm honey Lady adds to her cereal.

He ignores my words. "They're all going to hate you even more when you show up on my arm tomorrow night."

The thought of walking in at Davyd's side and seeing their faces is far too appealing. "I thought Lady—" I trail into silence because he's grinning that satisfied grin. He never actually said whose idea the whole me-going-to-the-ball thing was. "This was your idea?"

"The important thing is Mother thinks it was her idea and she was the one who convinced Huckle."

It makes sense. He promised he'd get me to the Control Room and there's no better time than when his colleagues are distracted by a party. It's brilliant and bold and he's made it look like he's simply fulfilling his mad mother's whim. Except…

"How?"

He blinks. "You'll see."

"I'll be seen. Everyone will be watching me. Lifers at the ball aren't a common occurrence."

I've given him pause, but then his assured grin slips back into place. "You're imagining some fairytale ball. The reality's a lot more sordid. Beyond the initial stir of you being there, those people will be far too interested in themselves to notice what happens to you."

Is there a threat in his reminder of my place in this world?

I need to remember how clever an opponent he is for the day when our goals no longer align.

Chapter Fourteen

[Blank]

"What the hell did you think you were doing?"

Keane growls the question. His fists are clenched as he stalks around the station's big open kitchen. The lights hanging above chase the echoing cavern back into the tunnels that lead off in every direction. His glare swings from me, where I sit on a chair, to Megs who leans against the long bench. "He's mental, but you? I thought you had a brain."

She shrugs, unperturbed by his anger. "I thought it was a good idea at the time."

He turns back to me. "Why?"

It's a good question. "The girl didn't seem so bad." The explanation's lame, and I know it, but I can't find the right words. Something in me couldn't walk away.

Keane jabs my arm, just below the tape the medics put on my strained shoulders when we made it back to the station. His finger strikes the telltale green mark of a Q hit. "Was it before or after she tried to kill you that you decided she *wasn't so bad?*"

His imitation of my accent at the end gets me on my feet. "Would you have let her fall?"

Keane turns away. "She's the enemy."

"*Your* enemy." The words I don't say hover over us: Not mine.

Megs' eyes shutter but not in time to hide the hurt I've caused. Keane shakes his head as though I'm a lost cause.

I rub at my aching shoulders. "Look, I don't like what I've seen of the Company but I couldn't leave a young girl to die." No one says anything and I stand in front of Megs, waiting until she meets my gaze. "You were there. You helped. Don't make this out like it was something I did against your cause."

Megs sighs, and looks to Keane. "She was just a kid."

He pulls up a chair and collapses into it. "You're right. When we become the kind of people who'll let an unarmed kid fall to her death we might as well hand the city over to the CEO."

It's as close as I'm going to get to an apology.

Something's been playing on my mind. "They're in trouble if that girl's a sample of their defense against the aliens."

Keane's head jerks up. "I told you. There are no aliens. And as long as they have the Q they keep us in check."

"But why keep up the pretense of an alien attack for all these years?"

"I don't know. To scare people into joining their city."

Since I don't have any better ideas, I shut my mouth but it adds to the list of questions building in my mind. Only I doubt getting my memories back will help.

No one speaks much as we help ourselves to the pot of stew left warming on the stove. The painkillers the medic gave me for the cuts and scrapes are making the high corners of the room become fuzzy. My stomach revolts at the smell of the rich, creamy gravy, but once I force a mouthful down I realize I'm starving. I clean the plate, mopping up the remnants with some bread.

Megs and Keane eat as heartily.

While we eat a few others enter and take seats on the other side of the room. One is Gan's, from the gaming bar, familiar face.

Megs sees me looking. "He passes through sometimes," she says. "And gives us work when he can."

A few people I don't recognize grab food but they sit at the other end of the room, leaving us in privacy. Nothing important is said.

The rest of the day is for recovery. We don't speak much about what happened on the cliff. I don't know what to make of Megs sticking by me when she made it clear she doesn't trust me with the rebellion's secrets. I'm too wimpy to ask her.

I sleep some, and go with Megs to visit Janic. There's no change in his condition. Standing at the foot of the bed, I again imagine Megs in his place. The chills racing across my skin aren't from the painkillers.

Keane doesn't ask for my decision but the pressure to decide is immense. A few times I catch Megs looking at me with a question in her sad green eyes but she doesn't put it into words.

I try not to think about what might happen if I say no to the procedure and even less about the ramifications of saying yes.

Even though Megs stays with me through the night, I don't sleep much. She keeps her distance so there's no chance of waking with her in my arms. Part of me would prefer she begged me to let Keane mess with my mind. It would be better than the awkward silences between us where before we got along so well.

Early the next morning, Keane stops us in the hallway after breakfast. "You've had a chance to recover," he begins, looking at me.

This is it, decision time. I wonder if he's the procedure ready to go or if I'll have to dread it for a few more hours. I wonder whether it will hurt.

"Wait," says Megs before I can answer. "You saw New City yesterday. Before you decide, you need to see our city." She turns to Keane, bright for the first time since we returned from trying to save the Company girl. "I'll have him back soon."

Keane flashes a rare smile. It's because of Megs; when she's happy, her spirit's infectious. He waves us away. "Don't be too long." His gaze fixes on me. Heavy. Demanding. "But every day the Company gets stronger and more people go to New City and never come back. I need your decision today."

I nod, faking confidence. "When we return." Deep down, my decision was made the moment I set out to find answers, maybe when I awoke in that garden.

Do whatever it takes.

But I want to put off the possible brain damage for a little longer. The chance to go somewhere with Megs seals the deal. She takes my hand.

I tamp the familiar guilt down and enjoy her touch. Soon enough I'll know why I feel bad every time I respond to Megs. For now I want to pretend what I did before we met doesn't impact my feelings for this amazing girl. I squeeze her slender fingers in mine. "Where to?"

Instead of heading back to the garage we left from yesterday, she leads me into the heart of the building. She opens a door next to the stairs we used to visit Janic and reveals another stairwell. Older and darker. The only light creeps in from the poorly fitted seals around the doors and from gaps in a trap door above our heads. The rays splinter in filled with dust and smog, each particle reflecting a tiny beam of sun.

"No one comes this way much," says Megs, with a grin. "There are sentries on the roof but they use the new stairwells at the end of the building."

"I can't imagine why."

The wooden steps creak beneath my weight. The spider webs that are probably holding the staircase together stick to my feet. We climb up. I grip the rail with my free hand, ready to take off my weight if the whole thing gives way. Megs still holds the other.

We step out into a breeze that tugs at my t-shirt but isn't enough to dislodge the early morning fog. Megs waves to the sentries at either end of the building. We head toward the three old brick chimneys rising from the middle of the building.

She sits between the two chimneys in the least disrepair, on the edge of the roof, and tugs me down beside her. "Here."

I sit and swing my feet like Megs. The tap of my heels against the crumbling concrete beneath makes pieces of it break off and tumble to the street below. I get the feeling that the whole thing could collapse at any moment. But instead of being scared it makes me feel more alive.

A glance over my shoulder shows us completely hidden from the sentries keeping watch on the street. We're alone.

"What do you see?" she asks.

I've been so focused on Megs I hadn't considered the view. I look out. The destruction I saw from the back of the bike is worse through the fog and the heavy brown stench that coats this part of the city like the pillow Eliza tried to use to smother me.

"Ruins," I say. "Buildings missing their rooftops or several walls. Bits of concrete that might've been roads once. Black shadows I'm guessing are cracks in the earth." I stifle a shudder at the black hole that took the Company girl. I never want to end up in one of those.

"Anything else?"

I look closer. She must be testing me. "There's no people, no plants other than the mossy weed that grows over everything, no signs of life."

"Really?" She takes our joined hands and points toward the roof of a neighboring building.

I follow the direction she's pointing. For a second I don't see she wants me to look at. This building's the same as the others. Gray and grimy, with the moss growing in the damp cracks.

Until in the far corner…"The bit of green?"

She flashes a grin that makes me feel like I've said something brilliant. "Exactly. Someone's growing something there. Sometimes when I come up here, I see an old lady out watering that little patch."

"What do they grow?"

She shrugs. "It doesn't matter."

"Then why bother?" I don't understand what she thinks I should be getting excited about.

"Because she's trying. To make a life free of the Company. If the food grows she can trade it for something else she needs, like making sure she keeps electricity in her home. The hungry and the desperate are easy prey for the lure of New City."

"Why do so many here wear the green robes?"

"A small symbol of defiance." She grins. "And someone found a huge stash of the material in one of the old buildings."

"But the Company has control. What's to stop it from shutting everything left in this city down?"

"Manpower. But as Keane said, they'll outnumber us in time. New City began as an alternative to the devastation left by the Upheaval, but we're not being left alone as promised by the Company. They're more open in their attacks."

"What then?"

She slides her hand free of mine, and twists the end of her purple hair. "We have plans."

"Like?"

She's silent. We're shoulder to shoulder, but in her mind she doesn't believe it's safe to let me too close. It's the same point at which she stopped Keane talking on the mountain. She's afraid to reveal the rebellion's master plan in case I'm Company.

I lie back, close my eyes and rub at my aching temples. "Look, I get it. I get why you don't want to tell me."

Her hands slip over mine.

I open my eyes and she's kneeling over me, her light weight settles on my stomach. Every part of me aches to press her even closer. The usual guilt fights a losing battle against how much I want to kiss her.

My hands go to her thighs, bare from her cutoffs. Her skin's warm and smooth. I trail a path of Goosebumps on her skin. "You're pretty close to the edge," I manage to say past a dry throat.

Her eyes are shadowed as the sun behind her begins to burn through the fog. "You won't let me fall."

From thighs, to waist, to her jaw. My hands move on instinct. Her breath catch. I answer the smile on her lips with one of my own.

And then I pull her down. Slowly. As though we have forever, when in a few hours I might be her enemy. Anticipation ramps the ache in me to painful, alongside the whisper of a memory.

I promise. Forever…

"Megs." I say her name to drown out that other girl in my mind. Gravel from my feet tumbles down the side of the building as I shift.

She shakes her head. "If you don't kiss me soon…" Her mouth's so close, her breath, sweet on my lips.

Then the kiss. And it's everything. Her mouth, her taste. I deepen the kiss. Her lips part beneath mine. I tangle my fingers in her hair and arch up to press closer.

She pulls back a little. "Blank," she murmurs.

My name on her lips reminds me of the decision ahead. I never want to stop kissing her but the shadow of what lies ahead hangs over us. When she pulls away again we're both breathing faster. Her cheeks are flushed pink and her eyes are hazy. Her fingertips return to my temples.

"Do you have the answers in there?" she whispers.

My gut clenches. "Is that what this is about?"

She pales. "Of course not. I thought…"

I lift her off me, making sure she's well away from the edge of the building. Then I bring up my knees and wrap my arms around them to stop myself reaching for her again. My hands are fists. "I don't want to hear it."

Angry heat burns my cheeks. At myself. These people are at war. Would they trade a kiss to get the answers they want? Megs made it clear how much she wants revenge on the Company.

How stupid to think she actually wanted to kiss me.

"Blank?" Her voice pleads.

I won't look at her. I refuse to feel bad. Like I need more guilt. "I wish I'd never followed you to the warehouse."

"Don't say that."

"Why?"

"Because then Janic wouldn't have a chance."

I laugh. I got my hopes up. Thought she might've been glad we'd met for me. But no, it's because I'm the freak who doesn't get hurt by the Q and was strong enough to bring her brother to safety.

"I'm just a means to an end for you people."

She's silent.

I scramble to my feet, dangerously close to the edge but I'm past caring. Fall. Not fall. Whatever. At least a fall would put an end to the million questions in my brain.

"I'll do it." I'm shouting but I don't care. "That's what you want, isn't it? That's the reason for this whole performance?"

I stare at her then. Daring her to argue, still somehow hoping she'll tell me I'm wrong, that she brought me here because she likes me. Not just what I might be able to do for her friends.

She hasn't moved from where I put her. When she looks up her eyes shine with unshed tears. "I can't lie. I did bring you here to help you decide." She stands and walks over to stand right on the edge with me. Her hands wrap around my fist, her touch warm and soft despite my anger. "But kissing you. Damn it, Blank, if you don't know why I kissed you then you really need something done to fix your brain."

I want to believe her.

"I could die." It's the closest I come to admitting I'm scared. It's funny how a few days of a life already seem important enough to cling to.

She nods. "I'd miss you terribly."

"But you still think I should take the chance."

Her hands move to clasp around my neck. She rests her head on my chest, against where my heart pounds hard from her nearness and from the procedure ahead.

"More importantly, you do," she says into my t-shirt.

She's right. I want answers. I want to know who did this to me and why. I want to help Megs if I can.

I hold her close. "We'd better find Keane."

She hesitates. When I look back she's biting her lower lip.

"There's another place."

Her words are so soft and spoken so quickly it takes a second to make sense of them. "This is your secret?"

"A community over the Upheaval Mountains, out of the Company's reach."

She's given me the greatest gift by trusting me. "I won't let you down."

This time we use the new stairs. They're clean and brightly lit. As I expect, we head toward Janic but turn off the corridor before the one leading to the Recovery center.

Silently we pass closed doors and silent hallways. And then we stop. Megs squeezes my hand in front of a plain white door, no different to any of the others we've walked past to get here.

"Here."

I knock. Keane opens the door but he's not smiling. "You've decided?"

I nod, looking past him, but there's not much to see beyond a hallway opening into a larger room beyond.

"You need to say the words."

"Yes. I want my memories back."

He smiles then, but it's a grim twist of his mouth. "You'd better come in."

"Now?" I'm glad the question doesn't come out as a squeak.

"No point wasting time." He heads inside, leaving the door slightly ajar.

Megs pulls me close in a brief hug. "Good luck."

This is when I should drop her hand and stride away. I linger. "I'll see you soon."

But the simple farewell isn't enough. I meet her gaze and am selfish enough to hope the fear in the green depths of her eyes is for me. I lean close and press a hard kiss on her mouth.

I walk into the room without looking back.

The door clicks closed behind me with a finality that should terrify me. Instead I'm calm again for the first time since I made my decision. Soon, I'll have answers. Or be so brain damaged it won't matter anymore.

I expect something similar to the Recovery center, but the room beyond the entryway is shining white and sterile. More like the Doctor's rooms in my memory banks. The rest of the station might be run down but they obviously don't mess around with medical procedures.

There's a hospital bed in the center of the room beneath bright directional lights and Keane waits beside it. I cross the few feet in a blink. I avoid the metal tray with medical devices on it. Scalpels. Needles.

I gulp. "Here I am."

As I speak, a trim, dark-skinned woman enters through another door. She's holding a machine that's the stuff of nightmares, with wires and probes and a crapload of buttons.

"This is Charley. She's our senior medic."

I attempt a smile. "Blank."

"Hopefully not Blank for long," she says with a warmth that reminds me of Megs. Even in tossing her long dark, curly hair over her shoulder, this woman exudes skill and confidence.

Some of the tension in me eases and I breathe for the first time since entering the room.

Keane points to the orange stubble on my head. "At least we don't need to shave you down."

I swallow past a constriction in my throat. The ID picture back at the gaming bar showed me with longer hair. Whoever modified my memory must've cut my hair, and in the back of my mind I sort of knew it. But the idea gives me the creeps. Almost more than what they did to my mind. Was I conscious at the time? Did I struggle? My gut flips. Maybe I'll know soon.

"Do it," I say, before I lose my nerve.

Keane nods to Charley. She pats the bed. "Take a seat."

I do as she asks and she raises the back of the bed so it supports my spine. "Should I take off my shoes?"

"Whatever makes you comfortable."

I take them off, not thinking about whether I'm delaying what's about to happen.

She attaches the probes at regular intervals across my scalp. Each one's cold and damp when it first touches me, but once they're there I hardly feel them.

"Ready," she says to Keane when she's finished.

He pulls up a chair and straddles it, facing me. "Last chance to wimp out. Are you sure you want us to try this? The fact that you've remembered nothing in days suggests that whoever did the operation on you knew what they were doing."

My neck muscles tighten and my ear tips burn. That I remember nothing isn't exactly true. I mean, I've remembered a girl's voice a couple of times and there's the nagging guilt whenever I'm around Megs. But did I take such an instant liking to Megs if there was already someone special in my life? I've been here for days and there's been no sign of anyone from my past looking for me.

Anyway, I don't want to reveal everything to Keane. He saved my life but it doesn't mean he won't sell me out for his cause. He's made no secret that bringing down the Company and their mysterious CEO comes first.

I take a deep breath and lift my head to look him straight in the eye. "I'm sure."

He nods. "We'll begin with a local anesthetic."

"I thought you'd knock me out."

"It's important you're awake so we know whether it's working."

"Will the memory part hurt?" I ask, managing to keep my tone level. Showing fear is showing weakness.

"The probes will enter your brain using nano-fine needles. You might not even feel them."

I haven't seen the whole Station but nothing about their setup suggests they have the capability to make nano-anything. "How did you make—"

"Let's just say we borrowed some of the technology," Keane explains, cutting me off.

"At considerable expense," Charley adds.

They mean lives. People died to get this. The weight of the experiment settles heavily where each part of the instrument touches my scalp. If the procedure works the rebellion might be able to reclaim their own people. It's about so much more than me.

But I'm the one who's taking all the risk. "Okay, so you jab me and the nano-things go in my brain. Then what?"

"It's hard to explain, but we believe the memory change is achieved by literally blocking some of the pathways in the subject's brain and creating new ones." While Keane speaks, Charley's busy with the machine and I don't know who to watch. "We use special frequency waves across those pathways to break them open."

"Break?"

"I didn't say this would be fun."

He didn't and I never thought finding the answers would be easy. "Give me the local."

Keane and Charley share a look over my head.

She fumbles with the side of the bed and I hold my breath. Long, gray straps like the ones Eliza used are attached to the side. She looks apologetic. "First we have to tie you down."

"But I won't move."

Keane places a heavy hand on my shoulder. "You might not have a choice."

There's more to it than moving from pain. It's about what happens after. If I'm a trained Company spy then unlocking my memories might be dangerous for everyone in the Station. Just because I understand doesn't mean I like it. But it's a too late to start complaining about the details. I lie still while they strap my chest, each foot and my hands.

"Are you comfortable?" Charley asks when they're done.

"Does it matter?" They don't respond and I regret the childish outburst as soon as it leaves my lips. "Let's get this over."

At Keane's signal, Charley prepares an anesthetic patch. I tense, bracing for the sting as it hits the side of my neck. Then everything above my shoulders is numb.

"Can you feel this?" Charley presses a needle behind my ear.

"Yes. But it doesn't hurt." My words are slurred. It's hard to control my mouth with the anesthetic.

"Good. We'll give it a minute or two to make sure it's working and then we'll begin."

Over the next few minutes she tests my whole head using the needle trick. My heart rate escalates with every passing second. Drool pools at the corner of my mouth and I clench my useless hands.

The saliva builds and spills over my numb lip, dribbling down my jaw.

"Huwy up," I manage.

I try to swallow but gag on the liquid in my mouth. Charley frowns and wipes at my chin with a cloth. When I'm cleaned up, she flicks a switch and the probe points tingle. At first it doesn't hurt but then there's pressure. Lots of pressure.

My eyes squeeze shut and a moan escapes from deep in my throat. I put everything into keeping my eyes open despite the overwhelming need to let them close. I want to see what they're doing, like somehow that gives me control.

The low hum of the machine disappears beneath a rushing in my ears. I strain to hear what's happening around me. Charley's eyes widen and the faint lines around her mouth become crevasses as she studies the small screen.

"I don't know," she says to Keane.

Or at least I think she does. It's hard to read lips with my eyes squinting. Not the words I want someone messing with probes in my brain to say.

A pulse ticks in Keane's jaw. "Begin the procedure."

Every breath I take feels rusty, and the beating of my heart becomes the clamoring of my memories trying to break free.

Still, Charley stares at the screen. "He's not responding as I hoped."

I can't move my eyes fast enough to catch Keane's response but I know what it must be. He hasn't gone this far to stop now. I think tears run down my face but I'm not meaning to cry. The pressure on my head is just so, so...

My eyes give up the fight and squeeze shut.

And pressure becomes pain.

I scream but make no sound.

I arch against the straps and feel them snap one by one.

My bladder gives way.

And my head. My head explodes on a wave of black, icy light that sweeps everything in front of it. I sit in a pool of my own piss with the stench of memories I wish I'd left unfound.

"I am Samuai."

Chapter Fifteen

[Asher]

Kaih keeps her promise, sending my dress up in the kitchen drawer late afternoon on the day of the ball. However, I'm so busy dealing with one of Lady's attacks I don't get to open it until five minutes after I'm supposed to be ready to leave the apartment.

"Hurry up, Asher dear," Lady calls from the front door.

"Leave her here." Huckle's words slither under the door.

I freeze, straining to listen.

"You promised." I know that tone; Lady's on the edge of losing control.

But her husband doesn't read her as well. "Lifers don't belong at the ball, except to serve," he says.

"She will serve me." The words are almost a screech.

"Like the last girl?"

My stomach contracts. The servant Mother warned me about.

"I couldn't save her." Lady sounds almost sad.

"Maston won't approve." Now there's panic in Huckle's voice. Did he hope he could placate her by agreeing and then she'd forget when the day arrived?

There's a long silence. What's happening? I move closer to the door. Then I hear it, Lady laughing, genuinely, all tension gone.

"Maston will say nothing."

How can she be so sure? Does it have something to do with Davyd being so close to the head Naut?

"We're leaving, Lifer." This time it's Davyd calling. I picture him standing, impatient, at his mother's side.

Nerves dampen my hands as I hurry to open the plastic sheath encasing the material. If it doesn't fit I'll be attending in my Lifer uniform. Or not at all. I banish the wishful thought of curling up here and hoping it all goes away. How I look is irrelevant. Tonight's about the Control Room. Nothing more.

I will succeed. Or I will die trying.

This time the packaging tears open beneath my fingers. It frees the lightest, silkiest white material I've ever seen. It floats in my hands, gossamer like. I take a deep breath before stripping my Lifer uniform, and pulling the dress over my head. Careful, so I don't tear Kaih's creation.

The fabric's nothing more than a whisper against my skin. A single, thin strap loops around my neck and supports the whole thing. It falls over my body in waves, hugging my breasts and my hips, flaring out to brush the floor.

I stare at the girl in the mirror. Her shaved head and lean figure mark her as Lifer but beyond that she has nothing in common with me. Somehow, Kaih's made me almost beautiful. A hundred images of Samuai reflect back from the walls behind me. He never saw me like this: fresh, clean, wearing a dress.

My gaze fixes on one of his warm smiles, I twirl on bare feet. "What do you think?" I whisper into the dead silence.

I hold my breath for a heartbeat but of course there's no answer. Samuai's been gone for weeks. And Davyd waits.

He and Lady stand by the door leading out of the apartment, talking softly. Huckle's nowhere to be seen. Suddenly shy, I pause in the doorway, waiting for them to look up.

Lady sees me first; her powdered face cracks into a big smile. "You look so lovely," she cries. She crosses the room to envelop me in a squishy hug.

But the whole time I'm waiting for Davyd. Waiting for him to look at me. Waiting for him to comment. He does neither, pressing his wrist to the scanner to open the door and lead us down the hall.

It isn't disappointment that makes my eyes burn and my hands shake because I didn't dress to impress him. I know he didn't dress to impress me but his plain charcoal suit fits his broad shoulders so perfectly I struggle to look away. The gray of his shirt reflects the ice of his eyes and, although he's not bothered with a tie, he's anything but casual.

My feet drag as we approach an area of the ship I've only heard about. The Commander's Lounge belongs to Maston, the head Naut, and he will play host for the evening. The hallway's deserted but neither Lady nor Davyd seems concerned that we're late.

Davyd scans his wrist and the doors open with a soft swish. I smooth my hands down the sides of my dress. Nervous fingers encounter something strange. Small pockets hidden in the folds of the material. If only I'd known before we left the apartment. Maybe I could've carried a weapon instead of relying on my wits. And Davyd.

I brace for stares at the least. No Lifers but me are allowed inside tonight; even the serving will be done by low-level Fishies and the Nauts' special servants.

Inside, Fishies stand on plush carpet, clumped in groups around candlelit high tables. The flickering flames that are the centerpiece of each one are reflected a hundred times in the sparkles affixed to every second female's dress and many of the men's ties. The effect is a kaleidoscope of color.

I expected a quiet formal affair, but the noise is so loud and the conversations so self-absorbed that not one person looks up when we enter, and my fears of being the center of attention evaporate on my exhaled breath.

As we move into the room, the air thickens with a dozen different perfumes. Flowers scents like Lady's but sweeter, thicker somehow. Other scents of rich foods and heavy sauces. Spice and sour. Each one's stronger than the last. By the time we reach the bar and Huckle, the stuff coats my throat. I'm not sure it's any better than the unwashed stench of the Lifer quarters.

I think of the celebration below and miss my mother and my friends more than ever. But I can't wish myself down there. Not after all I've done to be here tonight.

When I think of the Control Room, my gaze seeks Davyd's but he isn't looking my way. He speaks to his mother in a low voice and then gestures to the person working behind the bar. I take the opportunity to appreciate the simplicity of his suit compared to the lime green Huckle chose and some of the other ridiculous color combinations.

"You look lovely." It's Huckle. He's standing so close to me that his rancid breath hits my face.

I stifle a shudder. "Thank you."

There's no evidence in his demeanor of the stress I overheard earlier. His red face shines and his eyes are hazy, like he's not quite seeing me. He rests a heavy arm across Davyd's shoulders. "You could have made more of an effort though. What will Maston think?"

Davyd's lip curls and he shrugs the arm away. "You won't remember what I'm wearing come morning at the rate you're sucking down tubes."

That explains it. I've heard the Lifers who set up the room for the ball talk about the tubes we're not permitted to touch. Then I see them for myself, hundreds of small black vials filled with clear liquid are stacked behind the bar along with other drinks.

"Want one?" Huckle asks, pointing a stubby finger in their direction.

"No, thank you." I need to keep my head clear.

As it is I'm struggling to keep everything about the setup and the crowd straight in my head to report to Mother.

"Another for me then," says Huckle so loud that those Fishies closest to us turn.

Each of them grins wide with the same hazy look in their eyes. They don't look twice at me. If only Mother knew. Tonight's the perfect night to make an attempt for control of the ship. Most of the Lifers' opposition is out of their mind on whatever drug fills the black vials.

Davyd hands over the tube and Huckle's damp arm slips around me as he throws his head back and gulps loudly. He reeks of the clear liquid, bitter and sour combining to make my eyes water and distaste crawl a slimy trail over my skin.

"We know it's planned for tonight," he says conversationally.

"What?" I hope he's too intoxicated to notice my flinch.

Has Davyd betrayed me already? When I look to him for answers, he's disappeared into the crowd. Leaving me alone to face Huckle. Huckle who seems far too jovial for a man who's uncovered my plans to break into the Control Room.

"Neale attempted to kidnap my wife and hold her hostage." I stare at him dumbly until he adds, "The rebellion will be thwarted thanks to the listening device you planted."

I think of Kaih, looking so excited. Is this what she meant by telling me to prepare? Then Huckle's words sink in. If this is Neale's plan, then it's a setup by Mother, but why?

He waits for a response. I adopt an earnest expression. "I'm glad I could help."

"Of course you are."

I'm curious but don't want to ask the wrong questions and make him suspicious. "Lady seems safe enough."

"Now," he says with heavy emphasis. "Their attempt won't happen until she retires to our quarters later."

"What do you mean won't happen? Surely you locked up those planning such a thing."

"Better to catch them in the act. Then it's a death sentence."

I don't have to fake my gasp of horror. What's my mother doing? An attempt on Lady would never work, particularly when the Fishies know in advance. A diversion, then. But why?

Lifers will throw away their lives tonight. But what will we gain from it?

I'm so caught up guessing my mother's true purpose that I don't notice Huckle's fat fingers slipping down my arm and lingering near my chest until Davyd drags Huckle's arm away.

"Hands off the help." His stony voice reflects the ice in his eyes. A faint pulse throbbing in his throat betrays his anger. Is it in my defense? I imagine he's come to my rescue like one of the knights in the recordings of old Earth stories they play in the recreation areas.

"Want a piece for youshself?" Huckle sprays saliva with every word.

Davyd's right hand curls into a fist. But only briefly. He relaxes, and even chuckles, like the idea of him wanting me is laughable. "No, Father, but I don't want to see a man of your esteem have your reputation lowered on such a night."

Father. The title sounds foreign coming out of Davyd's mouth. I don't think I've ever heard of him refer to Huckle that way. Again, I'm struck by how little either of Lady's sons resembles her husband.

"You're right," Huckle agrees. His chest puffs out and he

moves toward the bar, immediately calling for another black vial.

"Thank you," I say.

Davyd shrugs it off. "I just didn't want him making a fool of himself."

It was stupid of me to think he might have any other aim. I hope the confusion in my brain doesn't show on my face. The noise in here has increased since we arrived. Every few seconds there's a squeal of laughter and I wince. The tension of being here, of what's to come, of trying to work out why Mother plans to sacrifice Lifers tonight, of what the diversion is really for, it all compounds to make my head throb.

I must focus on getting to the Remote Device and finding out what happened to Zed and Samuai.

I glance around the room, appearing interested but not too interested in my betters. I would pick most of them for Fishies; they have that soft look about them. The only people I've never seen before, even in passing, are the men behind the bar, and they don't look special enough in their brown t-shirts and matching trousers to be Nauts.

"Where are our fine leaders this evening?" I ask Davyd.

"One of them would have opened the party, but they have better things to do than watch this crowd drink themselves blind."

He speaks so surely, like he thinks of himself as better than everyone here. Like he thinks of himself as a Naut.

"Like what?" I ask.

He ignores my question. "I think you're blushing." His palm grazes against the skin at the top of my bare shoulder. The contact's so light—he could be brushing away a crumb—except I haven't eaten anything here and his words are full of suggestion. "Are you thinking naughty thoughts?" he asks. He's trying to distract me.

It works. "Only of Samuai," I snap.

"He's not going to keep you warm at night."

I allow a slow smile to curve my lips. "But the memories—"

"You don't know anything about him," he growls, but some of the confidence from earlier is missing.

Without thinking, I curl my fingers around the lapel of his jacket. "Tell me."

He roughly dislodges my hand. "You'll find out soon enough."

His gaze meets mine. It's all heat and anger and I'm not sure whether he's going to haul me into his arms and kiss me senseless or slap me. But we're in a room full of his peers and Davyd is never out of control for long.

"Forget it," he mutters.

"I can't. I'm wondering whether you actually plan to keep your word or if this is an exercise in humiliating me."

"Your feelings aren't my concern."

"Lookee what we have here." It's Tesae, as drugged as all the others and looking as much like a sofa as Kaih suggested. The bulbous wings of her dress resemble the armrests and her chest two puffy cushions. "Hi ya, handsome." She runs pale fingers up over Davyd's chest, then behind his neck, leaning in for a kiss.

As her painted lips smear from his cheek to his mouth, he's looking at me. I look away.

With Davyd claimed, she turns her focus on me. "Did they run out of time to make your dress?" A tinkle of amusement follows the question.

I don't dare answer in case I say something I regret.

My gaze is lowered but I see her red-clad leg curl around Davyd's. She must be clinging to him to stay upright. "It almost makes me feel sorry for her," Tesae whispers loudly. "Except that she's scum who shouldn't even be here."

Don't, Asher. She's not worth it.

I count individual strands of the cream carpet and breathe

deeply.

"You're right," agrees Davyd. "The dress is terrible. The way it shows off all that smooth skin, that sheer skirt that reveals legs that could make a guy turned on if he looks too long. Don't get me started on her cleavage."

I look up to catch Tesae blinking, like she's not sure whether Davyd's agreed with her or not. But I know, because I felt every word like a rough caress. Laughter at the other girl's confusion mixes with something hotter in my chest.

Now I know what he thinks of my dress.

The tension breaks when Tesae forces him into conversation about some delicacy they served earlier and my stomach rumbles. I'm not going to be much use in the Control Room if I'm faint with hunger. Lady's a few feet away, talking to one of the Naut servants who balances a large tray of food in one hand.

I move to her side. "Can I help you Lady?"

Her hand takes mine, her nails digging into the skin inside my wrist. "I was just telling this boy he reminds me of my Samuai."

Apart from his brown hair, the servant looks nothing like her dead son. Would Mother see Zed's face in the unfamiliar features of a stranger? I don't wonder for long because the darting of Lady's eyes tells me she's close to having an attack. "That's nice," I say. If she falls apart here, I'll be straight back to the apartment at her side and the chance of going to the Control Room will disappear.

The servant says nothing. I take two plates from him, not dwelling on how wrong it feels to be served by another, and pile both with miniature catfish pies, the only food I recognize. "Would you like something to eat Lady?"

The distraction method's helped before. But I couldn't be that lucky tonight.

Lady reaches out past the plate. "Did you know Samuai?" she

asks the boy. "My son was so beautiful...so cruelly taken from his mother." Tears streak Lady's face.

The boy shakes his head, his eyes darting around for escape from the crazy Lady. He isn't much older than Zed. I try desperately to think of something to do that will let him flee before she starts thinking he's Samuai.

I bite into the light pastry. "This is delicious. You should try one."

Where's Davyd when I need him? I catch the thought before it grows. Now's not the time to rely on a Fishie.

"Delicious," I say loudly.

Lady looks at me like she's seeing me for the first time tonight. "Asher, I didn't see you there." Her gaze drops to the food. "They look lovely, may I try one?"

"Of course Lady."

As she takes a bite, I jerk my head to suggest the boy leave. He doesn't need a second suggestion, blending silently into the crowd. I exhale relief and bite into my second pie as Lady looks around in surprise.

Is she looking for the boy? I tense, ready with an excuse for him when she smiles a satisfied smile. "I'm glad to get you alone. Have you found out what happened to Samuai?"

We spend most of our days alone in the apartment and she's asking me here? "Not yet, Lady."

She drops the plate. The food splatters across the thick carpet as the white plate breaks. The pies are warm and sticky on my feet, staining my dress. Fishies look. Their gazes accuse. What did the uninvited Lifer girl do to Lady?

I force them from my mind. "Lady, do you need to rest?"

She lifts a shaking hand to wipe her brow. "A lie down would be lovely. The noise, you know."

But her words carry, because for the first time the conversation in the room's quieted to a whisper.

Huckle and five other older Fishies stagger to Lady's side. All of them have the hazy look of the tubes. I step out of the way as she's escorted from the room. A wicked piece of the plate bites into my heel. I bend to pick it up and then slide it into the fold of my dress. I'm not asked to go with my mistress; all the attention is on Lady, who bends over and vomits in the doorway.

What a performance.

Apart from Huckle, other Fishies follow her out of the room at a distance. Each of the men radiates excitement. They're expecting an attack from the Lifer rebellion.

"They're armed you know. I think there's a fair chance they'll take each other out." Davyd's smooth voice wraps around me. Unsurprised, I face him. With the distraction of the attempted rebellion, there's no better time to take me to the Control Room.

And the pieces click into place.

Mother guessed what my presence at the ball meant; this staging of an attack on Lady is her way of creating a diversion. My resentment's washed away on a grateful tide of understanding. Rather than doubting my courage, she's helping me in the only way she can.

Thank you, Mother.

Davyd's words register. "You're not worried about your parents?"

"My mother can look after herself."

No mention of Huckle. Now isn't the time to press him on their strange relationship. There's so much more politics to the Fishie existence than I observed in my years on the lower levels. Davyd insists that I didn't really know Samuai because of some secret; but secret aside, his life must have been so different from what he showed me in our forbidden meetings. Maybe Davyd's right.

Pain follows the thought, swift and sharp. I loved Samuai and he loved me. I have to stay strong.

Davyd takes my hand. I hope he doesn't notice it's damp. I don't want him to think I'm scared. Around us, the noise level rises as conversations start up again, everyone whispering about Lady's turn. "When we walk out those doors, there's no going back," he says. "Are you ready?"

My hand drops to caress the sharp edge of my makeshift weapon. "Bring it on."

Together, we walk out of the ball. No one stops us or points; nobody even looks our way. The biggest walk of my life and it might as well be a trip to use the toilet facilities.

"I'm not sure this is a good plan," I whisper a few minutes later.

"I am. And that's what counts."

I'm busy staring at the ground trying to appear subservient so I only hear the confidence in his voice.

He's brave, I'll give him that much. I expected something covert when we left the ball, but he leads me to the elevator and up to the Control Room level, brazen as can be. At each set of doors he swipes his wrist across the scanner and is granted immediate access. Our footfalls are loud in the silent corridors. I'm making mental notes to report to Mother. The hammering of my heart and swirling in my belly makes it hard to think at all, let alone remember details.

Keep going. For Samuai. For Zed.

I think of the young men I've lost when my knees threaten to give way and find the will to keep walking.

The hallway leading to the Control Room is no different from those on the Fishie level below. This time of night it's softly lit. We're the only ones here. The attempt on Lady's probably still occupying the Fishies. Still, I half expect to be stopped and questioned with every step I take toward our destination. My father died attempting this same walk.

Davyd leans close. "The doors at the end of the hall," he murmurs into the curve between my neck and shoulder.

"So close." My mouth dries and I misstep. I can't believe I'm walking to the place my father died trying to reach, the place my people have dreamed of reaching for so long. And I walk with Davyd. With only a piece of plate for a weapon.

He steadies me with his hand on the small of my back, sending tingles across my skin. I turn to face him. I don't ask aloud whether he's sure about this but he must read the question in my eyes.

"Hiding in the open Asher. All you need is guts."

I straighten my spine and lift my head high. "I'll be fine then."

His wrist presses against the scanner. "That's my girl."

I'm not your girl. I want to cry the words. But I can't, because the doors to the Control Room slide open.

I hold my breath.

Where I expected huge displays, and floor to ceiling buttons, dials, and screens, there's three ordinary consoles, not so different from the ones we use for watching the Earth recordings, a black leather sofa, and a couple of round tables. No Remote Device— not that I have a clue what it looks like beyond black and small and deadly with a button or maybe a switch.

There's movement. A Naut mans one of the consoles.

Crap.

Afraid to breathe in case he looks up, I back away. If I get out of here, I'll pretend this never happened and maybe I won't have my sentence extended to take up the rest of my natural life. Maybe.

I back right into the warm flesh wall that is Davyd. His hand wraps around my shoulder, intimate and strangely reassuring.

"Did you think there'd be nobody here?" he murmurs.

Somewhere in my brain I knew there would be someone monitoring the ship, I guess, but since I couldn't get my mind past getting to the Control Room, no, I didn't really think about it.

But I'm not going to admit that to Davyd.

"I thought you'd sort that out."

"I have."

He clears his throat loudly and the Naut looks up. Davyd pulls me even closer and gives an embarrassed laugh. "Sorry, I thought Maston had cleared this."

The Naut's an older man who reminds me of Huckle, except he's lean and hard where Huckle is soft and pudgy. He takes in our fancy clothes and the fact Davyd's pretty much carrying me because my knees fail me and makes his own conclusions.

His dark gaze runs over my body and his fat lips curl in a leer. "Don't blame you Davyd." He sniggers and wipes his nose with the back of his hand. "I'll leave now to give you two a little *alone* time."

Davyd winks. "Owe you one."

"Don't do anything I wouldn't." He licks his lips in a way that makes my already nervous stomach turn.

The Naut keeps his gaze on us as he logs off and moves toward the set of doors across the room. Playing up for our audience, Davyd's arms go around me and he nuzzles the side of my neck. I hold myself still against my nerves and against my body's traitorous response.

The nuzzling becomes a kiss on my throat. Then another. Then he meets my lips with his.

My eyes close. My hands meet around his neck as I press my body closer. Our kiss is gentle and sweet and wonderful. It's everything I've dreamed about when I couldn't even admit I was dreaming of this moment.

It's Davyd.

I open my eyes.

"He's gone," I say when the doors close behind the Naut.

"So?" Davyd kisses me again, the haze in his eyes reminds me of the other Fishies. I know he hasn't touched a drop from the black vials. "You seem to be enjoying yourself."

"Shows how much you know," I lie.

I hate that I force myself to push him away. I'm mourning someone who was truly worth my love. I shouldn't feel anything for this Fishie who I don't even like most of the time, who's made it clear how beneath him I am.

"I know," he says simply. His fingertips brush my mouth and it's all I can do not to lean toward him.

"Remember why we're here?" I say to remind myself as much as him.

He drops his hands like I'm poison. "How could I forget? Beloved Samuai."

"And Zed."

"Ah yes, the little brother who got in the way," he says with a sneer in his voice.

I stop moving toward the console but I snap my head around at his words. "What the hell does that mean?"

I'd put his snide comments about Samuai down to general nastiness, or something between the brothers from before the accident, but suddenly it all adds up. Maybe I never needed to come to the Control Room to get my answers.

"What do you mean saying Zed got in the way?" I repeat.

His arms are crossed. The haze is gone and his eyes are clear, gray and deadly. "Maybe you should ask your boyfriend."

"Funny. How exactly do you propose I question a dead man?"

In two steps he's closed the distance between us. He grabs my hand and drags me to the chair in front of the nearest console.

His heavy hand on my shoulder forces me to sit. "How did you plan to get any information from the cremation logs?" he barks. When I don't answer immediately, he reaches over and swipes a finger over the reader. "There, I've even unlocked it for you. What now?"

"I don't know."

"You must have a plan." He's shouting like getting caught doesn't matter.

I'm scared. Not of Davyd this time but of what he'll tell me if I have the courage to make him.

"I don't know."

What's happening here is out of my control. I can't think. Dread overwhelms the nerves and hot tears prick at my eyes. What if I've made a terrible, terrible mistake? Finding out what happened to Samuai might not be something I really want to know.

One thing is clear: Davyd has way more power in the Control Room than a mere Fishie ever should.

He spins me around and I see the truth in his eyes. How could I have ever thought they were ice? Rage seethes in their almost-black depths. He wants to tell me. All the sly comments, the bet he lost, everything that's happened tonight. It's all been leading to this. He knows what happened and he's desperate to tell me despite it being some big secret.

"You don't know anything," I say with a laugh.

He strides across the room and back, each step betraying his unrest. Finally he faces me again. "I know nobody died that day."

They lived?

My heart leaps and crashes in the space of a sickening moment.

"I don't believe you."

But the ache in my chest tells a different story. It fits with all the secrecy. But...

"If he'd lived he would have come to me."

Neither Zed nor Samuai would leave me without saying anything. "We're on a spaceship, where the hell could they have gone?"

He shrugs. "As I said, you'll have to speak to him about that."

"Prove it."

"Easy." It only takes seconds for him to bring up the cremation logs. But before I get a chance to read them, the doors to the Naut quarters swish open.

I turn, scrambling away from the console. It's a different Naut to the one who was here before. He's powerful, tall, with warm brown hair and his eyes are a familiar shade of gray. They match his one piece uniform.

"Maston." Davyd speaks the name I've already guessed as everything begins to make a scary kind of sense.

"What's going on here?" he asks. And his voice could be Samuai's.

My mouth can't form words. I stare helplessly at Davyd. He set this up; maybe he has a backup plan. But he's shaking his head sadly. "She seduced me into bringing her here. I thought she wanted some alone time—"

"No," I cry. "You're lying."

But Davyd acts like I haven't spoken. "I tried to stop her, but I'm afraid it's too late."

I stumble toward him. My hands outstretched.

"No closer," he says.

In his hands he holds the second Remote Device. My stomach lurches and I collapse to my knees. The hands that caressed me a few minutes ago now contain the ability to switch off any Lifer he chooses. All he needs is our unique code.

He keys something into the screen. "It's intimate in a way, to know your number."

"Please." I beg. I don't care about pride or winning an argument. This is what killed my father. "I don't want to die."

He glances over my shoulder, at Maston. For instruction?

I scan the room but there's no escaping the Device. I don't know its range but it must cover the ship, and he has my code. The piece of plate in my pocket isn't going to help me. If I run now, I'll die a coward. From somewhere I find the strength to rise on shaky knees.

I have lived my whole life as a servant but I choose not to die like one.

When he looks back at me he's almost sad. I think. Everything is blurring with the hot tears I refuse to let fall. But I see his finger on the switch. It's moving.

I lift my chin. *Launch it.* I've failed everyone I care about and put my trust in a boy who is about to kill me. How could I have been so damn stupid?

He flicks the switch. I stand tall and proud, refusing to die as anyone's slave. The last thing I hear is his voice.

"Sorry, Asher."

Chapter Sixteen

[Samuai]

Ipass out after my dramatic, and probably slurred, announcement.

Later, awareness trickles into my consciousness in the form of someone breathing nearby. The sheet's roughness against my skin, and the whisper of air moving over my face.

I'm Samuai.

The once-blocked memories crowd my brain in a rush and my stomach revolts. I curl on my side, heaving my guts but only tasting acid.

Asher…Zed.

Thinking about them sets off a burst of pain somewhere behind my eyeballs.

"What have I done?"

"Good question."

I know it's Keane before I force my eyes open. He's sitting next to my bed in a room like the Recovery center except I'm all alone. I've been cleaned up and moved here. Only the sight of his hard face keeps me from crying like a child. It's all there.

"You're not Company?" he asks.

It's only half a question. He must know already, but I shake my head to confirm.

"Who is Maston?" When I don't answer he adds, "You've been raving in your sleep. We know you blame him for everything that's happened."

If only it was that simple. But thinking about Maston doesn't hurt as much as the others.

"He's the head astronaut on the spaceship I called home." I gulp the water Keane offers but it doesn't help my papery mouth. "He's Company. Or at least he wears the same uniform and it's him who left me with Eliza."

"Spaceship?"

The pain in my head makes the room vibrate and makes it hard to focus on Keane's question. Something about a spaceship. "The Pelican. Escaping the alien threat after the Upheaval."

He turns toward someone near the door. "Check our records."

Then the black comes again and I don't think.

***

The next time I wake Megs is there, next to the bed. Gorgeous, caring, hopeful.

"Hey," she says, taking my hand with a smile. Her lips are painted the same shade of purple as her hair. On anyone else it would look silly but on Megs it's breathtaking.

I tug my hand away and roll over to face the wall. Facing her is impossible without memories of Asher flooding my brain. It was her voice I heard whenever I was close to Megs, her who I betrayed when I acted on my feelings for Megs.

Thinking of Asher brings the dark thoughts, the ones I'm learning not to think about. The truths that will make both girls hate me.

I welcome the darkness this time.

***

"Time to wake up." Keane shakes me into consciousness.

I blink, trying to adjust to the light. Trying to shake the images from my dream of the preserved tree in the garden that first day, but instead of the tree, I was held in the glass cage.

"How long?" I croak. As I speak I'm making sure Megs isn't here with a quick glance around the room. I exhale my relief when there's no sign of her. But we're not alone. Charley stands by the door and she offers a small smile when I catch her gaze.

Excellent, Keane's going to question me so hard they need medical supervision.

"Two days," Keane says. He passes me more water. There's an IV drip in my arm that wasn't there last time. "We didn't expect you to be out so long," he explains but there's shadow in his eyes.

I gulp more liquid to avoid answering. The aftereffects of the procedure aren't what keep me in this bed. The guilt makes my limbs heavy and muscles weak. But to put what I've done into words would give it a reality I can't bear yet.

"We've been looking into the spaceship." Keane has a pile of papers in his hand with schematics on them.

I nod.

He passes me a recent print out with an old date. "The Pelican with her cargo of people tools, and supplies to colonize a planet should be almost at its destination by now."

"I know." I don't want to read about it; I've lived it. But what happened over the last few weeks and what I believed for the first seventeen years of my life doesn't add up. Someone lied. This time it's not me. "Look, that's well and good, but fact is, I was on board a few weeks ago."

They all think I'm dead.

He puts the papers aside. "Tell me what happened for you to end up in that garden."

"I was tricked into leaving the ship. The meeting my brother promised wasn't what I thought. All I wanted was change for the people on board. I thought Maston was on my side." My gut churns to think of everything I shared with him, all my hopes and dreams.

"He wasn't?"

"No. The ship was close to landing, or so we thought. I believed we could start fresh. No more Lifers and Fishies separated by class, but colonists all together."

Keane's lip curls. "You thought that would work? Once people have power and privilege they don't take kindly to it being shared."

"I thought it was worth a try. Maston seemed to agree and I dared to hope for the first time of a different future. I didn't want people punished for their ancestor's petty crimes. You can't imagine what it was like for these slaves. They're dehumanized in every way and forced into menial labor, with no reward or hope of their lives getting better. Not even able to mix socially with those they served."

"There was a girl, huh?"

Am I that obvious? I ignore the dig. "Maston warned me there'd be risks. I didn't even know Davyd knew about my plans until he led me to the Control Room in the middle of the night. I should've known something was wrong, but I was desperate to change the future laid out for me as a Fishie." The future where I could never be with Asher. *She thinks I'm dead.*

I cough to clear my throat. "A young boy, Zed, followed me

in secret and was only discovered after Maston revealed the truth. Maston decided he'd seen too much. He couldn't have the people on the Pelican knowing it was all a lie."

My voice breaks and the dark memories threaten to bring the blackness with them. As if leaving Asher wasn't bad enough, I'd taken her brother too.

"Zed was the dead boy in the pond?"

"Yes." I brace myself for more questions. Charley is silent. I pick up the cup again and my shaking hand grips the plastic so tight it cracks. Water spills all over me and the bed.

Keane throws me a towel. "If you went to them by choice, why did they block your memories, give you money?"

"I never thought I'd step out of the long, dark corridor onto Earth." As I mop up the water soaking through my clothes, I replay that moment in my mind. Real soil, a gentle breeze, sunshine. The shock, the wonder and then the overwhelming rush of betrayal.

"I don't understand."

"Neither did I. Earth? It should have been impossible."

"But?"

"But I stood there and it was undeniably real. Everything I've brought up to believe was a lie. I never dreamed I was being held captive in some underground pretend ship. They wanted me to join them, but I wanted to tell those I'd left behind."

"Bit late for loyalty after you snuck away."

I can't meet his gaze. I'd wanted change, but I went like a thief in the night, without even saying goodbye to Asher.

"Maston thought so too." Being ungrateful was the least of my crimes. "He threatened to kill me, but decided this was better."

I leave out my suspicion that his mercy involved how similar we looked.

"And he's Company?"

He's asked the question before. He's checking me for consistency but my answers aren't going to change. I nod. "He wears the same uniform. All the Nauts do. They're the astronauts who run the ship but if we're not in space, then I guess that's all lies too."

"Probably."

"They took me to an abandoned building, drugged me, and shaved my head." I keep my voice even but the nightmare of those days makes it difficult. "Eliza was there one of the days but the rest of the time it was strangers. I don't know how long they argued over how to use me and then I woke up in the garden. Naked. I don't think I was supposed to be left alone."

"What did they plan?"

"I heard them say something about a test but that was moments before they knocked me out."

Keane rubs his head with both hands. "You lie there and expect me to believe you're from a spaceship, only it's not really a spaceship. And it's run by the Company who has somehow managed to keep everything secret for more than fifty years?"

The way he says it, the whole thing sounds like the imaginings of a mental patient. But it's what I remember. Or at least, some of it. "Yes."

"Then tell me where it is."

The question was always going to happen. The ache in my head forces my eyes closed, but I don't delay the truth. "I don't know."

"Convenient, huh?"

I scrunch the sheet in my hands and look him in the eye. "I'm telling you what I remember."

He's silent. I think for a second he's going to listen. He sighs and shakes his head.

"I don't believe it. Any of it." He holds up a hand to cut

off my protest. "You might think you were on this ship but it's impossible."

"It's the truth!" I shout but the words come out all strangled.

"Enough."

Charley speaks for the first time. Her voice rings with authority.

Keane shoots her a glare but sighs. When he stands, he doesn't seem as tall as before; there's a stoop to his shoulders. "Rest now and we'll talk more later."

He leaves before I answer. Charley smiles one last time and leaves too.

The memories slip and slide around my mind. I remember a kiss on a roof I never want to forget. But Megs' face becomes Asher's, and then turns into Zed, lying in the pond.

I don't care what Keane says. My memory might be fuzzy but I'm sure it's the truth. I walked off the Pelican and straight out onto the ground. An island in fact. I remember catching a glimpse of the sea in the minutes it took to realize we were being lied to.

An island, or at least the coast.

"Keane."

I call after him but he doesn't return and my croak isn't enough to stir anyone else.

The image of his face before he left entwines with the other memories my brain tries to keep a handle on. When he didn't believe me there was disappointment in his voice and in the new lines in his face. I don't know what he was hoping to find out through my memories, but whatever it was, I've failed to deliver.

Not only did I bring him ravings instead of new information, but he thinks the procedure failed too. His hope for those lost to the Company's New City has been destroyed by my flawed memories.

"You're wrong," I say. But there's no one to hear me.

A spaceship but not a spaceship. I twist the possibility in my mind. No wonder Keane thinks I'm crazy. So many people being fooled for years and years and all for some unknown Company purpose.

You don't keep people locked up for so long for no reason.

And Maston knew all along. My face heats as I replay the foolish hopes and dreams I'd shared when he allowed me special privileges working in the outer control room. He took an interest in me. I thought I mattered to the head Naut, but when it came down to me wanting to expose his secret, he wiped me.

As far as everyone on that ship is concerned I'm dead. Do they still mourn me?

How could they explain the lack of a body? Mother wouldn't be placated with near-truths.

Hope sparks. Maybe she's searching for me.

We talked often about being planet-side one day, of the garden she'd grow. I miss her, but at the same time fear twists everything. Shame burns my skin. What will she think when she knows I walked away?

Davyd knows already.

My brother's betrayal stabs deep. We always competed. In the training rooms, working for Maston, impressing girls—at least until I fell for Asher—but I never considered he'd want me gone. I cover my head with the pillow, but it doesn't help. The memories crowd my brain. I can't escape my actions. I long for black oblivion to return.

But I can do something about it. Keane will believe me if I find the ship.

Energized, I sit up and really look around properly for the first time. The bed I'm on is in the middle of a small room without windows, so it must be somewhere in the center of the Station. There's a lone door; only one way out.

At the end of the bed there's a small white table with a tray. Food. I choke down half a plain roll. My throat aches with every swallow but I need energy if I'm going to find the ship. The bed's damp from the spilt water and so is the hospital gown I'm wearing.

Someone stripped me of my soiled clothes after the procedure. Heat flushes my cheeks. Sure I had probes in my brain, but no one likes to wet themselves. Did they tell Megs? Her opinion shouldn't matter anymore. But knowing about Asher doesn't change what I feel for Megs. Just makes it a whole lot more screwed up.

Other than the table, the room is bare. There are no clothes, nothing I could use as a weapon. I hold no illusion that they're going to let me walk out of here. I don't even know if I can walk.

I stretch my rubbery legs out, testing my muscles' response, and then swing them off the side of the bed to touch the cold linoleum floor. I haul myself upright. They take my weight.

For a second.

I grab at the bed but the blackness beats me and I clutch air.

***

Megs is back when I next open my eyes. "They found you on the floor."

I shrug. "Happens."

"Were you trying to leave?"

There's concern in her voice but whether it's for me, or at the possibility of me somehow betraying her little rebellion, I can't tell.

"I wasn't going to the Company, if that's what you're asking."

She looks down at her hands. "Who are you?"

Blank.

The answer I want to say to this girl isn't the truth anymore. Part of me wishes I'd never let Keane go ahead with the procedure—or even better, he'd tried and failed. Without the brain damage. I could have made a life here as Blank, with Megs.

And leave everyone I grew up with trapped forever?

It's too late for the might-have-beens. The procedure worked and I'll live with the knowledge of what I've done, the memories that make me unworthy of breathing the same air as this girl.

"Keane told you the story of the boy who thinks he's a spaceman?" I ignore the way she flinches at the edge in my voice. My priority is warning those left behind on the Pelican, I owe them that much.

"I'm asking you."

How can I refuse? I take a deep breath.

"My name is Samuai."

...and I have a girlfriend.

But the words go unsaid. I don't want to hurt her more. If I never find the ship, if all I think I remember is a figment of my imagination, then I would be causing her unnecessary pain.

A smile teases her pale pink lips. "Samuai." Her accent stretches the last syllable. "It's a good name."

Of all the people here at the Station, she's the closest I have to an ally. I can't afford to alienate her.

"Somewhere underneath this city there's a spaceship with my mother and my brother and I will not rest until I find them."

"You think the Company's responsible?"

"Yes."

"Seems we have a common enemy."

I nod. "Once I've freed the people on board the Pelican, the Company will pay for what it did to my brain."

"In that case, you might need these." She reaches down to the floor and picks up a pile of clothes I recognize. I take the jeans and t-shirt.

"Thanks."

"Need any help putting them on?" she asks with an arched brow.

I crave the touch of her hands on my skin but I know she's only teasing. And there's my feelings for Asher. "I'll manage."

She doesn't ask me any more questions about the ship. We talk about Janic, who hasn't shown any signs of improving enough to wake from his Q-coma. She turns away while I dress.

Aware of Megs waiting, I move quickly, stripping off the gown, disconnecting the IV at the port, and slipping the dark green t-shirt over my head. Next are the jeans. It's while dragging them up that I notice my leg. It's almost healed. The only sign I had a deep, weeping burn there a few days ago is a pinkish discoloration of the skin.

I clear my throat. I'm happy to be sitting on the edge of the bed across from her, not the invalid I was a few minutes ago.

She turns with a grin. "I promise I didn't peek."

"My leg's better."

She doesn't look as surprised as she should. "I heard."

"Heard?"

"Keane might have mentioned something about it."

"I'm guessing the cream isn't magic."

"No." She presses her lips together like she doesn't know whether to continue. Her fingers go to the long strands of purple hair, something she does when she's unsettled about something. "Combined with the Q resistance, there's some odd stuff happening in you."

And Keane talked about it.

I think about the questions I posed for them, how much

stronger they'd be if they could be safe from Company officers wielding Qs, and then the drip in my arm and the two days I was in and out of consciousness makes sense.

Stomach tight, I search my arm. Next to where the drip went in there's the fine mark of a needle in my skin. I close my eyes.

"Did they take my blood?" I keep my tone level.

She's silent.

"Not just blood then. Other samples too?" My voice rises but it's nothing compared to the hot rush of anger inside me.

"I don't know anything for sure. I was with Janic and I heard him talking with Charley. I'm sure he was going to tell you about it."

"He had plenty of opportunity to tell me when I first woke up. Or he could've waited to ask my permission. Strange concept I know." I rub at my arm where there's the faintest spot from the needle. Just another violation. I'm so damn tired of being someone's experiment. Keane's made no secret of where I rank compared to his people but to take samples? "Sounds like something the Company would do."

Her head snaps up. "You can't compare Keane and Charley to the Company. They've saved people's lives and given you back your memories."

"Yeah, great."

"It's what you wanted."

I can't argue, but the tentative truce we'd reached strains. I look at the door, hoping she'll leave, or a change the subject from her allies taking pieces of my body without permission will come up.

It's hard to think around Megs. Every thought twists and changes because of my feelings, because of the crazy need to impress her and mostly by wanting to touch her.

My hands grip the edge of the bed and I rest my feet square

on the floor. "Help?"

When she moves beside me I inhale her Megs-scent. It gives me the strength to stand. Her strong hand in mine helps me balance. I don't want to end up with my butt on the floor in front of her. The first few steps I take might as well be on plastic legs. As sensation returns I'm able to walk alone.

"You're doing it." She claps her hands together like I've accomplished some brilliant achievement.

"It's just a few steps." I sink back onto the bed, the rubbery feeling in my legs gone.

"It's a good start."

The silence descends again. I'm fixated on the samples Keane took. Less now on what he did—I understand it, as much as I hate it—but on what he might find out from them. My hand drops to where the burn was and I press hard. It doesn't hurt at all.

Bang.

We're both on our feet and heading toward the door where the sound came from in an instant.

"What was that?" It's the first time I've heard anything from outside.

"I don't know." Megs opens the door and peers into the hallway.

With my superior height I'm able to look over her head and see two green robes running past. They have Qs drawn and ready. They head toward a barred door at the end of the hallway. Or at least I think it's barred. A woman stands close, with her back to us, guarding my door. She hesitates and then runs off to join the others.

Megs backs away from the door and closes it behind her. She frowns.

"Are there cells down there?" I ask with my hand on the

doorknob. She hesitates. "I saw the bars."

She nods and places her hand over mine. "It sounded like an explosion."

Her touch sends warmth up my arm. I'd like to think she's looking for comfort but I suspect she doesn't want me opening the door again. Several boots clomp at a run in that direction. "Maybe someone broke out. Holding many prisoners?"

"Just one."

"Eliza."

I shrug off her hand and drag the door open in time to hear an older woman call out from behind the bars, "She's gone."

The woman who helped mess with my brain and then tried to kill me has escaped the holding cells. I press my hands hard to my eyes, trying to stay on my feet. This feels important.

"I have to get out of here. What did she know?"

"They questioned her but she maintained her innocence." Megs' hand on my shoulder pleads for me to stay more than restrains me.

My aching head struggles to finish my train of thought. Eliza could be speaking to the other Company officers right now. "Does she know I have my memories back?"

"I don't know. We'll find Keane, talk to him."

If she knows I remember about the spaceship, then I'm in danger, the station's in danger, and everyone I grew up with is in danger. So many lies, so many people used and misled, so many killed.

I tense my muscles, take a breath, and rip the end of the IV from my arm. The sting's nothing compared to the pain inside me. I step out into the hallway, leaving Megs and my sickroom behind.

"Where are you going?" Megs asks. She's jogging to keep up. "Stop him," she calls from behind me.

I don't break stride. "You promised I could leave when I want. Now's the time."

The woman who was supposed to guard me rounds the corner at a run. Allowing the collision gives me the opportunity I need. I knock her to the ground and she scrambles to stand.

The Q she held is in my hand before she makes a threat. The green marks on my fingers tell me she tried to use it. I laugh. "Too bad."

Operating on guesswork I head downstairs, toward the garage we left the day we went to the mountain. The Q's light in my hand and my legs operate as they should.

Two sentries stand at the garage door. "You're not allowed here, Blank."

"The name's Samuai, and I'm not in the mood to ask nicely." I wave the weapon in my hand and both of them pale. "I'll use it."

But they're Keane's people and I know they won't back down easily.

I stop out of arm's reach, aware of Megs behind me. "I don't want to hurt anyone."

"Stop him."

This time the voice is Keane's. He's shouting from the floor above.

The woman sentry raises her weapon. "Keane said stop."

"Don't bother," I snarl. "It won't work. Thanks to the Company's special breeding program."

"He's telling the truth." Keane catches up.

I'm surrounded. But I feel no fear. I turn to face the man who created this hell in my mind when his experiment worked. "You're not having a great run with captives today. I have somewhere I need to be."

Keane shakes his head. "I can't let you walk out of here. What if you report straight to the Company?"

"Like Eliza? The woman you didn't believe could be a threat?"

Red tugs at the edge of my vision like an oncoming wave. I move toward the sentries. They stand aside.

My hand's on the door. All I have to do is get to a bike and I'll be on my way.

Keane's hand comes down on my shoulder. "Wait."

"Or what?"

"I don't think your rapid healing will help much if I slit your throat." The glint on the blade in his hand penetrates the anger buzzing in my brain and sends a stab of fear into my gut.

"If you don't let me go, I guess I'm going to find out."

"You're serious?"

"If Eliza warns the Company and something happens to those people because of me—"

My throat closing with emotion prevents me from finishing the sentence. When I turn to face him, his eyes reflect the guilt I feel inside. I'm responsible for the people I left back on the ship, like he is for his people here.

"You don't have any proof. It could take months to find anything if it even exists." He's trying to be reasonable, I hear it in his voice.

But it's far too late for reasonable. "I have my memories. I know there are people being held captive by the Company." I pause heavily. "Your enemy. I'll find them no matter how long it takes."

"Then what?" The question comes from Megs.

"We'll be united against the Company." The lie rolls off my tongue. Now's not the time to explain about the divide between Fishies and Lifers. When the people on the ship learn how they've been tricked, it will change everything.

Like we always hoped.

Keane rubs his head with the heels of his hands. The right

one still grips the knife. "What do you want from us?"

"Intelligence."

"We've done what we can for your brain, Sam." There's a hint of a smile on Keane's face.

"Hilarious," I snap, but for the first time he seriously considers about what I'm saying. "You must have information on the Company's movements. I saw a big stretch of water. All we need to find is strange goings-on near the coast." I project a confidence I don't feel. "The ship's out there somewhere."

He closes his eyes and then, finally, he nods. "We'll help you find the ship."

Chapter Seventeen

[Asher]

When I open my eyes, Samuai's warm brown gaze focuses directly on me. *Is this some kind of afterlife?* The thought lasts as long as it takes to blink my bleary eyes and realize it's just another picture. And if my memory's correct, Samuai might not be dead. Or Zed.

I fight the flicker of hope in my heart. It's been weeks without a sign of either of them.

I'm in Samuai's room and somebody's turned one of the memorial pictures on its side. Deliberately? If so it had to be Davyd.

Davyd, who kissed me with a gentleness I can't bear to remember. Who pointed the Remote Device at me, begging on my knees, and pressed the trigger. But somehow I'm alive.

"How do you feel?"

I sit up so fast at the lilting voice that my head pounds in protest.

"Lady, I didn't see you there." I stretch my arms and legs beneath Samuai's blanket. Everything works. I'm still wearing the white dress and the edge of the plate's cut into my thigh, but other than that, "I'm okay."

"Davyd told me what happened."

"Really?"

She leans toward me, all clear-eyed and intent. The dress she wore to the ball seems faded from the bright yellow of before and her lipstick's smeared at the edges. "You made the Control Room but Maston surprised you there." Her lip curls into a little smile at the mention of the head Naut.

No wonder. I remember Mother saying they once fought over a boy, I suspect Davyd and Samuai are proof that Lady won the battle. Does Huckle know his wife cheated on him for years?

"How did I get here? How long ago?"

"Davyd carried you in an hour ago." She says it like I should know, but her version doesn't mesh with what I remember. "He told Maston you reacted badly to too many tubes and you weren't yourself."

Only a father could be conned by that lame story. Could Davyd really have been pretending in order to protect me? It's hard to imagine him carrying my unconscious body through the halls. The idea of him killing me was easier to comprehend. I didn't know the Remote Device even had a stun function.

"Where is he?"

She shrugs. "He said he had something to do. Questioning the kidnappers or something."

The kidnappers. Lifers. My mother. "Was anybody hurt?"

"I'm fine. More importantly, what did you find?"

I close my eyes as the fuzziness in my head starts to clear a little. The words that her son could be alive get caught on my tongue. When I open my eyes she's staring at me. Expectant. Waiting.

Only the truth will do. "You were right. Samuai didn't die that day."

She doesn't look surprised. "The logs were fudged."

"Yes." This isn't news. All I've done tonight is confirm

something she already expected.

There's a hint of a smile on her face. "You know he has to be here somewhere."

"Maybe."

It's not in the existence of a Lifer to believe.

"He's with the Nauts. In Maston's quarters."

I hold up my hands to stop her following through to ask me something impossible. "We're never going to get past the Control Room. They have the Remote Device."

She grins in that crazy way I recognize. "They don't have this one."

In her wrinkled hands is the device Davyd pointed at me in the Control Room.

I shudder, unable to react with the glee I think she expects.

"Maston has another."

Her shoulders slump a little but I haven't completely deflated her. "We'll need some help."

"Who?" I ask, even as I'm thinking *Davyd*. But he knew about Samuai and Zed and didn't tell his mother. He might not have killed me yet but he's not going to go against Maston.

"I was hoping you'd have an idea." She stares at me. Wide-eyed and hopeful.

The weight of thinking mixes with the after affects of the Remote Device. The room's fuzzy at the edges. Something's wrong.

"Where did you say Davyd is?"

She brushes me off. "He said something about the cells."

Her obsession with Samuai doesn't leave any room for the son who's still here. Despite what he did to me in the Control Room, a twinge of sympathy tugs inside me. No wonder he didn't tell her what he knew.

I would tell my mother about Zed. I *will* tell her at the first opportunity. My mother! I hope the excitement sizzling through my veins isn't showing on my face.

"My mother could help us." The Lifers have been preparing to fight the Nauts my entire life. With Lady to give us access to every level of the ship we might have a chance.

It might mean revealing that she's the leader of the rebellion, but to reach the Naut's quarters we'll need control of the ship.

Lady hesitates. "Elex won't help me."

There's an edge of vulnerability in her voice. She's right to feel that way. My mother's in no hurry to forgive this woman the wrongs of the past. "But she'll help me. For Zed's sake."

Surprise lifts Lady's brows. "Your brother. He didn't die either?"

"No."

Part of me rails against someone being so self-absorbed that she didn't spare a thought for the other missing boy, but most of me expects it now. If we succeed in our attempt to get past the Control Room she'll have to change; my mother and the other Lifers won't return quietly to the levels below.

There will be change. The change Samuai and I once dreamed of together. The change that will let my brother grow into a different life than the one slated for him.

I thought I was dead an hour ago. Staring at a hot boy with death in his eyes changes the game forever. I'm no longer afraid. But Lady has more to lose.

"If we try to get into the Naut's quarters there will be no going back."

"I'm prepared." She stands and seems taller and straighter than I've ever seen her. The girl my mother remembers might still be there after all.

I throw back the covers. "We'll go now. While everyone feels the affects of the tubes." Hopefully the Lifers' celebration was more restrained.

"Yes. Huckle passed out twenty minutes ago." She sneers at the mention of the man she's emasculated their whole marriage. She flaunts the head Naut's sons without shame. Why has no one noticed?

Because it's easier not to.

I hope Huckle isn't the only one unconscious. Assuming Lady's right and Davyd's at the cells, he's on the far side of Farm level. If I get to Mother quick enough it might be all over before he returns.

"You're sure Davyd's down at the cells?" I check as she swipes her wrist for us to leave the apartment.

"Why would he be there?"

"Questioning the kidnappers."

"Oh. Yes. Everyone else is too intoxicated for the job."

We don't see a single Fishie on our way to the elevator. The late hour and the effects of the tubes work in our favor. As I walk next to the woman I serve, I think of a way to ask for the Remote Device that Lady carries. She might be on our side for now, but if Samuai isn't in the Naut quarters she could change her mind in a heartbeat. I don't want her taking out her loss on any Lifers.

The elevator doors are about to open on the Lifer level when I blurt the question. "Lady, may I look at the Remote Device?"

She raises it to eye level like she forgot it was in her hand. Her fingers curl around it. "I think I'll keep it for now."

Crap. Just what I need. I cross my fingers that Mother will be able to keep her scorn for this woman to herself and not bring up their falling out. If they refuse to work together we won't get as far as the Control Room, let alone beyond.

The doors to the Lifers' quarters swish open. The presence of Lady at the entrance creates a silent ripple of interest and tension in the low-lit space. Lifers lounge on beds in small groups stopped mid-conversation while others rest. This isn't a party. Lady sniffs the air beside me and I bite down on an apology for the smell. We don't have access to a clean room like she's used to.

I wait for Mother to join us. It's not my place to bring this woman any further into the Lifer's domain. Not tonight, when we're here to ask for their assistance.

It doesn't take long.

Mother strides across the room, bright-eyed and alert. She's the embodiment of the unrest in the air after the failed fake kidnapping.

"Asher, is everything okay?" She doesn't embrace me but her hand seeks mine for a brief squeeze. Her narrow-eyed gaze fixes on Lady.

"We've come to ask for help," I say with my head high. It feels strange to stand here united with a Fishie, especially the one my mother hates so much. I should be with the Lifers.

Mother doesn't look away from the woman standing just behind me. "What could we *lowlife scum* possibly have to offer Lady?"

"I should never have used those words to describe you," Lady says before I answer. "I never thought you were scum."

Mother folds her arms. "You're about eighteen years too late for an apology."

Lady steps forward to stand beside me. Her arms are crossed exactly like Mother's. "I didn't come here to apologize."

Mother looks to me and her eyes are shadowed. "Why did you bring her here?"

Neither of them lifts a hand in anger but I feel like I should step between them to stop a brawl. They need to grow up. This isn't about the past.

Our future hinges on these two women working together. I'll not fail because they'd rather bicker over the memory of a boy.

The small, imaginary, hands of my brother shove me as I step forward between them. Time to put everything on the line.

"We're here because I went to the Control Room tonight, in part thanks to your diversion." I pause to let my news sink in. Mother's mouth opens in surprise but she says nothing. Guessing my plan and helping is one thing, but no Lifer's ever gone there and returned. I search for pride in her expression but it's carefully blank. "And the logs showed neither Zed nor Samuai died that day."

Now she reacts. Her lips press together and the blood drains from her face. "They're alive?"

A murmur rises from the darkened beds around us. I'd almost forgotten our audience. Well, they need to hear this too. If we're going to breach the sanctity of the Nauts' domain, some of them will need to risk their lives alongside Lady and me.

"That's what we need to find out."

"How? We'll do anything."

Mother's back in control. She's the leader I counted on.

Lady holds up her wrist. "With my DNA I can open any door on this ship. But I can't fight whatever we find on the other side."

I take over. "The only place the boys can be is the other side of the Control Room. In the Naut's quarters. I haven't been to the meetings, and I don't know your plans, but with Lady's access we have our best chance at the rebellion finally succeeding."

Mother says nothing. Her eyes, so like mine, flick to Lady and then back to me.

I meet her gaze dead on. "It's our best chance."

She nods and I finally exhale a breath I didn't realize I held.

"We'll take control." Mother's gesturing to other Lifers before she's finished her sentence. She turns to face the room.

"Tonight is the night," she says. Her voice is strong and sure and carries to every corner of the Lifer's quarters. "Come morning we'll be in charge of the ship and setting a course for freedom and equality."

There's a cheer from those gathered on or next to beds. It's a wave of raw, hungry sound.

Lady's breath catches and I wonder if she's suddenly realized what she'll unleash tonight.

Kaih is first to Mother's side. She flashes me a grin. "Dress looks good."

I almost forgot I'm still wearing the white creation. The ball seems a lifetime ago. "Thanks."

"No, thank you." Her hand reaches into her pocket and comes out with the dead, dry petals of the flower I gave her. She glances down and then slides it away before I say anything. Then she's off at a run, following an order from Mother I didn't understand. Something about the material store. In Manufacturing?

A hand grips my wrist. Lady. Her other hand curls tightly around the Remote Device. I spare her a glance and there's naked fear in her eyes. Of the task ahead or of the Lifer force I'm not sure.

"It's too late to back out now," I say as gently as possible.

It's taken all of Mother's authority to keep some of the men down here from attacking before the Lifers were ready. They'll use Lady's wrist to get access tonight now whether it's attached to the rest of her or not.

"I know. It will be worth it to see Samuai again."

I nod.

Mother orders a group of Lifers to the care center where the smallest children are looked after. They must be protected from any Fishie retaliation. When she's finished delegating, she turns her attention back to me.

"I need details of the exact layout of the levels above." Someone arrives with parchment to draw on and I sketch a quick map while answering Mother's rapid-fire questions. "Did you locate the second Remote Device?"

This is where things get tricky. I take my time to answer, aware of Lady's hand ready for action and Lady's mind, always a delicate balance between rational and crazy.

"I did. And I learned it has a stun function."

Mother's brows shoot up. The memory churns my belly too much to go into detail so I shake my head at the question in her eyes. "We have it now."

"We?" Mother asks.

"I have it." Lady corrects me.

Mother's gaze drops to her enemy's hand then she sighs. "And you're keeping it like the traitor you always were."

Lady's fingers convulse. "He chose me."

"Look how well that turned out." Bitterness underlines every one of Mother's words. "He's keeping our boys."

Or not. I don't dare point out that Zed and Samuai might not be waiting for us if we succeed.

They stare at each other. Lady pushes the Remote Device into my hands. "Asher can have it."

The weight of the thing in my palm is almost enough to bring me to my knees. I don't show the two women watching me the affect it has, slipping it into one of the secret folds in my dress like it's nothing.

When Davyd pointed it at me I believed it was the end. I shake my head to dislodge the memory from my mind. I don't care where he is and whether he's okay.

Only a few minutes pass before an older Lifer approaches Mother. "We're ready," he says.

Mother looks to me. "We're ready," she repeats.

It's two words. Nothing, really, in the scheme of things, but tears well in my eyes. She's waiting on my command. The person

I admire most in the world is looking to me to lead.

A good leader wouldn't dissolve into tears so easily. I blink them back. "We need a diversion. The fewer Fishies standing between us and the Control Room, the better, and none must be free to attack from behind."

"Fire," Mother says simply.

The chill spreading across my nerves is hard to ignore but I manage. "It could kill us all."

Mother nods. "Yes." She gestures to a nearby Lifer who holds out a strange looking cube. "But we'll burn these instead of the ship."

My nose wrinkles. The dark green and brown material reeks of rotting food. I take one from her. They *are* rotting food, dried and compressed into hard bricks. "Food scraps?"

"It's taken months to collect the ingredients but they burn with lots of smoke and respond well to a bucket of water."

Dangerous, but not insane. I hand it back. "Distribute them outside Fishie doors. Don't let the ship catch alight."

"You heard her," Mother says. "Will she open the intercom panels?" Mother barely looks Lady's way.

"She will," I answer for her. I don't look at Lady, feeling a weird tug of guilt by reporting back to Mother. "What will that do for us?"

"The intercom system links to the main life support functions of the ship. By hacking in we'll disable the sprinkler systems on the Fishie level, and we'll create more fear there with less widespread damage."

"Good. It would be nice to have a ship intact at the end of this."

"Trust us," Mother says.

"I do." Mostly because I don't have a choice.

I pause to think about the layout of the Control Room

itself and the small hallway I glimpsed when Davyd convinced the Naut to leave. "There are thirteen Nauts and they have one Remote Device. What weapons do we have?"

Mother gestures to a waiting girl and it's Kaih. I've been so focused on planning I didn't see her approach. She steps forward and holds out her hands. One contains a wickedly long knife and the other a club made from a piece of old pipe. "We've been storing them behind the material for a long time." Her anger the day I nearly knocked a pile over makes sudden sense. "There aren't enough for everyone."

I nod, taking the offered knife and feeling its weight in my palm before handing it back for someone who might be able to use it better than me. "I've seen the training rooms. I believe we'll take most of the Fishies with our bare hands." Except Davyd, but he's occupied with Neale in the holding cells.

Mother and Kaih flash knowing grins. Those who've returned to wait for the go ahead chuckle in appreciation. They're all looking at me. Looking to me.

I clear my throat. "It's time. The herding point for the Fishies is a large room above Manufacturing where they had their ball earlier tonight. The room's called the Commander's Lounge."

I hesitate and then add, "These are people too. Use no more force than necessary but don't consider defeat."

There's another cheer and I grin. Being a revolutionary is addictive.

I lead the way to the elevators. From the training levels we use Lady's access to open the emergency stairs between levels and the Lifers follow me up like a wave of navy-clad vengeance.

There's pushing and shoving on the stairs. My shoulder slams into the wall as people push behind.

"Pain."

"Blood."

"Payback."

The murmurings below rise in volume. Mother, Lady, and I increase our pace without needing to confer. Despite my hatred of serving them, I hope the Fishies won't resist the rebellion and there will be no lives lost tonight on either side.

Lady opens the doors at the top of the stairs. An old Fishie wandering down the hallway dressed in a deep violet suit stumbles in surprise at our appearance. Bushy eyebrows fly up and he opens his mouth to speak. Before I say anything, two Lifers push past me and grab him.

"What the—" he begins in a slurred voice.

Gerrard swings the club and cuts off the Fishie's question. Blood from an open cut on his forehead runs down his stubbled cheek and soaks into the violet lapel. Gerrard grins.

I look away, stomach heaving. What have I started here tonight? Freedom better be worth it.

Mother inhales, ready to speak, but my hand on her arm stops her. It's my problem.

"Gerrard, take a brick and start the fire," I order. "Far end of the hallway." I point in the opposite direction to where the Fishies will be contained.

He drops the old man to the floor and wipes blood off his hands. "Happily."

I look to the other Lifer. "Take the old man to the Commander's Lounge at the end of the hall."

He nods and drags the body behind him, leaving a trail of blood on the floor. The smell of burning food overtakes the fresh floral scent of the hallway before the prone Fishie's halfway down the hall. Alarms ring through the ship.

It has begun.

Huckle's one of the first out into the smoky hallway. "Why aren't the sprinklers working?" he shouts. Then he blinks and sees the flood of navy-clad people with knives and clubs. He backs away. Gerrard's closest and catches his arm.

"We're taking control of the ship." I speak loud enough to carry to some of the other Fishies stepping out sleepily.

My cry's taken up and echoed through the entire level. "We're taking over the ship."

Huckle's as brave as I thought. He submits without struggle. He glares at me when Kaih leads him past. "You'll pay for this, bitch."

I meet his hate-filled eyes. He must know something wasn't right about Samuai's apparent death, but he helped to cover it up. He's not smart enough to have been involved, but I have no doubt he chose ignorance.

I've faced the Remote Device. I've lost people I love. He doesn't scare me. "All we want is freedom and truth."

His laugh's like a trail of slime across my skin. "Be careful what you wish for, baby." Then he sees Lady. His jaw drops. "You're with them?"

She steps forward. "I'm doing what I need to find my son."

Huckle shakes his head. "You should've let it go."

Lady steps forward with her hand raised but Mother stops her. "We need to make it to the Naut's quarters first."

Huckle's dragged roughly away with the other Fishies. His laugh snakes down the hall behind him.

"Mother?"

She turns with a smile that tells me she believes victory's close. But I know that the Fishies are nothing but pieces we need to move aside to get to the real enemy: the Nauts.

"Do you know what struck me most about the Control Room?"

She waits.

I prepare to put into words the thing that's bugged me since

I woke but until now I couldn't put my finger on. "There was nowhere to see the stars."

"You weren't there for long."

"No."

"You probably missed the portal. Or it was closed."

"Probably," I agree, but the gnawing sense of something wrong in the Control Room won't leave me.

To distract myself, I check the progress of the four burning bricks along the hallway, moving a little away from where we're supposed to be waiting for the all clear. They're more smoke than flames at this point but it's hard to resist putting them out. Logic overrules the instinct I've grown up with. We need the Fishies to be afraid. The buildup of smoke from these fires and the others lit in matching hallways across the Fishie level stings my eyes and coats my tongue. Grains and leaf matter sizzle and burn.

The end of the hall is hazy now from the smoke but I see more Fishies walking toward the ballroom under the prodding of Lifers behind them. Fear of the fire mixes with intoxication and the Fishies panic.

There's a scuffle at the end of the hall. A Fishie girl breaks from her Lifer handler. She sprints toward us through the smoke. Her red dress flaps behind her. Tesae. The piece of plate's in my hand. I'm moving without thought to block her path.

"Stop," I cry.

She doesn't.

I brace for impact, taking in the fact she's unarmed, but her eyes show the effects of tubes. There's madness in her bright red cheeks and dilated pupils. She's not hearing anything and can't be reasoned with. Mother and Lady stand somewhere behind me. If she gets past me they'll be under threat.

"Stop," I say again.

She swings wildly at my head with a clenched fist. Crunch.

The blow opens up the skin below my eye and sends hot, shattering pain through my cheek and into my teeth.

No more time for talking. I plunge the long slice of plate into the chunky flesh of her thigh. She clutches at her leg and falls to the floor, writhing in pain.

Mother is there. "Are you okay?"

"Fine," I lie.

Mother uses her sleeve to wipe at the blood on my face. "Not against the fight anymore?"

"Only if the cause is worthwhile."

Two Lifers drag the howling girl back to the ballroom. I watch her go.

"She'll be fine," Mother says. "You used the least reasonable force to stop her."

"That's what I'm afraid of."

There's still no sign of Davyd and much less resistance than I feared.

Kaih returns a minute later at a jog. "I think we have this level under control."

"Fires out now." I look to Mother. "Our backs are covered. Time to go."

Mother gives the Lifers guarding the Fishies their orders. Soon we're ready to ascend to the upper level with Lady to provide access.

The whole thing only takes a few minutes, but it's long enough that my nerves ramp up and the strain across my shoulders finds a matching ache in my head. The pounding of my heart nearly drowns out the sound of footfalls on the squares. I spin.

Davyd.

He appears relaxed and unconcerned despite having literally walked into a fire. He takes in his mother and mine both flanking me and holds up his hands in surrender, although no one has threatened him. Yet.

"Good night for it," he says conversationally.

As though he didn't aim the Remote Device at me hours ago. As though he didn't kiss me before that.

Why didn't you kill me? Do you know Maston's your father? Do you know any more about Samuai? Zed?

I don't ask any of my questions. It's a waste of time when I won't believe a single answer. Davyd is playing something here and he's as likely to help us as fight us. Depending on whether what we're attempting aligns with his twisted goals.

I pull the Remote Device out from the folds of my dress and pass it from hand to hand. "Going pretty well so far."

His gaze flicks to my hand and then back to the side of my face where Tesae punched me.

"If you're going for the Nauts, you'll need me to get through the door."

Lady shakes her head. "I have access throughout the ship."

Davyd takes another step closer. I tense my legs to resist stepping back. "Not the second door. Asher, you know the one."

My name again. In his mouth it's a rough caress and my body sways the tiniest fraction in response. "I remember everything."

He ignores the emphasis in my words. "Let's go." He takes a step left to the Control Room level, then pauses and looks back over his shoulder. "Scared?"

I feel my mother's questioning gaze on me but I don't want to talk about it. There'll be time for explanations after this is over. Maybe.

"No," I say. I take the lead.

Mother and Lady follow behind with a backup force of Lifers not required to keep the Fishies in lockdown or the fires under control. Kaih's among them. I don't dwell on the danger my actions are putting everyone in.

Instead, I think over the challenge in Davyd's words. I would've denied being afraid on principle but it's true. Facing the Nauts should terrify me, but now it's here I just want it over. I want to know what happened to my brother and Samuai even though I don't hold much hope of finding them alive. I want the rebellion to succeed and a new order to begin before we land. I want it all.

Walking down the hallway's different this time. I don't cling to Davyd's hand. I don't look at him or wait for him to lead. I know where I'm going and I'm not afraid of what I'll find.

Davyd swipes his wrist across the scanner and the doors swish open. Out of the corner of my eye Mother gazes hungrily around the Control Room. It doesn't interest me. I want to know what's on the other side.

"Ready?" Davyd asks. It's an echo of his question at the ball a few hours ago.

I think about what I did last time. I refuse to look at him. What if he sees in my eyes that I remember, and thinks it means I care?

"Yes."

Holding my gaze with his own, he hesitates over the scanner. He swipes with a flourish.

Nothing happens.

I exhale in a rush. "Why?"

"It's locked from the other side." He's unconcerned.

"Okay, how does it open?"

He gestures toward the panel next to the doors with a satisfied smile. "We'll need the Remote Device."

I'm not going to hand over the device he was willing to use on me without hesitation. I step forward and click it into the only place it fits. The doors swish open. Beyond there's a short hallway and four large rooms. There's a door marked 'Engine' and a soft hum comes from beyond it. The space is light and airy and fresh like the Fishie level, but rich wooden boards cover the floor and the walls are an opulent burgundy. Each of the main rooms stands with its doors open wide, revealing sleeping, relaxing and eating quarters.

Empty quarters.

Lady rushes past me, my mother close behind. They're united in their search for their lost sons.

"Samuai," one woman calls, desperation lining every syllable.

"Zed," the other echoes.

I don't move. Davyd's similarly still beside me. A glance at him shows his icy and impassive expression. How much of what we'd find here did he know?

Mother and Lady return together. They've been in every room, even poking their heads into the whirring, throbbing engine room. The hope that had them running has drained, leaving each of them dragging their feet. My mother, so dark and tall and lean, Lady, blond and plump. For the first time they look horribly the same. It's the matching sadness and fresh grief in their eyes.

Mother puts into words what I guessed from the moment we opened the doors.

"They're gone. They're all gone."

We've won, only it feels like I've lost all over again.

Chapter Eighteen

[Samuai]

Keane was right. It would have taken me months to figure out the location of the Pelican alone. When he realizes I'm serious about combing every inch of coast, he uses the green robes' resources to help track down key areas of unexplained Company movement. One includes an island and two others are old ports from before the Upheaval.

We sit around a table in the big kitchen area of the Station with Megs and Toby. I don't know whether Keane's cleared the meeting time with the rest of the green robes but no one bothers us. It leaves plenty of tables free to spread out maps with what looks like hand scrawled notes and numbers.

While we talk, I eat some more stew from the big pot that's always on the stove. It reminds me of Farm Level and the limited diet we had on the ship.

But we always had spices. We always had the special alcohol at the End of Year ball. We had things that were impossible if we were really in space.

I just never questioned.

There will be a reckoning.

I piece together the scraps of memory in my head.

I'm standing with Maston. It's foggy, as always in the early morning here. And high up. There's a patch of water in the distance. And flowers.

"There have to be flowers," I blurt.

Keane, Megs and Toby all turn to look at me with matching frowns.

"I remember yellow flowers."

Toby tugs at his left ear in a thoughtful pose. "There ain't no flowers left on the mainland."

"Then it's an island." I lean over the map.

Keane's stubby finger comes down hard on one of the drawings. "This is the one. It's a small island that used to house a notorious prison back before the Upheaval. Now it's one damn big mountain sticking out of the water."

"How long will it take to get there? Darkness is probably better, right?"

Megs is perched on the closest chair but doesn't speak. She plays with her hair. She's been so quiet since my memories were returned. Maybe Samuai doesn't interest her like Blank did. Each movement screams her worry but I resist telling her everything will be okay. It already isn't.

Keane and Toby share a look. The older man gathers up the maps.

"We'll go before dawn when anyone on guard will be at their most vulnerable." Keane glares at me. "It's only a few hours. Promise you'll wait until then."

With Eliza gone, the passing of time grates on my every nerve. I think I could find it myself, but I'd probably waste time I could sleep instead.

"Okay."

He pulls something from his pocket and flips it to me. "From the game."

I catch it. The silver token glints in the light. "Why?"

"Hopefully you have the answers I promised now."

I slip it into my pocket. "We're square."

"It will be reconnaissance in the first instance. We need to see what we're getting ourselves into."

"Fine by me." Keane can call it whatever he likes, but once we find the place I'm going in. Whether they're with me or not.

***

I've barely closed my eyes when Toby wakes me. "Time to head out."

I take thirty seconds to splash water on my face and then follow him down to the garage. Keane's waiting with Megs. There's a small pack of basic supplies for each of us, including a Q and a knife like the one Keane threatened me with earlier.

Keane's not smiling.

"We'll take two bikes to the dock and a small boat across the bay."

"Sounds good."

"You didn't have to come," I say softly when I climb on the bike behind Megs again. This time it's even harder to resist pulling her close.

"I wanted to."

No one bothers with a blindfold this time. I don't know whether that means they've accepted me or that I won't be released from their sight any time soon. The bikes roar through empty streets. Keane and Megs easily avoid chasms and debris along roads they must know well despite the darkness.

We kill the engines and coast down the hill to stop at an abandoned toy warehouse by the water. The faded sign hangs off the front and is still cheerful in the dim light. Another bearded man wearing a familiar green robe waits for us in the shadows. "Boat's ready," he says to Keane.

We board the small boat with its noisy, diesel-spewing engine and cross the choppy bay without anyone speaking much. I join Toby behind an oar for the last hundred feet. Ten minutes later, the boat bumps silently against the rocky shore.

My turn to lead. I disembark, followed by Keane, Megs, and Toby. There are no noises from the surroundings to suggest we've been seen. Moonlight through a gap in the clouds reveals an empty wooden dock nearby with a small dinghy similar to ours moored to it. Morning's still a good two hours away.

"Anything look familiar?" Megs' whisper is almost lost in the crashing of the water against the rocks.

"The entry to the ship is higher up," I say. Which is true, and hopefully helps cover up the fact I don't recognize anything here. I glance back over my shoulder, hoping to match the dark expanse of ocean with the scrap of blue sea I do remember.

Nothing.

I shiver in the early morning sea air.

"Here." Toby pulls something from his pack.

I take the material in my hands and shake it out. "A green robe?"

He shrugs. "Might suit you."

We take a few minutes to anchor the boat around the coast behind some rocks and metal debris. It's not perfectly hidden but someone arriving or leaving the dock might not see it.

I'm hesitant to use the trail leading away from our landing point but each side's the cracked, jagged rock typical of the Upheaval, only interrupted by the odd tree with a ghostly white trunk clinging to a patch of soil. I exhale in a sigh.

No yellow flowers.

Leaving my doubts behind, and refusing to look at anyone, I stride ahead along the trail with my Q in my hand. The Nauts are Company and they've shown fear of the Q. They must not have the advantages of breeding that I do.

The ship is on this island, in this mountain. It has to be.

As we climb higher, more soil covers the rock face and the trees are joined by undergrowth. No flowers interrupt the dark tangle beneath the overhanging branches. Waves break the silence behind us and salt in the air scents each breath I take.

Slap. Slap. Slap.

A new sound adds to the water. I stop to listen. Could it be an animal? It sounds like—

"Someone's coming. Get off the trail."

Moments later, we lie flat in the undergrowth. Megs between Keane and I, and Toby on the other side.

"What did you hear?" Megs' whisper sounds loud in the night.

The approaching footsteps carry clearly through the trees. They're coming from above. But there's a puzzled frown on Megs' face.

"They're coming." I listen again. "At a run."

From their confused expressions, I add superior hearing to what's different about me. Thinking back to the game at the warehouse, maybe it wasn't just the *Focus'n* that gave me advanced reflexes.

Megs' eyes widen, showing white as though the noise that's been so clear to me reaches her at last.

"Quiet." It's Keane and he's glaring at both of us.

We don't move. I hold my breath, thankful for the green robe that makes my body disappear into the dense undergrowth. The noise gets closer and closer and then there's a blur of approaching Company uniforms moving through the trees.

Megs tenses beside me. I look for familiar Naut faces above the uniforms of the green robes' enemy. There's one. He used to work in the Control Room. A flat line of fear has replaced Ike's usually sleazy grin.

I was right. Relief chases the last of my doubts away. The ship's on this island.

Four Nauts go past us. When it's silent again Megs moves to stand. "There should be thirteen," I whisper.

We wait a few minutes more in silence but nobody else comes down the trail. From below we hear the sound of the dinghy engine starting up and then moving away across the water.

The others look at me to make a decision. Keane glances up at the lightening sky through the fog. "If we wait much longer it'll be light."

I stride ahead. "Stay off the track."

I pick my way between trees, looking up the trail and straining to hear anyone else approaching. There's nothing. The fog increases until we're more outlines than identifiable people. With no need to talk there's plenty of thinking time.

What made the Nauts so afraid?

I'm sure Maston wasn't among those fleeing down the mountain but it doesn't mean we've avoided the man in charge. He might be waiting ahead.

Streaks of gray break up the black sky by the time we approach the top of the mountain. I stumble to stop myself at the edge of the small clearing. My pulse thuds in my ears.

This is it.

Nausea squeezes my gut in a nervous fist.

Where there should be celebration there's only dread, the dread of trying to explain to a ship full of people they've been lied to. Trying to explain why I left. And trying to explain what happened to Zed when I still can't think about it.

There are no signs of guards or any other people, just a heavy metal door in the rock. It squats beneath a serrated overhang, deep in the night shadows and fog. The thick trees have been cleared, leaving a kind of undulating meadow around it. The long grasses are filled with flowers. Despite the fog and the dark, the smudges of color are undeniable. Yellow flowers.

"Bush poppies," Toby says, stopping beside me in the shelter of the last tree.

Keane and Megs don't say anything but Megs' slender hand slips into mine. She's warm and real. Even though I know now Asher's only feet away, I cling on for a last touch before everything goes to hell.

"That's the door." My observation is unnecessary but I need to say something and 'I told you so' seems a little childish. Part of me can't believe it's real, even though I have memories to tell me so. The simmering anger against the Company bubbles like bile into the back of my throat.

Keane runs his eye over the layout of the space. I know he's thinking about the killing zone between the trees and the safety of the door. "We'll need reinforcements."

But I never planned to stop here.

"The door isn't closed properly." I point to the seal that sits out a finger's width from the flush rock face.

Megs' fingers tighten in mine. "We don't know what's in there."

"I do." I tug my fingers free. It shouldn't hurt as much as it does to let her go. I couldn't hold on forever.

"We're not going any further." Keane speaks for all three.

Megs and Toby move to his side, leaving me alone closest to the edge of the clearing. I'm reminded that they might have lent me a robe but I am not one of them. I belong with those on the ship.

"My people are inside." I take a deep breath and smell smoke.

"There's a fire." The cramp in my gut becomes painful. "There's a fire and that door's the only way out. No wonder the Nauts ran."

Keane stares at the door, sniffing the air, but he doesn't take a single step in that direction. "They probably have it under control. No one else has followed."

I shake my head. "Don't you get it? They think they're on a ship. There's nowhere to go." I strain to listen. "Did you hear a scream?"

I've taken two steps into the open. No one joins me but they don't try to stop me either. I glance back. "It's probably better I go alone."

Megs stares at me with an unreadable expression. But I can't worry about her now. She chose to stand with Keane.

Keane looks toward where the sun will rise in less than an hour. "We'll wait as long as possible."

"Thank you." I don't know whether I'm talking about them waiting, or the memories, or the robe but he seems to understand.

"Hurry," whispers Megs.

My head down and heart galloping, I cross the meadow at a crouching run. I dodge and weave, reminded of the way I flew in the warehouse game. I'm braced for shouts or shots or something but my feet squishing on the damp grass is the only sound. I'm breathing heavily when I reach the door. I glance back to where the others wait in the shadows but am unable to see them.

Regret lances through me. I might never see Megs again and I didn't even say goodbye. I lift my hand in farewell but there's no movement to indicate they saw. Or that they're even still waiting there as promised.

The smell of smoke is stronger here and it's definitely coming from behind the door. There's no obvious handle. The panel set into the rock face has a familiar ID swipe mechanism. But it's slightly ajar.

I manage to slide my fingers along the edge and pry it open further.

Smoke drifts out, catching the early morning breeze. I drag the heavy door wider and step into the darkness, picturing the layout from when I was last here. The pain of the procedure to wipe my memories has left this time a little blurred. If I didn't need to find my way, I'd be happy to leave these memories permanently buried.

I went to the Nauts for change. Maston encouraged me, and when the moment came it was Davyd who led me to the Control Room and praised my courage.

I asked questions, of course. But the answers were caught up in promises of secrecy and Maston telling me he was protecting me for my own good. I hate now how important and special he made me feel. I don't know what I expected. Another ship, a chance to petition all thirteen Nauts? I don't even know how Zed even managed to follow but he was the most brilliant kid I ever met.

Maston opened the door and the natural light and the lush green hurt my eyes, but before that it was darkness and noise and a narrow twisting path between pumps and wires.

Now, the throb of what I once believed was the ship's engine fills the darkness ahead. Following instinct and scraps of memory, I let the door close behind me but prevent it clicking completely shut in case I need to leave fast. I step forward, turning sideways to squeeze between two huge vents, alert in case someone comes from the other side. First it's left, and then right, and then left again along a path that isn't really there. It lies between what's probably nothing more exciting than the ventilation systems for the levels below.

When Maston first led me this way I commented on how big the ship's engines were. He'd laughed. I guess living in a mountain for three generations was pretty funny to someone from the Company.

Here the smoke mingles with the warm oily smell from the machines. It's noisy enough to drown any sounds beyond. It's warm but not the heat from a raging inferno. The sprinkler systems so carefully maintained after the fire in Manufacturing must be working.

I drop the ground at the sound of a door being flung open and the accompanying burst of light. The thudding of my heart matches the throb of the machines around me. There are scrambled voices for a second then, as fast as it opens, it closes again and the darkness returns. My steps slow. I edge toward where the light came from. Through the door are the Naut quarters but there was something more familiar about the woman's voice.

I replay the moment in my mind. The voice was older, about Mother's age but not her. Someone I know.

Not *my* mother but Asher's. Elex. I'm sure it was her and she said, "Not here."

What is a Lifer doing in the Naut quarters? Who is she looking for?

Zed. It has to be. She's looking for her son.

I freeze between two racks of wires. I press backwards to disappear against a hard metal shelf, even though there's no one in here to see me. The vibrations of the pump behind me reach deep into my chest and find a rhythm with my panting breaths. I know what happened to him. I was the last to see his body after I stripped off his clothes and left him submerged in a shallow pond. How can I face this woman?

My nails bite into my palms as my hands form useless fists. The anger inside me has no outlet. It's directed at me. But there is no going back.

I force my feet to move. First left and then right. Step by

painful step I approach the door. There's no panel or special lock here. The metal handle's cold to touch but gives easily under pressure. There's a click and the door seal breaks.

I blink at the light as I open the door a crack. My nose presses to the edge and I peer into the short hallway beyond. There's a blur of movement. Navy uniforms mostly. More Lifers in the Naut quarters.

There's no sign of the Nauts in their Company clothes.

There's hustle and activity but no panic. The smoke seems to dissipate as I watch. Whatever caused the fire must be under control now. I scan the people who walk past, looking for a Fishie or at least a familiar face. I've given up expectation of seeing a Naut. The four who fled down the trail must have been the only ones on duty. And then I see her.

Asher.

She's not the girl I remember. Not the same as the girl I've loved since before I knew the difference between girls and boys or Lifers and Fishies. Something about her has changed. It's not the flowing white dress clinging to her body where I've only seen her in navy before, or the bruise under her eye, but the way she holds her head. There's command in her voice when she barks an order at a passing Lifer.

The girl whose voice was strong enough to penetrate the procedure Maston performed on my brain is in charge here.

Then, inexplicably, she looks toward where I hide behind the crack in the door to the engine room. My hand tightens on the handle but I don't move. There's no way she should be able see me here in the darkness. But her eyes widen and the color drains from her high cheekbones.

"Samuai." My name is a silent cry on her pink lips.

And then she's stumbling straight for me on bare, blue-swirled feet just like her brother's. The feet I left beneath the water.

My gut twists.

The pressure on my chest reminds me of the force on my brain when Keane gave me back my memories. I can't breathe. I can't move. I can't think. I simply stand and watch.

She's moving closer. There's a single tear on her cheek and her eyes shine brighter than any stars I saw in the city. I feel the sting of matching tears in my own. I never thought I would see this girl again.

The heavy door swings open beneath my hand as though on the lightest breeze. I don't care about warning anyone, or the Company, or what has happened to give the servants control. I just need to hold this girl in my arms again.

She fits perfectly. My arms go around her like they remember how it used to be.

"Samuai. Samuai." She whispers my name over and over in the lilting way it was meant to be said. She looks up at me. Her fingertips brush the orange stubble on my head. "Your hair…I can't believe it's really you."

"I'm here."

There's a booted step behind me, at the doorway I just came out through. My hands drop from Asher and I turn with her still half in my arms.

Megs stands in the doorway to the engine room with darkness behind. "This is why you didn't want us to come with you."

More guilt adds to the weight inside me. "It's not like that."

Her gaze skips over Asher who's still buried against my chest. One eyebrow arches. "Really?"

Megs' presence must penetrate Asher's shock. She looks up at the other girl and then edges away from me, crossing her arms across her body. "Who's she?"

I get her confusion. She believes we're on a ship and strangers are not in her life experience.

My hand reaches out to comfort her and Megs' lips flatten. I bring my hands together instead. Two brilliant girls and neither of them will be mine once they know the truth.

I breathe in smoke and Asher and Megs and try to get the words in the right order.

"Asher, meet Megs. She's from Earth."

Chapter Nineteen

[Asher]

"She's from Earth?" I repeat Samuai's statement to make sure I heard him correctly. His once familiar voice now stretches the vowels in a way similar to the girl's in the doorway.

A stranger.

I don't know whether to stare at the living ghost of the boy I'd given up for dead or the girl he's brought back from the grave with him.

Earth? It's impossible...unless the government sent another ship after the Pelican.

"Yes." He stands awkwardly between us. "It's hard to explain." He looks past me toward the Control Room where people are trying to understand the ships' systems now that there are no Nauts to run things. "What happened here?"

"Rebellion. Revolution. More importantly," I peer into the darkness behind the girl where there should only be engines to run the ship. "Where's my little brother?"

Samuai's clasped hands grip each other so tight the knuckles whiten but he doesn't answer.

"Where's Zed?"

The girl by the door looks from me to Samuai. "The boy in the pond?"

I know a pond is a small pool of water from history lessons but we have nothing like that here. Zed can't swim. What would he be doing in a pond? "Samuai?"

His name comes out strangled. The hope that flared within me at the sight of him fades.

There's a screech behind me. I don't turn to see Lady running. She passes me with her elbows flapping with joy. Then she takes her boy in a tearful embrace. "My baby," she croons over and over. She touches his face, his arms, and his legs like she wants to make sure he's not an apparition.

Red blooms in the tips of Samuai's ears but he suffers the maternal affection, holding his mother close for a minute and calming her tears. "Don't cry, Mother."

Her sobs only increase. "I never gave up hope."

I feel Davyd stop behind me. As usual my whole body is attuned to his presence.

"The prodigal son returns," he murmurs for my ears only.

And then my mother's with us. No flapping run like Lady, but an energized stride across the wooden floors. "Zed?" The hope in her voice hurts my heart.

Tears I don't want to cry burn my eyes. I blink hard to get myself under control. Surely Samuai would have told us good news by now. I take Mother's trembling hand in mine.

"Samuai was about to tell us."

Everyone looks at the boy we believed was dead. His gaze skims me and Mother and then lands somewhere on the floor.

"He didn't make it."

Mother convulses silently at my side. My strong Mother sways and it's only through clinging to my hand that she stays on her feet.

"What the hell does that mean?" I clench my free hand into a fist to prevent closing the distance between us and shaking him by the shoulders. Davyd's hand brushes the small of my back. Supporting, taunting. I don't know anymore.

And I definitely don't know this orange-haired boy Samuai's become.

The girl, Megs, moves to his side in silent support. Her body angles to his, showing they're close. Their unspoken communication confirms it. The hot shaft of jealousy through my chest takes me breath. It's crazy I've grieved for Samuai. I should have let him go. Hours ago I enjoyed kissing his brother.

The room spins. I close my eyes.

When I open them, Samuai's head is up and he's looking at me with his warm brown eyes awash with tears and pain. "I'm so sorry. Maston decided he'd seen too much."

"Maston?" Mother's question is raw and filled with anger. She's shaking with it.

Samuai nods. "Zed followed us. There was—" he hesitates. "There was nothing I could do."

"Sure." Davyd's word is no more than a whisper but it's clear to me.

Samuai might have changed, but he liked Zed, I'm sure he did, and the pain in his eyes is real. "What did he see?"

"The truth." Samuai hooks a thumb over his shoulder. "Beyond the machines is another door."

"Where does it lead?" Davyd speaks for all to hear.

He moves a little closer behind me and when I glance up to look at him his gray gaze is locked with his brother's. There's a challenge and something else I can't read.

Samuai looks away first.

"To a mountain." He pauses then adds, "This ship never went in space."

Hot then cold. Goosebumps rise on my skin and my knees threaten to give way.

"I don't believe you." Mother speaks first. Four words filled with grief and all the anger of a lifetime of servitude.

We could have walked out at anytime. The new life we've been promised with a fresh start for humanity was a big trick. Everything we've lived with for three generations is a lie.

Launch it all to hell.

"No."

"It's true," says the girl by Samuai's side.

It fits with the pond, with the strange girl, with Samuai and Zed, and the Nauts disappearing off a ship in the middle of space. It's why I couldn't see the stars.

My brain can't mesh everything and come up with something that makes sense. "But there's a countdown."

Samuai shrugs. "I don't know what they planned for when it hits zero."

"They?" Mother picks up on his words. "You know who did this to us."

There's movement behind Samuai and two men in green robes step through the engine room door. More strangers. One is stocky and dark-haired with a blockhead and a grim expression.

"You call them Nauts," the man says. "We call them Company. Either way they're the enemy."

"Who are you?" I ask, because everyone else seems too shocked. I'm aware a crowd of Lifers has gathered in the Control Room. Whispers pass on the news about the ship to each new person who arrives.

I wonder whether the Fishies contained on the level below us know yet.

"My name's Keane," the man says. He gestures to the man at his side. "This is Toby. We are part of a rebellion on Earth against the powerful Company that's kept you imprisoned here for their own ends. Samuai came to us with no memory of you, or this place. He risked his life to find the answers and then again to warn you."

"Hero," Davyd says under his breath.

"Warn us?" I say loudly to drown out the doubts raised by Davyd's sarcasm. "We've been safe here for generations."

Samuai seems to consider. "The Company might know I'm here and they're known to be ruthless when people go against their wishes."

"They shot my brother in the back because he wore a green robe," Megs adds with a tremor in her voice. "He's just a kid."

Like mine. My eyes meet the Earth girl's. Despite her purple hair and strange clothes, I feel kinship between us. It disappears as she breaks eye contact and Samuai refuses to meet my gaze.

The gathered crowd of Lifers waits for a decision with a buzz in the air. Earth. Freedom. Walking around under the open sky is something we've all longed to do. But the ship's our home and we've just won control of it.

I look to Mother to lead but she's staring into the darkness behind Samuai as though Zed might still walk through the door. Lady's attention is fixed on her son and she's in a kind of happy trance. The Fishies are locked up and the Nauts are gone.

The weight of the next move settles on my shoulders.

Mine and Davyd's. I never thought it would be him I'd turn to when I couldn't be sure whether to trust Samuai. His gray eyes are unreadable.

"What do you think?" I ask in a low tone.

I don't really expect help from him but asking will give me time to think. He was close to Maston and he didn't exactly faint with shock when Samuai explained that the whole ship thing is a lie.

He smiles that slow, charming, irritating smile. "I think you'd look sexy in sunshine."

Heat climbs my throat and I glance around at Samuai and Mother and the Lifers. Did his words carry? No one reacts, and I exhale a shaky sigh. His sheer audacity breaks the stress of the moment. I can think again.

I have no interest in being a dictator here. The rebellion was never about swapping one tyrannical ruler for another. "We'll gather the whole ship and vote."

While I spoke to Davyd, the second man, Toby, I think he was called, limped through the doors and returned. He clears his throat and the smile he offers is more like a grimace. "Whatever you do, you'd better make it fast. Company officers are waiting outside."

"So you say." Mother spits the words. Her eyes dart around the room, taking us all in but focusing on nobody. "They say all this but we don't know they're telling the truth." Finally, she fixes on me. "Zed could be out there."

The pain in Samuai's eyes and voice when he spoke was real. I'm sure of it. "He's gone, Mother."

She shakes her head. Hard, jerky movements of denial. "No. They're lying." Tears well in her eyes. "They have to be lying."

She grabs a club from the nearest Lifer. The metal pipe appears so dirty and big in her slender hand. Then she's pushing past the men at the door and into the engine room at a run.

There's a heartbeat of shocked silence.

"Mother, stop!" The cry rips from my throat but she's beyond hearing me.

I'm first to follow through the machines and the dark twisting path. My feet slap on the floor, in time to my thumping heart and racing pulse. But she's way too fast.

The door at the end bursts open, streaming light into the greasy dark space. She's out into the morning sun before I reach the threshold. I glimpse a green meadow with Lady's yellow flowers.

Samuai was telling the truth. But I can't even take in the sky because Mother has my focus.

Twenty figures lift their weapons to shoot.

"Mother."

I step after her but I'm dragged back by a fistful of dress. Davyd.

"Let me go," I scream. I fight him. My nails rip at the bare skin of his arms and face but he's too strong.

All I can do is watch.

"Fire," the tallest man calls out.

As one they flick the switch on their weapons.

"No. No. No." The emotion clogging my throat makes the cry a squeak.

For a second, nothing happens.

She's closing the gap, screaming something that sounds like my brother's name. Tears blur my eyes and my pulse is loud in my ears. They're stepping back, looking at each other in confusion.

She reaches them with club swinging. Crunch. The pipe sends one slight figure flying with a spray of blood. Another swing. I feel the impact through my own body.

Maybe she'll make it. That's two down. But there are too many. Way too many. Then she's surrounded. They fall on her like a swarm of ship moths at the light.

They drag the club from her hands but she fights on. Kicking out with bare blue-inked feet. Thud. One strike lands in a woman's stomach and she doubles over.

But now they have her club. And I need to get to her. I have to help.

"Mother."

But Davyd won't let me go. His arms imprison me when I need to be free. "You dying won't save anyone."

My heels connect with his shins but it doesn't make any

difference. "Don't you understand?" My voice scrapes from my throat. "I don't care."

I fall to my knees as they drag her to hers. My hands go to my head with the first blow of the club striking her skull. Then it's on her jaw and bone juts through the mangled flesh and pooling blood. Then she's down among them, and their fists and feet are flying.

Acid burns my throat. I need to be sick, but I can't look away. "Mo-ther."

Davyd drags me backwards despite me fighting to stay. The door closes. We're in darkness again.

Chapter Twenty

[Samuai]

We sit around a table in what was once the Control Room. We know now it did little more than run surveillance and air-conditioning. Megs and Keane are on one side. My mother, Davyd, Asher, and another Lifer I don't know sit on the other.

We told Asher she didn't have to be here after what happened to Elex but she insisted. She's cried no tears since she returned through the engine room door, leaning on my brother's arm, but she's pale and silent.

Toby stands guard at the door with two Lifers I don't know.

"Seems it's not going to be as easy to get out as it was to get in," I say into the silence. "A traitor from the city warned the Company I would come here." I avoid the might-have-beens of hitting Eliza harder in our fight. "They're armed and waiting outside."

"What's this Company?" My mother's voice is strong and sure. "Why do all this?"

Her question echoes the million I've had over the last few days. The unique Q weapon, the aliens, the lack of a real army.

Why?

Guilt muddies my thinking and makes the air hot and heavy in my lungs.

I can't sit still a second longer. The screech of my chair pushing back makes both Megs and Asher flinch. I pace the room from the table to the console.

"The Company is the remains of what government pulled together after the Upheaval," Keane explains. "It ran the propaganda to get resources for the big launch of this ship."

"Their officers wear the same uniforms as the Nauts, but they carry a strange weapon. I seem to be immune." I lift my shirt to show the green marks still on my skin. "Shots like this are what left Megs' brother fighting for his life. I think everyone on board is resistant. It's why they couldn't bring Elex down easily. I'm guessing they weren't sure their experiment worked or they wouldn't have come armed with Qs."

Asher says nothing but recoils at the sound of her mother's name.

"But you don't know." Davyd's non question is filled with skepticism.

The perpetual smirk on his face triggers my hands to ball into fists. He led me to the Control Room. He wanted to get rid of me. Now he's sitting next to Asher like he owns the place.

I grab the Q from my pocket. Stride around the table. And fire into the skin of his bare arm. A green mark forms in seconds but he doesn't even flinch.

"There. Guess confirmed."

Davyd jumps to his feet and grabs a handful of my t-shirt. "Whatever you have to say, just say it."

I smack his hand free. "Who says I have something to say?" But the memory of the last time I saw him won't go away.

"Me." His brows go up all innocent-like and I almost punch him. "I'm not surprised you'd prefer to skulk in the shadows. After all, that's how you left."

Every eye in the room is on me. "I believed I could help."

"By running away?"

"You know an awful lot about what happened for someone who stayed behind." I wave my hand around the table. "Yet, I suspect you didn't share anything with anyone here."

He hesitates a beat, but I'm the only one who notices. "For weeks you and Maston had these secret meetings, clamming up whenever anyone was around. I was working late when ordered to bring you to him. You weren't surprised that night to be woken and then you disappeared with him." He swallows as though the words are hard to get out. "When Maston returned, he reported your tragic death. I'd just lost my big brother. Who would blame me if I didn't want to tarnish your memory?"

He sounds so sincere, but he's not. There was the smirk for starters—it's the last thing I saw on the ship as Maston led me through the door. And he's too ambitious not to be involved. Our whole lives he resented me for being older and being the one Maston chose for Naut work, leaving him with Huckle. He's playing us, playing all of us and I don't have a shred of evidence to prove it.

I glance around the table and see sympathy for the position Davyd found himself in Asher's beautiful face. Damn him to hell, I never thought he'd have her conned.

"You knew," I say. But there's doubt in my voice and I hate that there's still so much going on with Maston that I don't understand. "You're probably still working for them."

Davyd holds out his hands. "I didn't." He even manages to have his voice catch. "I want the same as you. Freedom, equality, all of it."

I shove him back so he lands heavily in his seat. I feel Keane's eyes on me but I don't want to look his way and see censure. Instead, I return to my place and stare at the table.

Keane takes over again. "We're guessing it's something they're putting in the air or the water here deliberately."

Mother waves her arm to speak and then waits for Keane to nod his head. "All children on the ship get injections. Maybe there's something in those."

I zone out when he talks about the green robes and rebellion. I've heard the spiel before. None of it will bring Asher's family back. Maston and his CEO must have a stake in all this. Having seen their fledgling New City, I know they don't have resources to throw away on keeping a pretend ship running.

"Could the aliens be real?" Keane asks. His brows are lowered and he's jiggling his right knee like the rapid thoughts in his brain need some kind of outlet.

I slap my forehead. "That's it."

Davyd leans forward in exaggerated anticipation. "Wow us, oh brilliant brother."

I ignore him and look to Keane. "The Company doesn't need to recruit an army."

"Because they're breeding one." Asher's soft words finish my sentence.

I nod. Obviously her silence was less wounded and more thoughtful. She's become so strong. The girl I knew would've given up after her mother died.

"Yes. It's us. We've been created to be immune to the Q, the greatest weapon in the Upheaval."

"We need to get away." Asher's voice is strong and sure. "Now, while we outnumber the Company."

Davyd nods. "I agree."

Keane and Toby share a glance. Keane stands. "The world out there is unstable. Resources in the city are few. Leaving's fine but where will you go?"

Megs clears her throat. "We could take you beyond the mountains." She's speaking to everyone but her gaze is on Asher.

She's trying to help.

I remember the place Megs talked about that day on the roof. It could be a fresh start for everyone on the ship.

Keane frowns. "We're not ready to move."

"On this ship we have farmers and tailors and mechanics and cooks." As I speak I'm aware I'm listing the jobs of the Lifers. The Fishies don't have much to contribute. "We have skills. If you're making a new start we could help. Work together."

"Together?" Keane asks. He pins Asher with questions in his eyes. "What about those you've captured below?"

She drags a hand across her eyes, then looks at all of us. "Get past the Company and we all get a new start. They'll have the same choice: stay here in the shell of a spaceship or start fresh with you."

Keane nods. "You'd be welcome."

"Let's get this over." Asher shoves her chair back and stands. Incredibly fragile, incredibly strong. She turns to the Lifers, her face ice. "Everyone gather in the ballroom."

They move at once to obey her command.

***

"Listen up," I call to the Fishies and Lifers squeezed into the ballroom.

I don't look for her but I know Asher's behind me. She's the one who made this decision when she could have left the Fishies to rot. But it's up to me to speak.

The weight of her brother's loss and now her mother's is a wall between us. If she knew the truth…

I tamp down the memories. There'll be time to tell her,

sometime when we're safe from the Company and its plans, in the place Megs told me about beyond the mountains. But we have to get through a wall of Company soldiers and off this island first.

The crowd of Lifers and Fishies look to me and the weight of expectation in their eyes almost freezes my throat.

Almost.

"The Company has a specially developed weapon. It will take down anyone from the city but those of us from the Pelican are immune."

"They still have fists and feet." Davyd glares at me like I was disrespecting Asher's mother. He stands at her side and despite Megs—despite the fact I left her—jealousy rears in my chest where I held her image close to my heart for so long.

I stare my little brother down. The one who betrayed me to the Company to get me off the ship. I don't know whether he planned to get closer to Maston or Asher, but whatever his reason, I know he has Zed's blood on his hands too. There will be a reckoning between us but not at the risk of more lives.

I owe too many people to be sidetracked now. "I will go first." My emphasis is deliberate. I know he can't stand to be thought chicken.

But it's Asher who responds first. "These people from the city have freed us to a life on earth." She stares out over the crowd. Touching them all with her gaze. "All we have to do is take it."

And I see the girl I fell in love with all those years ago. Strong and determined. She has lost more than all of us, but is willing to fight for what she believes in.

The Lifers close rank around her. Even before Elex's death they followed her as leader but I don't think she's realized her power yet.

I find myself looking to my people, the Fishies, in the hope they'll step up to the battle. For several long seconds there's nothing. I'm aware of those from the city observing and shame spikes within me.

Then Davyd moves from Asher's side. He saunters through the Fishies' crowd like he's heading to the bar. Soon they are all looking at him. He halts in front. "We're with you. Wouldn't want you showing us up."

In an instant he's spoken for everybody and claimed them as his own.

Davyd and Asher become a blur of action. Keane and Toby confer about the best approach once they open the door. They work together easily, finishing each other's thoughts. They direct those who will stay and care for the wounded and children, and select those who will join us in the attack.

Other than answering a few questions about the weapons and the layout beyond the door, I'm not needed. So much for coming in to save the day.

"Davyd's your brother?" Megs asks.

Asher and Davyd had my attention and I didn't notice her approach. I turn to face her. "Yes."

"And Asher?" Her tone's casual but her arms are folded.

There's no point in lying. "She was my girlfriend."

"You couldn't have mentioned her?"

"No memory, remember?" But the excuse sounds as hollow spoken aloud as it does in my head. When I remembered nothing else, I remembered Asher's voice. I've had plenty of time to tell Megs since my memories returned.

"What is she to you now?"

I glance over at Asher, the girl in the white dress, who hasn't spoken to me properly since Megs walked through the door.

"She's an old friend," I say eventually. It's the truth, but so inadequate to describe my feelings.

Megs leans closer. I breathe in her scent of open air and fog and freedom.

"What am I?"

"A new friend."

It's lame and weak and we both know it. If only there were some way to love them both without hurting them more.

She offers a sad smile and walks over to Toby and starts talking about ships to ferry everyone off the island once we've neutralized the waiting Company force.

A hollow feeling takes up residence in my gut.

It's with relief rather than fear that I stride through the engine room when Asher calls for the attack to begin. She carries a jagged piece of pipe, a twin to the one Elex had in her hand earlier.

We gather at the heavy metal door that leads outside. It's cramped, dark, and smelly in the small space. Others wait in the engine room to follow us out into the meadow where Elex was killed. I pass my Q from hand to hand. The safety's off and I'm ready to fire. Davyd carries an identical weapon. I wonder which of the city visitors gave it to him.

Megs wanted to fight but Keane and I agreed she had to stay behind. One Q shot and she'd be like her brother.

Asher pauses and looks at each of us one last time.

"There were about twenty of them. Mother took down two." She's so matter of fact it makes me ache more than if she dissolved in tears. "We will do better. Those with the city weapons, fire at will. The rest of you will need to get closer." She stands straight and tall. "Do not throw your lives away."

That is all. There is no count, no hesitation. The door's dragged open.

I move with the others into the open air. My gut cramps at the sight of the row of Company officers. They learned from Elex. In two waves they throw fist-sized rocks. One hits my shoulder but I raise my Q and take the officer down with one press of the switch.

Something moves past me in a white blur.

Asher.

She's in amongst them before I fire again. Davyd's close behind. He drops another officer a second later. She swings with madness like her mother. But she's sane. Deadly. Light on her feet, she dances out of their reach. Fine drops of blood trail down her dress. She takes a blow to the kidneys without flinching and opens up the officer's neck with a swing of the pipe. He's on his knees, clutching at flapping skin as she finishes him with another blow to the nose.

A Lifer screams. I drag a woman I've never seen before back to the door. Blood streams from a slash to her chest. When she's being seen to, I return to the fray. Beneath the tall, swaying trees, Asher swirls like an angel of death, uncaring for her own safety.

A flick of the Q I hold brings another officer down.

My ear rings and pain shoots through my head. I turn and raise the weapon but the Company woman's strong. She holds my wrist in a clawed, desperate grip. Her knee lifts and my balls are on fire.

Eyes watering, I free my hand and swing at her nose. The sound of the impact's lost in the noise of the fighting around me but I feel the bones give and smell blood. The officer cries out. Both hands clutch at her face and she runs toward the trail.

I hold up the Q but can't bring myself to shoot her in the back. A scan of the fighting shows a killing field. At least eight officers are motionless and three Lifers too. Asher or Davyd are nowhere to be seen but we're definitely winning. It's only a matter of time.

There's too much death in the air for me to rejoice.

I follow the fleeing Company officer as she weaves down the

trail. Her sobs carry behind her. My legs ache. I don't know what I'll do if I catch her but I can't let her bring reinforcements. Twice I fall and scrape my knees on the rock. But I force myself back to my feet.

The shouts and sounds of flesh hitting flesh disappear behind me as I get further away from the killing meadow. I hear wind through the trees and smell the salt from the sea.

The officer turns to face me at the foot of the trail. "Don't come any closer," she shouts, her words slurred by the bright red blood pouring into her mouth from her mangled nose. There's a rock in her hand.

I take three deliberate steps. "Go on."

I might not be willing to shoot a woman in the back but these people messed with my brain. I'll take one down in a fight.

She backs into the water. Then her bloody mouth curves into a smile.

My heart stops. *Bang.* Something hits the back of my head. The pain takes my knees from under me. I bring up the Q but my hands are jelly. A man takes my weapon from my nerveless grasp.

Still, I fight. I didn't go through everything to die here when victory's so close.

The man pushes me toward the woman in the water. The rock in her hand becomes a club. My hands come up to protect my face but only momentarily. The man in the Company uniform drags them behind my back and holds them there.

One blow, two. Then I'm under the water. It's shallow water. My knees hit the sand. But they're holding me down. I taste salt and try to hold my breath.

And hold my breath.

And hold my breath.

Images swim in my brain. Asher and Megs. Mother. My

favorite apple pie, hot and steaming, on the bench. Green grass soft beneath my feet. Stars. I'll never see them again. My lungs burn, my head pounds.

Until I can't hold my breath a second longer.

Chapter Twenty-One

[Asher]

I'm fifty feet down the trail in a skirmish when I glimpse Samuai in trouble. Dodging a kick at my knee, I see him ambushed by a large Company man through a gap in the trees. I turn on my foe with renewed energy, shoving the officer as hard as I can. He stumbles, falling backwards into a crevasse in the rock. I glance over the edge. It's a long way down. Although he's moving, he's not climbing up anytime soon.

I wipe my face and taste sweat mixed with blood. Only some of it's mine.

I need to help Samuai.

Down by the water, a woman officer joins the man and strikes Samuai's head with a rock. He sways. They force him face first into the shallows, and then stand over him while he struggles. I hit the trail at a run. My bare feet slip and are sliced on the rocks. Pain stabs at me with every step but I stopped feeling the moment Davyd dragged me away from Mother. All that matters now is the boy in the water.

I'm level with the last trees where rocks mix with sand when he stops moving.

"No," I cry. "Get up."

But the boy I loved lies face down in the waves and the

Company officers are walking away.

It only takes seconds to reach the water. I wade out, uncaring whether the officers will return for me. I will not let another of those I love die.

Waves lap at the bare skin of my ankles, then my calves. Part of my brain wonders at the sensation of so much water, but Samuai's my main focus. I drag in a salty breath. He hasn't moved.

"Duck," commands a familiar voice. Davyd.

Launch it. I throw myself to my knees.

The woman who held Samuai down seconds ago stumbles over my head. Splashing and cursing from behind tells me Davyd's wrestling with the man who must have returned too. I move forward, prepared to fight the officer for my friend's body, but she's motionless. Blood flows from her nose and a wound above her eye where her forehead hit some half-submerged rock.

Free again, I turn Samuai face up. He's heavy and limp. My muscles protest as I take two fistfuls of his top and yank him over. His skin has a pale blue tinge and his lips are turning gray. I stumble backwards toward the shore, dragging him with me. A few feet feels like forever but I tug on his legs with everything I have. My progress is agonizingly slow. The whole time I watch him for signs of life.

There are none.

Suddenly, Davyd's at my side. "He was the last of them. No more Company officers will bother us."

What I couldn't do alone, I manage with Davyd's help. We drag Samuai's unmoving body from the water. Like back on the ship with one of Lady's attacks, we work together, putting Samuai onto his side and opening his mouth to let the water escape. It floods out on the sand but he doesn't regain consciousness.

Davyd rocks back onto his heels. "He's not breathing."

"He has to."

A faint memory from the Earth films I used to watch instead of going to the training rooms springs to my mind. "I'll breathe for him."

Davyd shakes his head. "It won't work."

I don't want to hear it. With both hands, I push Samuai onto his back and kneel next to him on the wet gritty sand.

More Lifers join on us on the beach. Davyd's right. The fight's over, for now. One of the onlookers is Kaih. Blood is smeared across one cheek but she's still lovely. "How can I help?"

"Stay alive."

I take a breath, press my lips over Samuai's, and fight a shudder at how cold they are beneath mine. I cover his nose with my left hand, and exhale into his mouth as hard as I can. My gaze is fixed on Samuai's chest. It rises. I move back to let the air escape, and then breathe for him again.

Two more times I do it.

And then a splutter. I roll him onto his side. He vomits. Over and over until there's nothing left and his whole body wracks with the spasms but he's breathing.

Twice I thought him dead and twice he's returned.

His eyes open. "Asher—"

I press my fingers to his mouth. "Don't try to speak."

The color returns to his lips. They curve. "Thank you."

***

While the others celebrate our victory over the Company and the sheer thrill of looking up into the sky, I escape to one of the rocks a little way off the trail. Each gust of wind carries the scent of the sea. I imagine the tang of blood. I balance near the edge, over a long drop, and wrap my arms around my knees. Every muscle aches and my left eye's nearly swollen shut. My tongue darts out to test the split in my lip. It still stings.

I can't rejoice with the others. Too many lives were lost for me to believe we won anything.

All of the Lifers and most of the Fishies are eager to come with us to the place Keane talks about, beyond the Upheaval Mountains. We know there will be more fighting to come.

Their CEO won't be pleased to have the private army they were breeding escape. I hope the data Toby takes from the Control Room will answer some of the questions about exactly what's been done to us, beyond resistance to their Q weapon and the fast healing that Samuai talked about.

Fast healing didn't save Mother.

As I expected, we found her body in the killing meadow. She died on a bed of yellow bush poppies. I still can't decide whether she would have loved or hated that. Maybe I'll never make up my mind. The pain of thinking about it doesn't let me consider the question for long.

Twelve other Lifers lost their lives in the battle and a Fishie passed away from injuries sustained during the rebellion. None of the Company officers survived to tell their superiors what happened here, but I guess they'll know soon enough.

The Remote Device still hidden in the folds of my tattered dress pokes into my thigh. I dare not leave it where a Fishie could get hold of it, since their anger at being duped for so long by the Nauts encompasses us Lifers too, for daring to change our status.

A familiar figure sits beside me. Samuai. The boy who died twice.

His friend Megs was the first to his side when we carried him back to the ship. She threw herself into his arms and he held her close. The jealousy I would have felt a few hours ago burns out from inside me. I'm hollow.

Now he stares out over the water, his dark gaze fixed on the blurry shape of the city where the Company rules.

A million questions fight each other in my mind to be asked first. The biggest, impossible one wins.

"Do you think there are aliens?"

He sucks in a breath like my question wasn't what he expected.

"The memories they gave me when they took away mine tell me there are. It's the only reason to explain the whole pretense of the ship."

"To breed people resistant to their weapon?"

He nods. "As well as the fast healing and whatever else they've done to us."

"You think they'll follow us over the mountain."

It's not a question but he answers anyway. "Yes." He hesitates then blurts out, "Did you know they found Neale dead in the holding cells? His throat was slit."

The hairs on the back of my neck lift. I shiver despite the mild breeze. Neale, the pretend ringleader of the attempt on Lady. Neale, who Davyd was questioning when the rebellion took place. Neale, who would have preferred to count uniform creases than raise a weapon.

Davyd will have an explanation, I'm sure, but it reminds me that a shared kiss and standing together on a battleground doesn't make us friends.

I can't tell friend from foe anymore.

He points to the half-finished blue line on my ankle. "Was that for me?"

Heat flushes my cheeks. "I was interrupted."

He nods without censure. Now I'll have Mother's memory to mark on my skin. Hopefully there will be time when we make it to the other place.

I angle my body toward Samuai's and wait until he faces me. As usual his eyes are shuttered and I still can't get used to the shock of orange hair. His mother moans about how her little boy has come back different. She should be so lucky. His hair's merely the outward difference. Everything between us has changed.

"Why did you leave me?"

It's come to this. All of Davyd's snide comments, all the wondering, all the secrets. Piecing together what he's admitted over the last few hours, one thing becomes clear. He didn't ask to come to Earth, but he sure as hell chose to leave the ship without even a goodbye.

The silence stretches and an ache cramps my chest. Part of me still hopes he'll deny it. If he'd loved me as he'd said, he would never have walked away.

"I wanted change," he says eventually, ducking his head. "The same as you."

I close my eyes. Not like me. I would have shared the secret conversations he had with Maston. I would never leave him behind.

Maybe Davyd was right. I didn't know this boy. If I didn't really know him?

"Was any of us real?" I whisper.

His hand cups my face, rougher than Davyd's, and I hate that I'm comparing the two of them. I open my eyes and see the pain in his.

"I cared for you...I care for you."

He's close enough that his breath tickles my lips. Once this would have led to a kiss. But he's not the only one who's changed.

When we're together there's rightness to the world, but I know it's an illusion. Caring means pain. If I let myself feel again, everything will fall apart.

I stand and pull him to his feet. "We have some mountains to cross."

The killing meadow stretches before us as we return to prepare to leave the ship for the last time. Yellow poppies sway in the breeze and somewhere a bird chirps in a tree. Samuai holds my hand tightly in his as we walk through the tall grass together. We are equals.

THE END

ACKNOWLEDGEMENTS

It takes so many people to take a book from an idea through to completion and then into the hands of readers and I've been lucky to share the journey with an amazing group. Many thanks to Georgia McBride for seeing something in Lifer, and to the rest of the team at Month9 books who've been so great to work with. Also to Ashlynn Yuhas for helping bring the story to another level.

To Ali McDonald for her continued support despite some difficult real life circumstances.

To the amazing scientists of Lab 220. You guys inspired and awed me all at once. It was a privilege to discover with you and of course to have morning tea.

Writing friends are like gold and I have some who are particularly shiny. Thanks to Rachael Johns for not only reading Lifer but for the million daily emails that keep me sane. To Helen and Sandii for welcoming my adventure into something unlike anything I'd written before. To Maggie Gilbert for feedback on a different story that told me I could write this one. To Ro for your time and support on this, as always. And to Natalie Hatch for your read through and comments. Also thanks to the lovely ladies from SARA and RWAus who have inspired me so much.

To all my family and friends. My sisters are the best. Fi and Kirst, I'm looking at you. Mitch and Chloe, you're my favourite teens and I appreciate the times you've answered a call and my questions. I wouldn't be who I am without my family including Dad, Lyn, Dick and Shirley. I have some incredible friends who have heard me talk about this book for so long. In particular Caroline, the girls from mum's group and the school mums. I couldn't have done this without you and I'm so grateful to you all. Thanks to Mum for always believing in me.

And to Dave and my three amazing children. You guys are my world. I love that you're my biggest fans. Thank you for everything. Love you.

BECK NICHOLAS

I always wanted to write. I've worked as a lab assistant, a pizza delivery driver and a high school teacher but I always pursued my first dream of creating stories. Now, I live with my family near Adelaide, halfway between the city and the sea, and am lucky to spend my days (and nights) writing young adult fiction.

Find her online at http://www.becknicholas.com/
Facebook: https://www.facebook.com/beck.nicholas
Twitter: https://twitter.com/becknicholas
Pinterest: http://www.pinterest.com/becknicholas/

OTHER MONTH9BOOKS TITLES YOU MIGHT LIKE

BRANDED

INTO THE FIRE

A MURDER OF MAGPIES

FIRE IN THE WOODS

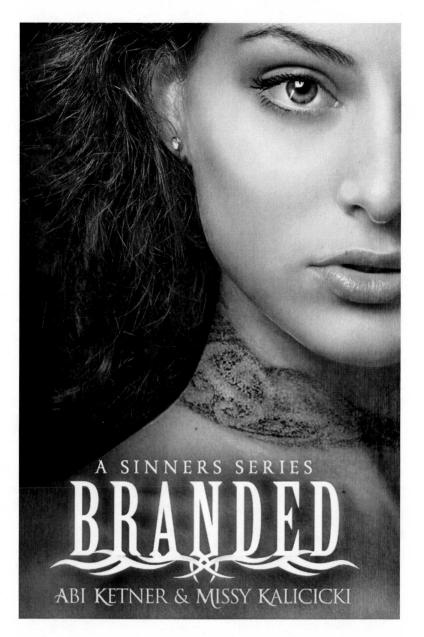

A SINNERS SERIES

BRANDED

ABI KETNER & MISSY KALICICKI

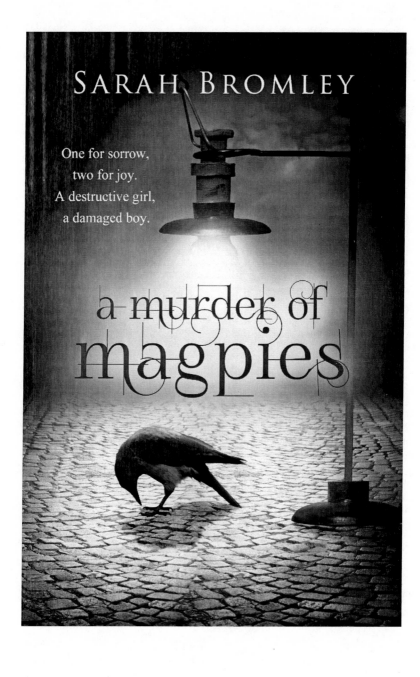

SARAH BROMLEY

One for sorrow,
two for joy.
A destructive girl,
a damaged boy.

a murder of
magpies

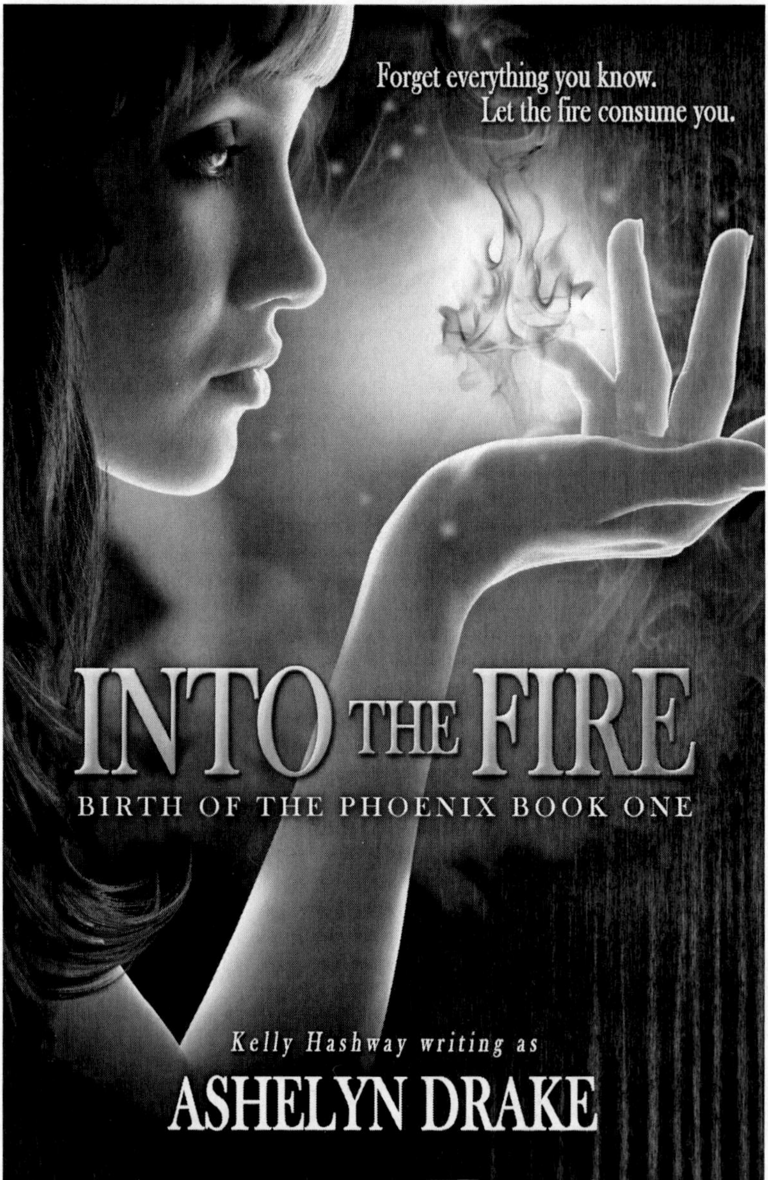
Forget everything you know.
Let the fire consume you.
INTO THE FIRE
BIRTH OF THE PHOENIX BOOK ONE
Kelly Hashway writing as
ASHELYN DRAKE

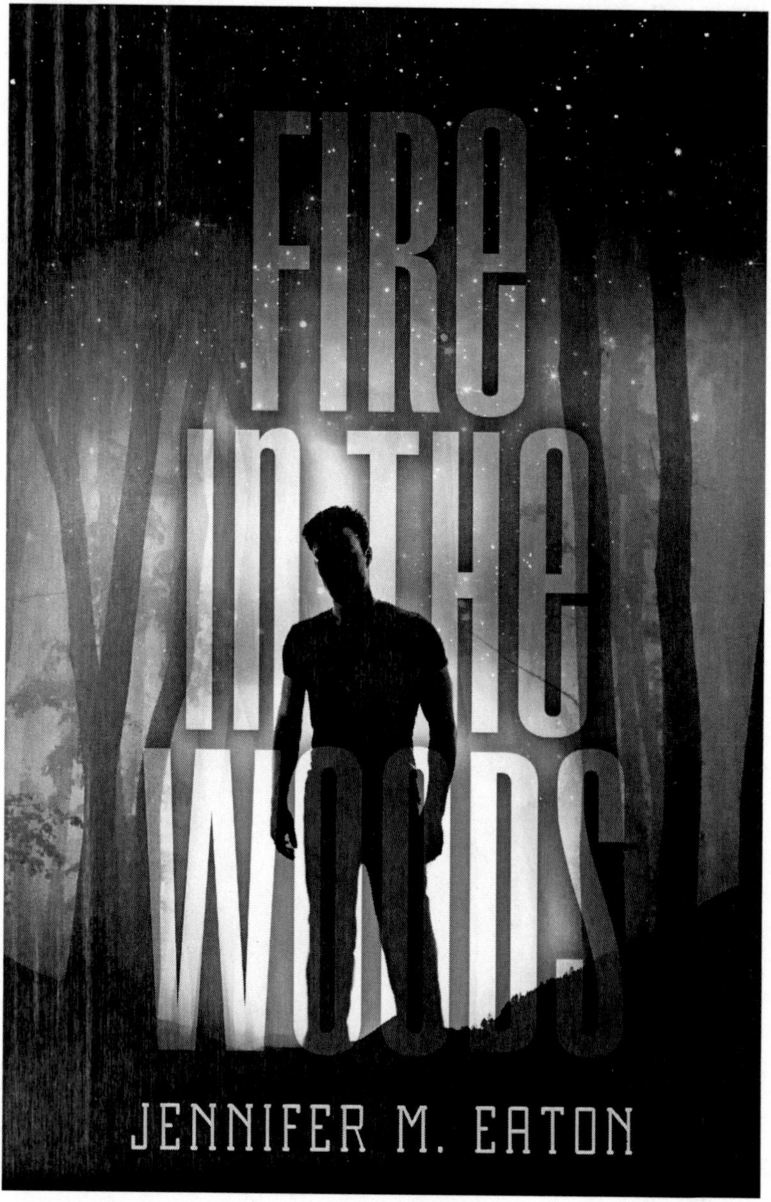
FIRE
IN THE
WOODS
JENNIFER M. EATON

Find more awesome Teen books at Month9Books.com

Connect with Month9Books online:

Facebook: www.Facebook.com/Month9Books
Twitter: @Month9Books
You Tube: www.youtube.com/user/Month9Books
Blog: www.month9booksblog.com
Request review copies via publicity@month9books.com